Luz

Luz

a novel

Debra Thomas

SHE WRITES PRESS

Published 2020
Printed in the United States of America
ISBN: 978-1-63152-870-5
ISBN: 978-1-63152-871-2
Library of Congress Control Number: 2019918531

For information, address:
She Writes Press
1569 Solano Ave #546
Berkeley, CA 94707

She Writes Press is a division of SparkPoint Studio, LLC.

for Mom and Dad
who always put us first

I tell you this
to break your heart,
by which I mean only
that it break open and never close again
to the rest of the world.

Mary Oliver

Darkness cannot drive out darkness,
only light can do that.
Hate cannot drive out hate,
only love can do that.

Martin Luther King, Jr.

Foreword

by Alma Luz Villanueva

When I was first contacted by Debra Thomas to perhaps read through, with commentary, her novel *Luz*, having to do with the immigrant experience (Mexico, Central America), those crossing the border to the United States, risking their lives, many dying, that dangerous crossing—I was hesitant. Debra is not a Latina. And so, I replied that I needed to know more about the impetus to write a novel with these immigrant themes—her concerns, the whys of the desire to write this novel. Debra responded fully in a passionate email, which is now in an Author's Note at the end of the novel. When I read that she's worked with immigrant communities in Southern California for decades, is an immigrant rights activist, has toured with Amnesty International to the US/Mexico border (speaking to people both sides of the border, including Border Patrol agents), and left jugs of water—the Blue Flags Water Station Project in the Imperial Valley Desert—for immigrants who would otherwise die of thirst and heat, and thousands do, I agreed to read this novel. And I'm so glad I did. This novel and all of the characters continue to resonate within me.

Of course, I was struck, first of all, that her main character is Alma; her daughter Luz. I laughed out loud, as I'm Alma Luz. Then the opening of the novel with Alma and Luz leads to Recuerdo . . . ("Memory"), and from then on, I was carried like a soft wind, then a strong wind, to a stronger wind, to a tornado wind. The final crossing into the States, a brutal attack (which I had to put down a few times in order to read it through)—millions of immigrants experience this brutality daily, globally. I told myself, keep reading. As it is with every scene, chapter, dialogue, each character—it was absolutely necessary.

The love story of Alma and Manuel is a very tender central theme. Of course, the most driving central theme, what forces Alma and Rosa, her sister, to leave Oaxaca, Mexico, is their father's disappearance in el norte. He always returned after working the farming seasons, but not this time. He told stories of the courageous farm worker leader Dolores Huerta to Alma, igniting her imagination. Part of Alma's quest is to find Dolores Huerta once she's in el norte. She does find Huerta at last, after a journey that would have killed most of us. With Dolores is news that leads back to that tenderness.

This is a novel of great tenderness and great brutality. Debra is right inside of her characters' minds, bodies, spirits, and souls, and she doesn't spare the reader either tenderness or brutality. This is crucial for these characters/people/immigrants, for their stories, their lives, to be passed on in an authentic human voice. The voice/voices are nailed to the page, speaking, truly, for millions of the life/death immigrant experience worldwide—the Mexican, Central American, this Turtle Island continent, as well as all of the Turtle Island continents globally.

Debra's novel is focused on these so *alive* Mexican, Central American characters. You will be immediately drawn into their lives as I was. You will journey with them and laugh at the light moments, sigh with the tenderness, recoil with the brutality. You will witness, via this novel, Martin Luther King's words (that Debra quotes in the opening): "Darkness cannot drive out darkness, only light can do that." You will experience Dar a Luz . . . to give birth, to give to the light. Believe me.

Alma Luz Villanueva
San Miguel de Allende, México
We are one humanity
April 7, 2019

Alma Luz Villanueva is the author of four novels, most recently *Song of the Golden Scorpion*. Her *The Ultraviolet Sky* received the American Book Award.

Prologue:
Los Angeles: 2015

"You don't know anything!" my daughter Luz shouts, stamping her foot in defiance. At fourteen, she thinks she knows everything. Yesterday it was about a boy who is old enough to drive a car—a car that she will never ride in unless he is willing to wait until she is eighteen. Today her anger is fueled by yesterday's argument as she tells me that I know nothing about the Central American children who are fleeing poverty and crime and have been detained at the Texas border. If she only knew what I *do* know—but I can't tell her. Not everything.

We had been watching the news when the screen filled suddenly with young brown faces and a headline "The Kids Are Back," referring to the previous year's migrant children desperate to cross the border and those newly arrived. Despite the government's attempts to handle the crisis, children were still coming. I wanted to take them all in my arms. Those with eyes full of fear and worry were clinging to each other, but there were others seated slightly apart, some with sagging shoulders and empty eyes, and one with arms crossed, chin lifted and a cold piercing gaze. I had seen these eyes before. All of them. I had whispered softly, mostly to myself, "God bless you, pobrecitos, perhaps you should have stayed home," when my daughter jumped up from her chair and exploded with her "You don't know anything!" remark, followed by, "Just because you crossed the border a long time ago, you think you know what's happening today?"

She is standing above me, hands on her hips, leaning forward. Gone is the gentle face of my sister Rosa whom Luz resembles in her sleep. In its place are my stubborn squint and firm pressed lips. As always, I search for traces of Manuel, but right now I see mostly my younger, angry self, as Luz continues with her lecture on my ignorance. "Many of them are just little kids; *you* were older. They have no one to help them like you did. Some have no parents anywhere; *you* had a mamá back home. Some are trying to get to a parent who is working in the United States, not missing like your papá, but actually there. This is not like you at all. They can't just 'stay home.'" She flips back her long, thick hair and lets out an exasperated sigh. My Adelita warrior!

A long time ago? Not so long, though to her it *is* a lifetime—I was just a couple of years older than Luz when I made my journey, and then she was born. Her unexpected anger has stopped the tears that welled up in my eyes at the sight of these children. I yank out the yarn of my crocheting, for I have lost count.

"I didn't mean it that way, Luz. I'm not saying they shouldn't have come. I just meant . . . well, I know the hardships they must have endured."

"Not worse than the hardships they are fleeing," she says, her nostrils flaring like Manuel's when he was angry.

I suppress a slight smile at this familiar sight and sigh, "Maybe. Maybe not. It's complicated."

I look up into her dark eyes. There is much I wish I could tell her, but she is so young. I have always thought that maybe one day, when she is older, I will tell her more. I want her to know me, who I was, who I really am. But now, as a flood of memories sends a chill that turns my hands ice cold, I tremble with the knowledge that she will never know my true story but will always live with the safer one that I have given her.

Perhaps this is the way of mothers and daughters. What, after all, did I ever really know of my own mother?

"Complicated?" Luz is saying, with a hint of sarcasm in her voice as she gathers up her schoolbooks and hugs them to her chest. "I'm going to my room. My math homework is 'complicated,' but I want to figure it out myself. I don't need your help."

This last bit is said to spite me, but I let it go. This is not her usual behavior. This is really about yesterday . . . about a boy . . . and we have tossed enough angry words about this apartment for one night. No more.

I pick up my yarn and begin to count again. Ten single crochets, skip a space, ten more. Should I have stayed in Mexico with Mamá? The thought alone makes my stomach turn. But if I had stayed, if I hadn't searched for Papá . . . I think of Rosa, of Manuel, of the night of the blinding stars. Maybe Luz is right. Maybe I don't know anything. But one thing is certain: Luz can never know the truth of my journey. My precious Luz de Rosalba can never know.

Recuerdo . . .

1

Oaxaca Bound

My father disappeared in 1997. My precious papá, who knew me better than anyone else, who saw not only who I was, but more importantly, who I could be. He was the one who praised my schoolwork, spoke with my teachers, and made me dream beyond our simple life in Oaxaca. Never my mother. Papá encouraged my fascination with numbers, and at a young age I learned exactly why he traveled so far, for so long, to support our family. I remember vividly the two of us hunched over a table by candlelight, my small fingers clutching a fat pencil, as we created three columns listing the cost of monthly expenses and comparing them to what he earned in el norte and what he would earn doing the same work in Mexico. I understood well enough to see the staggering reality. Numbers always tell the truth.

I was thirteen when Papá left for el norte that year like he had countless times before. For over three decades, he had worked on farms throughout California, arriving at each at designated times. He would stay for a season, sometimes longer, then return home for a couple of months. But this time his departure was followed by a chilling silence. No boxes arrived with T-shirts, toys, stickers, and stars. No first Sunday evening of the month telephone calls at the Cortez house, for we didn't have a phone. No word at all made its way back to us those first weeks, that became months—and then, as the season ended, no money, no Papá.

Mamá must have been terrified.

I think that now, but I didn't then. I thought only of myself and Papá.

Mamá let me stay in school that first year without Papá. Of course, I gave her no choice, throwing a fit until she said I could at least try to combine school and work. I was beginning the first of three years of secundaria, similar to junior high in the United States, but unlike my older sister, Rosa, who had decided not to finish her third year, and unlike most young girls we knew, who never went on to high school, I dreamed of going to preparatoria, and maybe even university one day to become a math teacher.

Papá had always said that nothing is impossible. He had learned this as a teenager, when he first began working the fields in Central California and met the leaders of the farmworkers' movement, Cesar Chavez and Dolores Huerta. Oh, how he talked about Dolores! He had never seen a woman quite like her before—small, but mighty, and so determined. He would often tease, and instead of calling me Alma, he'd call me his pequeña Dolores . . . his little Dolores, which made me feel very proud. But because of what he saw over those years, the long struggle and ultimate success of the farmworkers, he had learned that with patience, hard work, and a deep belief, anything could be achieved. And so, he had encouraged me to pursue my dreams—of course, I could become a teacher one day.

Because of this, staying in school was a must for me. But that year, unlike previous years, I had to hurry home to help Mamá and Rosa prepare tortillas. Mamá had found work with a taco vendor named Mundo, who was also an old friend of Papá's. The more tortillas we made, the more money he paid. So, we worked late into the night, mixing the masa, rolling a ball, and then flattening it between hands with a pat, clap, slap. Mine came out perfect each time because I measured the ball's diameter using my finger as a ruler. Then, after clapping each back and forth exactly ten times, I would finish with three slap, slap, slaps and onto the fire. Once done and stacked, they were wrapped and packed to go.

I could not get to my schoolwork until late in the evening, but I didn't mind. I came to like this nightly routine of Mamá, Rosa, and me, sitting by the fire in the center of our one-room, dirt-floor shed behind Mundo's house. My little brothers, Ricardo and José, then seven and five, would play on a blanket beside us until they fell asleep, while the three of us worked quietly by the fire. Clap, clap, clap, slap, slap, slap.

I felt in my bones that it was temporary and that Papá would return. There had to be a good reason why he did not come back for a visit that summer as he promised. Perhaps he had sent us a message that we didn't get, and he didn't know that we didn't get it. All I knew was that when he did come home, he would explain, and we would all understand, and then this nightmare would be over. How proud he would be of my schoolwork, especially my math exams. How proud he would be to see how I was helping Mamá. So, as we sat there, clapping our tortillas, I felt certain that everything would be okay.

The months passed. December, January, and then February came and went with no sign of Papá. These were the months that he always spent with us, finding odd jobs in Oaxaca before the spring took him back to the farms in el norte. It wasn't until the following summer that I began to worry when I heard Mundo speak of the increasing dangers of crossing the border. What he said made no sense, for he spoke of the gringos' anger that men like my father were crossing to work in the fields. Yet he had worked for the same farmers all his life, worked hard and made money to clothe and feed us. Now, Mundo said, they were putting up fences that pushed border crossers east to the desert where many died, or, if they made it, many were arrested and held in a prison called a detention center before they were finally sent back. Was Papá in such a prison, or worse?

While my own spirits began to deflate, Mamá's beautiful black hair began to show threads of gray, and her soft, round face became thin, as deep lines appeared around her eyes. She began to have headaches that, some days, kept her curled on the blanket with a pillow over her head to block out the light. So, when she told me I could not continue with school, even I did not have the heart to fight her. At least not that second year. Rosa and I took to the streets of Oaxaca by day, selling the tacos and even tamales that we made by night. Seven days a week, we all worked; even my little brothers helped the best they could, day and night, until, one by one, each of us would fall asleep beside the fire.

It was during the summer that marked two years without Papá that Mamá's distant cousin Tito, who smelled like sour beer, came up from Chiapas, the southernmost state in Mexico. The two of them, Mamá and Tito, would take long walks in the evenings, leaving Rosa and me to tend to the boys and the tortillas. They sometimes spoke in the Tzotzil language of her family, a language I did not understand, so their murmurings in this foreign tongue added a secret intimacy that infuriated me. Mamá rarely used her native tongue, for she left Chiapas at a young age after her mother died. Papá spoke only Spanish and some English. Only Rosalba, who was her firstborn, and whom I called simply Rosa, was taught a few words of Tzotzil, even a little poem or song, I believe, but when I was born two years later, Mamá never used Tzotzil. In fact, she rarely talked about her life in Chiapas, only that she came to Oaxaca to take care of an old aunt, who died shortly before she met my papá. This last fact was always part of her answer whenever I asked how she and Papá met; the old woman died, and she met my father at a wedding shortly after. It had always struck me as odd to link the two so purposefully, but as I watched events unfold, it began to make sense.

Over the next weeks, Mamá's headaches slowly disappeared. Two months later, she told us we were moving with Tito to Chiapas.

I hated Tito. I hated Mamá, and I hated the thought of Chiapas. As long as we stayed in Oaxaca, I felt there was hope—hope that Papá would return from el norte, and we would live once again in a cinder block house with a cement floor. Mamá would smile and decorate the walls with colorful fabrics—and I would go back to school.

"Go!" I shouted at my mother the morning she began to gather our few belongings. "I am staying right here. And when Papá returns, I will tell him where you are and what you have done!"

Mamá turned slowly, her shoulders hunched forward. "Papá is gone, mi hija. He is not coming back. Either he is dead or dead to us." She could not look me in the eye, but kept her head down.

"What does that mean . . . dead to us? Papá loved us. He worked hard for us. Everything he did was for us!"

"Not just for us," she said, finally lifting her eyes to mine.

She was referring to Diego, his son by a first marriage. Diego lived in Los Angeles with an aunt who had raised him after her sister, Papá's first wife, died in childbirth. I remember hearing Mamá and Papá arguing once about money, and Mamá saying that if Diego had a better life in el norte, then why did Papá have to give him any of *our* money. Papá's voice had cut sharp in response. "Because he is my son!"

"So, you think Papá is in Los Angeles?" I asked, my heart racing at the possibility, yet breaking at the same time, until I remembered. "But Rosa spoke with the aunt twice, Mamá, and they are as worried as we are! No one has heard from Papá since he left!"

"That is what she says, but people do not always speak the truth."

"Like Tito?" I couldn't stop myself. "Do you believe Tito speaks the truth? He's your cousin for God's sake!"

The disgust in my eyes was met with a hand slap across my face as she hissed, "Tito is here, now, with me! And you'd better treat him like the step-father he will be to you. ¡Con respeto!"

Before I could recover, my sister Rosa, who had been standing behind me, grabbed me by the arm and yanked me outside. I was about to spit fire, but Rosa released her grasp and leaned in as if to tell me a secret. I held my breath, thinking of the secret that I had, but she said very simply, "Mamá needs us; she needs us more than she needs Tito, only she doesn't know it."

She didn't say, *Papá is gone and he's not coming back.* She didn't say, *Stop being so difficult and stubborn.* She didn't say, *You can't live alone here in Oaxaca, because I'm not staying with you.* She said, "Alma, we must make a home for Mamá and the boys. We must keep our family together. That's what Papá would want."

That's what Papá would want? I looked at Rosa, so much prettier than I, slender and graceful. She wore her long braid wrapped up in a bun like a ballerina, accenting her swan-like neck. Boys always looked at Rosa when they passed, a slow, lingering look. Yet I was Papá's favorite. Everyone knew that. So *I* should be the one who knew what Papá would want.

But I wasn't so sure. Not when I thought about the letter. So many times, I almost told Rosa, but something kept my lips sealed. My secret—in a way Papá's and mine—a letter neatly folded and tucked in the corner of his wallet. I had opened his wallet to place a school photo of me in the front. That's when I saw the folded paper. I never got to read beyond the first few sentences:

Forgive me, Juan. I am so deeply sorry. There is no easy answer for us. What else can I do? I never thought I was capable of such a thing, but love can overpower our reason and lead us down unexpected paths.

It was written in Spanish, in small, round, perfect script, clearly not Mamá's writing. Mamá barely knew how to print her name, and even then, it was in large, childlike letters. What unexpected path had Papá taken? Did his disappearance involve this letter?

Rosa was stroking my hair like the little mother she was to all of us. "Don't cry," she whispered, wiping tears I didn't even know were falling down my face.

"But I don't want to leave Oaxaca," I sobbed. "It's our home. It's where Papá will look for us. Please stay with me here. Please!"

Rosa's face hardened; her eyes, like slits, were barely visible. This was the extent of any signs of anger that she ever showed. She didn't shout or rage, not even when the boy she liked made a baby with another girl and quickly married. No, she held it all in. Though she would never speak the words, I know she blamed herself because she would not let him do the things that made the baby. That's when I realized there was another reason Rosa didn't mind leaving Oaxaca, for to see him again with his new family was too much for her.

I had no choice but to pack my things and say goodbye to Oaxaca.

I sat in the back of the small dirty bus, away from them all, and cried until my chest ached from dry sobs. Like Mamá with her headaches, I curled up tight, burying my face behind the faded red rebozo that Papá had given me for my tenth birthday. "The color suits you, my little Dolores," he had joked, for he told us that Dolores often dressed in red, the color of love, passion, and sacrifice. I clutched it to me and wept, my eyes shut tight. I could not bear to see my precious Oaxaca City through the filthy bus windows.

How I loved the gentle energy of this city. Though I would come to know much bigger cities, at the time this was large to me, especially compared to villages that I had seen with Papá. Though we always lived on the outskirts, I enjoyed traveling by bus into the heart of Oaxaca City—to the old zócalo, the magnificent centuries-old

Cathedral of Our Lady of the Assumption, and the colorful Mercado Juárez. I especially liked watching the tourists from all over the world with their strange sounding languages. At a young age, I realized that there was a whole world out there that I couldn't wait to explore, but traveling south to Chiapas was not what I had in mind.

Bumping along in the back of the bus, I tried to block vivid images of Oaxaca City from my mind, but all I could see behind my closed eyes was color, color everywhere! Streets lined with buildings in varied hues of gold, blue, and peach; paper flags strung across streets and along walls, red and green, pink and yellow, fluttering like glorious butterflies; and of course, at the Mercado de Benito Juárez, the city long block with colorful displays of food and fabric, trinkets and toys. ¡Los colores! All of these images blended and burst forth like the kaleidoscope Papá brought back for Ricardo years ago. I was certain there was a rainbow of tears streaming down my face.

It was a long tortuous journey, first by bus, then by pickup along winding mountain roads, and finally on foot up steep mountain terrain. There was color here as well. Green hills, trees, and brush, blue sky with thick white clouds hugging the tops of distant mountains, and brown, lots of brown, especially as we climbed higher and reached the stick house with a tin roof that Tito called home. Surrounded by dirt on all sides, it stood a few yards from a dilapidated chicken coop, its chickens running amuck. Goats bleated in the distance. A clothesline was strung between the house and a tree, and hanging from it were two faded men's T-shirts and a ragged pair of pants, which matched the pair worn by a bare-chested, disheveled man who stepped out of the doorway, rubbing his eyes and approaching Tito with an outstretched hand. He was a friend, Tito joked, who was happy to get away from his wife and kids, while he kept an eye on Tito's place. At the edge of the dirt yard, stacks of wood served as the base of a long table made from the same metal as the tin roof. Several buckets were scattered about the yard, as well as a few upended plastic crates that looked to be used as stools. In one far corner, a few white calla lilies stood tall and proud in the midst of this dreary sight. I was so physically exhausted and numb with emotion, I couldn't cry. There was nothing left.

Rosa turned to me and swallowed hard. "We will make it a home, Alma. We will do our best." Then a flicker of hope as she added softly, "At least for now."

Our third year without Papá, we worked from dawn till dusk on this sad patch of land where Tito grew corn along the hillside and raised a few goats and chickens. He promised Mamá that he would build a better house one day. I don't know if she believed him. I don't even know if she really loved him. All I know is that she let him do things beneath the blankets at night. My head would pound, pound, pound as I held back my own screams of anger. How could she betray Papá?

I clung to Rosa like Mamá clung to Tito. There was nowhere else to turn. No Papá. No school. No future. Each day was the same. Tending the goats and the chickens, fetching water, cooking, washing. It was Rosa who suggested I teach the boys their numbers since even they were not attending school that year. Mamá promised that maybe in time she would enroll them in the schools of nearby Zinacantán, but for now, nine-year-old Ricardo and seven-year-old José were my pupils. So, for part of each day, I would sit them down in the dirt with sticks, stones, branches, and leaves, and work on addition, subtraction, and division. At night, once we were wrapped in our blankets in the dark, I would make them repeat the times tables over and over until Tito would curse for me to stop, and I would smile to myself and chant one more time: 3 times 2 is 6, 3 times 3 is 9, 3 times 4 is 12 . . .

How I wanted to leave, to return to Oaxaca and work for Mundo and wait for Papá. I said this to Rosa day after day, pleading with her to end this nightmare of a life.

One morning I threatened to leave on my own, telling her that she would wake up to find me gone. "Papá would be furious if he knew Mamá brought us here," I said. "No one *comes* to Chiapas. They *flee.* There is nothing here but poverty and civil war and misery. We are strong young women, Rosa. We can find work and make our own lives. If you won't see it, then I'll go by myself!" The chicken that I was holding much too tightly let out a squawk and leapt from my arms.

At the same moment, Rosa said sharply like a school teacher, "Sit down!"

Startled, I immediately sat back on the slope of earth beside me. A large lizard slithered around my bare feet, finding refuge beneath a small pile of rocks. Rosa remained standing, hugging a basket of eggs to her chest. Gazing up at her, I thought how beautiful she was even in her tattered gray pants and dirty white blouse. Everything about her was long and thin, her nose, her legs, her slender torso—not short and wide like everything of mine. Rosa would soon be eighteen, a woman—a woman who deserved much more than the life we were living.

"You have to stop," she said, looking away for a moment and then turning wet eyes to mine. She continued, "Papá is gone, Alma. He is not coming back. You have to accept that."

"We don't know that for sure!" I insisted. "He could be sick or injured. He could be in a detention center. He could be in Los Angeles."

"We spoke to Diego's aunt twice. They have heard nothing. He's not there."

"Mamá says she could be lying."

"She has no reason to lie."

"Everyone has reasons to lie," I said, jumping to my feet.

Rosa shook her head. "You think Papá would deliberately stay there and let us starve? Do you really believe that? You of all people? He adored you!"

I thought of his face when he appeared in our doorway after months away. The relief. The joy. How he'd scoop me up in his arms. Then I thought of the letter. *Forgive me, Juan. I am so deeply sorry . . .* I wish I had never seen it. Though I had no idea what it meant or who wrote it, I knew it was something sacred to him. Sacred and secret.

I bit my tongue. "All I know is that he is not here. So, he is either *dead*," the word caught in my throat, "or he is somewhere. And rotting in this pit of Tito's is not going to get us any closer to an answer."

"Well, neither will starving in Oaxaca," Rosa said, setting the basket of eggs down and closing the door of the chicken coop.

That is when it occurred to me. "We could go to el norte!"

"El norte! Are you crazy?" Rosa shook her head. "That's not possible. We are two young girls with no money, no connections. Impossible! ¡Estás loca!"

"Impossible? Nothing is impossible, remember? How many times did Papá tell us the story of the farmworkers, of Chavez and the fiery Dolores? How they struggled year after year, the strikes, the pilgrimage, then the fast, until they succeeded!"

"Oh Alma, those were stories."

"True stories, Rosa. You know that!"

Even now, I could see Papá's face in the firelight as he told us about his life when he was just our age. How inspired he was by Cesar Chavez and mesmerized by Dolores. At a time when he had no one depending on him, only his own stomach to feed, he had worked up the courage to leave the fields and join the picket line, and later, to join in the long march to the state capital. In fact, faded and torn, in my little wooden box, was a photo from an American newspaper of Chavez and Dolores, and behind them, third small head to the right, my father's young innocent face, grinning ear to ear. How proud he was of that photo, and how honored I was to keep it safe for him.

Whenever Papá spoke of this time in his life, he always brought it back to one message. "You have only one life, Alma," he would tell me. "With persistence, faith, and that stubborn streak of yours, you can do anything, mi hija." Whenever I was afraid to try something new, like jump off the rope into the river or stand in front of my class to read aloud, I would picture Dolores, how Papá described her, tiny as she was, standing proud before a tall gringo police officer, refusing to move and pumping her fist in the air, "¡Huelga! ¡Huelga! Strike!"

I grabbed Rosa by the shoulders. "Dolores!" I said as the idea sprang into my mind. "We can go find Dolores Huerta. She is a famous woman. I think she's still alive. I remember Papá said that Cesar Chavez died, but Dolores was still living. We can find her, Rosa. She will help us find Papá!"

The thought alone took my breath away, and I stumbled against Rosa, who grabbed my arm and held me steady. We stared at each other, and I saw her eyes widen for just a moment and then, like her mind, they closed.

"Oh, Alma, you are such a dreamer. How are two poor girls in the highlands of Chiapas going to get all the way up to el norte, not to mention across a border? And then what? Take a limousine to the house of Dolores Huerta?"

Desperate, I cried, "Papá was our age when he did these things. Our age!"

She let go of my arm, shaking her head. "This is our life for now, Alma. Here with Mamá, she needs us—now more than ever." She paused, then gently added, "She is going to have a baby."

"What?" I could taste the bile that rose in my throat.

"Yes." She nodded then gently took my face in her hands. "Mi hermana, put it in the hands of la Virgen de Guadalupe. She will guide us."

Rosa and her Blessed Virgin. The bile practically overflowed.

"Guide us where? Look where she's led us so far." I glanced around and motioned to Tito's pathetic excuse for a house.

The most Rosa could say in response was, "Please, Alma, try to accept what we cannot change, at least until we figure out what else we can do."

I pulled away, about to protest, and then I heard Papá's voice in my mind. *"Be patient, mi hija. Difficult as it is, some things take time."* And so, I picked up the basket and headed up the path. At least the seed of an idea had been planted. Even in this godforsaken place, it just might sprout.

Months passed and a new year began—in fact, a new millennium. I wrote in the dirt the numbers 2000 over and over, mesmerized by this futuristic sight. Anything could happen in the year 2000. And it certainly did that summer.

It began on a particularly warm day for August, April and May being the warmest months in Chiapas. The fog had disappeared, and the sun managed to cast its heat even into the deepest shadows. Rosa and I had just finished washing clothes on the stones by the stream, but before heading back to the house to hang them on the line, we decided to bathe. We had stripped down to our underwear and were splashing water along our arms and neck, when we heard a muffled groan and then the bending and cracking of twigs.

"What is that?" she asked, looking into the thicket of bushes. We had been warned of two specific dangers in the highlands—jaguars and Zapatista rebels.

I had just dunked my whole head in the water to wet my hair. Shivering, I shook the water out of my ears and listened. Silence. Quickly, we dried ourselves and dressed.

Rosa called out a few times, "Hello. Is anyone there?" but the only answer was the raucous call of the black chachalaca.

As we made our way home along the dirt path, the basket of wet clothes bumping awkwardly between us, we laughed nervously, but kept glancing around. The sight of Tito up ahead was, for once, a welcome sight. We ran to him and told him what we heard. Reaching for the basket with one arm, he put the other around Rosa and pulled her close. I saw her stiffen at his touch.

"You are safe now, chiquita," he whispered in her hair. "Don't worry. Next time tell me, and I will go with you." He smiled down at her, and she quickly pushed herself away from his grasp. The guttural sound of his voice vibrated down to the pit of my stomach. As we headed up the path, I reached for her hand, but she hurried ahead without a glance back.

The next morning, I woke as light was just creeping through the cracks in the stick walls. I could see Mamá was still sleeping, and as I turned to see if Rosa was preparing the morning meal, I saw Tito outside, looking in through the small window beside us, his hungry gaze resting on a sleeping Rosa whose leg was exposed outside her blanket. There was a jerking movement to his body as he watched her. When it dawned on me what he was doing, I gasped, and Tito's eyes met mine and widened in alarm. In a panic, he backed away from the window and stumbled over something that made a loud crash. Cursing loudly, he startled everyone awake. In seconds, Mamá, Rosa, and the boys were up and running outside to see what caused the commotion, everyone except me. I couldn't move, my heart racing as I now understood exactly who was watching us bathe the day before.

Tito was the first one to come through the doorway, limping slightly and refusing Mamá's help. Then he turned toward me with narrowed eyes. As I sat up and started to speak, he grabbed my little brother José as if to steady himself, but his hands swiftly shifted from my brother's thin shoulders to his neck. Tito's eyes bore deeply into mine as his fingers flexed, until I closed my mouth and he released his grip. Neither Rosa nor Mamá noticed a thing.

I knew I should tell Rosa, but I didn't want to frighten her. As for Mamá, what could I say? Even if I did, would she believe me?

"What is wrong with you?" Rosa asked several times during breakfast. "You are so quiet. Why aren't you eating anything?"

I couldn't look her in the eye. My head swirled with the thought of Tito touching himself and looking at her. Where would this lead? What would happen next? Mamá had to know, but would Tito really hurt the boys?

Tito stayed close to the house that day, using his twisted ankle as an excuse. He left no opportunity for me to be alone with either Mamá or Rosa. I could feel his eyes on me, like a snake watching a mouse scurrying up the path. That night I couldn't sleep. I kept as close to Rosa as I could. Once I heard Tito snoring, I managed to relax and doze off a bit.

The next morning, while making breakfast, Mamá asked me to take the boys to the well to fetch water. Tito was still asleep.

"Come with me," I said to Rosa, who was mixing masa.

"No, no, I need her here," Mamá said. "Hurry. Fill all the buckets."

Hurry, I did. But by the time I got back, only Mamá was in the house.

"Where is Rosalba? Where is she?" I asked, looking anxiously around.

Mamá tilted her head, "Ay, Dios mío! You can't live a minute without your sister?" She shook her head.

"Mamá, you don't understand. Where is she? Where is Tito?"

"Tito decided to go into town to get a few things. He's still hobbling on that ankle, so he asked Rosa to go along with him to help."

My heart sank. "No, Mamá, no!"

"What do you mean, No? They'll be back before dark."

I paced wildly, my heart racing at the thought.

"How long ago? When did they leave?" It took half an hour to get down to where he kept his old pickup, and with his ankle, perhaps even longer.

"What is wrong with you?" My mother stopped folding the blankets and turned. She lifted her chin. "What?"

"Oh, Mamá. I saw him. Saw Tito . . . looking at Rosa, and . . ." I glanced toward the door where the boys were playing outside. "I saw him . . . touch himself."

Her eyes widened.

"Mamá, he might hurt her. I have to go. I have to find them. I have to stop him."

"Stop him?" Her eyes flared. "Stop him from what? What is your problem? You are the one that has to stop. Jealous! Always jealous! Of me and Papá. Of Rosa and Papá. And now, Tito? This has to stop. ¡Inmediatamente! All of this has to stop!"

Just as I feared, she didn't believe me. Couldn't believe me.

Desperate, I continued. "But I saw him, Mamá! First, down by the river when we were bathing, and then yesterday," I pointed toward the window, "over there, I saw him looking in the window at Rosa and touching himself, before he fell!" I could see his face, his eyes glazed over, the slight upturned smile, his body jerking with each movement. As I turned back to Mamá, I was met again by a fierce crack across my cheek, this one much fiercer than before.

"Get out! Get out!" She screamed, spit flying in my face. "How dare you destroy the life I am making for myself. How dare you?"

I stumbled back against the wall. The boys were standing in the doorway with wide frightened eyes.

Mamá was breathing hard, tears streaming down her face. "Always complaining! You appreciate nothing! You just make my life harder and harder. Papá. School. Oaxaca. Well, you are a woman now! Let me see what kind of life you can make for yourself in this world! ¡Ahora! Go!" Throwing the blankets at my feet, she flew out the door, the boys scurrying after her. "You better not be here when I get back!" were the last words I heard her shout.

Sobbing, I slid to the floor and looked around the small dark room.

Then I remembered Rosa. I had to get to Rosa! I took a deep breath, struggled to my feet, and set to work. I grabbed my backpack hanging on the wall and, hurrying about the room, I stuffed in anything I could find. Some clothes, my red rebozo, and last, my little wooden box of stars, a gift from Papá that contained a few prized possessions, but hidden under a fake bottom, a small amount of money—money Papá had given me to save for school, money that I had never told Mamá about even in the darkest times. How often had I cringed with guilt? But now I knew, this was what it was for.

Quickly I pulled on a pair of socks and my old brown shoes and hurried out the door. Outside I could hear the sounds of José crying and Mamá scolding up beyond the house in our garden. Up there she would be able to see me heading down the mountain. I stopped to fill a plastic bottle with water from the bucket, took one last look at the ugly stick house, and ran down the dirt path. No voice called me back. I imagined her tight-lipped, arms crossed, watching me slip and skid on the steep, twisting path until I was out of sight.

I had never walked down this mountain path by myself. Rosa and I had accompanied Tito down twice to go to the mercado in Zinacantán, and our whole family had gone once for a festival. Rosa and I had explored the mountain a bit on our own, but I had never been alone—alone with the snapping of twigs behind me or the sudden movement in bushes or trees. Every turn, I expected to find a snake, or jaguar, or worse, a man. These mountains could hide the shame of poverty or crime, not to mention ski-masked rebels or paramilitary soldiers. Though nothing of that sort had happened in the year we had lived here, there were always stories of other villages, of other mountain hideouts.

I ran as fast as I could, sticking with the flattened path that lame Tito must have taken. The side of my face that my mother had slapped throbbed. I could still hear her voice, "Get out! Get out!" Did she mean it? Was she crying now? Would she run after me, as I was running after Rosa? The disgust in her eyes, was it for me or was it for Tito?

I was halfway down when I heard a woman's high-pitched plaintive voice to my far right. I couldn't make out the words. I scrambled up a boulder and saw them, Tito and Rosa, beside a stream. His shoe was off, and he was hopping on one foot toward Rosa, who was backing away. I jumped down and made my way in their direction, climbing over rocks and pushing through thick brush. I slipped, catching myself as I fell and scraping both hands. By the time I was able to see them again, Tito was on the ground holding his ankle and moaning in pain. Rosa was leaning forward, her arm extended to help him up. I shouted, just as he grabbed her and pulled her down, but her own scream masked mine. "What are you doing? Are you crazy?" she was saying. Absorbed in their struggle, neither heard me as I charged toward them.

Next thing I knew I was kicking Tito in his side with my thick brown shoes, as Rosa, wide-eyed, struggled underneath. Stunned, Tito turned and our eyes met just as I stomped my full weight onto his ankle. He let out a piercing scream, like that of a wild monkey. I stumbled and fell but rolled away just as he lunged at me. In that instant, a key flew out of his pocket at my feet. I snatched it up and shouted at Rosa, "Run, Rosa, run! Let's go!"

She hesitated, her open mouth, as wide as her eyes, so I grabbed her arm and pulled her forward. I glanced back only once to see Tito fall as he tried to bear weight on his injured foot.

By the time we reached the truck, I had told Rosa what I saw the morning before and then what Mamá had said today.

"How can we leave her?" she kept saying. "And the boys?"

"How can we stay?" I answered sharply; then I reached out and gently touched her upper arm encircled by a dark bruise.

"He held it so tight the whole way down, saying he needed to steady himself." Rosa shook her head, and continued, "We stopped by the stream so he could soak his ankle, but he started rubbing my back and playing with my hair. Why would he do that? Why *did* he do that?" Her voice rose in anger, "What is it with men. All of them! ¡Animales!" Her cheeks were blotched, her eyes fearful and wild.

Then she began to weep softly. "Oh, Mamá," she whispered, rubbing her face with her hands. When she looked up, she gasped, "Alma, did she hit you?"

Reaching toward my face, she gently touched my cheek. I flinched. "It's nothing," I said, thinking of Mamá's angry face and realizing I never wanted to lay eyes on her again. "We have to go, Rosa. Now!"

"But Mamá . . . and the boys," she pleaded again.

"Mamá will be better off without us. She will have Tito all to herself. That's what she wants. She won't leave him, and we can't stay there—not now. And think of it," I added, as the fact occurred to me, "they will have two fewer mouths to feed. Just the boys to worry about."

"And a baby," she said, more to herself than to me.

"Tito's baby," I reminded her, and she winced. I continued, "Rosa, it's not forever. We will see them again. Maybe we will find work and send them money, or make a home and bring Mamá there. Or maybe we will find Papá." Not waiting for an answer, I unlocked the truck door, handed her the key, and climbed into the passenger seat.

As Rosa slid into the driver's seat, the image of Tito showing her how to drive made me shiver. I hadn't thought of it at the time, but now I could see him in the middle leaning into her, his arm resting along the seat behind her shoulders, his hand on the steering wheel helping her steer. While she clutched the wheel nervously, his leg kept crossing over hers as he demonstrated the accelerator and the brake.

"I don't know if I can do this," Rosa said now, her hand trembling as she turned the key. The engine sputtered and coughed.

"Keep turning!" I said. "Tito did this, many times, remember, until it worked?"

"But I'm afraid to drive. I don't really know how, Alma, not really."

"You can do well enough. Just get us down to the paved road and then look for 190. I remember that number."

The engine finally roared, and as she shifted, we lurched forward and began a rough bumpy ride on the dirt road. When we finally reached the 190, she stepped on the brake.

"Which way?" she asked, tears streaming down her face.

"Not left. No, we need to head toward Tuxtla and Oaxaca. I think that would be right."

"Alma, what in God's name are we doing? This is crazy!" She wiped the tears from her cheek, paused for moment, and then looked at me with a hint of composure. "Think about it, really."

I sighed deeply and thought of Papá. What would he want us to do? Surely not go back to Tito. Then I thought of Mamá and what she had said about making a life for herself.

"Rosa, I think Mamá will do the best she can with or without us. Now we are old enough to take care of ourselves."

Rosa bowed her head, perhaps in prayer. We sat quietly for a while, the motor running. When she finally lifted her head, she said softly, "Tito might look for us in Oaxaca, you know, and he will certainly be looking for the truck."

When I turned to meet her eyes, I saw the fear. I desperately wanted to reassure her, but I was terrified myself. "You always say, trust in la Virgen. Put it in her hands. Well, let's do that. Just drive. Maybe she'll take us beyond Oaxaca, maybe even to el norte, and Papá."

Rosa moaned, "Oh, Alma." But she stepped on the gas, sending us on a hard turn to the right. We fishtailed a bit until the truck evened out, and then we were on our way. I let out a long sigh and hoped that la Virgen was indeed with us, riding shotgun.

2

Into the Fog

The mountain road twisted and curved sharply. Rattling along, the truck swerved from side to side as Rosa struggled with the wheel. Just as she straightened the truck, another curve, then another and another. It seemed to go on forever. At one point, clouds were hugging the side of the mountain and enveloping the truck in a thick gray mist. We could barely see the road ahead. Rosa slowed to a crawl, and we chugged along, both leaning forward, our eyes glued to just beyond the hood. For all we knew we were heading to the edge of a cliff. I could hear Rosa softly praying, and a part of me joined in as well. Finally, we turned a corner, and it was completely clear ahead. We screamed with joy and settled back in our seats. I think it was at this point that Rosa relaxed and became more confident in her driving, for the truck began to move smoothly, keeping to the right lane. Fortunately, there were no other cars on the road until we got closer to Tuxtla Gutiérrez, and then they whizzed by honking and speeding around us, often barely missing oncoming cars.

On the outskirts of the city, we pulled into a gas station to use the restroom and to check the truck. We had seen Tito pour water into something under the hood each time we had driven anywhere; as for gas, we didn't know where to begin. While we were fumbling to open the hood, a young man, who was cleaning the windows of a small orange truck, turned and asked if he could help. He was wearing a T-shirt with the words "Gracias a Dios" curved above hands in prayer.

Of course, he was speaking to Rosa. Even with strands of hair falling around her sweat-soaked face, she attracted attention.

Calmly and with an air of self-possession, Rosa said, "It needs some water."

He nodded. "Ah, radiator. My Papá's has a slow leak as well." Within seconds, he had popped the hood, unscrewed a cap, and poured water from a plastic bottle into the opening until it was full, then screwed it back on tightly, all with Rosa and I leaning over the hood and watching his every move.

"Need gas, too? I'm happy to help. No hay problema." Looking down at her hands, he added, "You don't want to get those lovely hands all dirty." When he smiled, two dimples appeared, giving him a boyish look.

Rosa glanced at me while she spoke to him, "I think we do. The line is below the half-way mark. But how much do you think we need," she paused, "to get to Oaxaca?"

"The state border or the city?" he asked, for Oaxaca was an entire state and Oaxaca City its capital in the center. We knew we were close to the state border, but the city itself was quite a bit beyond that.

"The city?" she asked, still looking at me.

"Oh, you'd need to fill up a couple of times. It's a good seven to eight hours from here, maybe more in this old thing." He began to walk around the truck, kicking each tire and examining them closely.

"Maybe we could get a bus in Tuxtla?" I said to Rosa, but before she could answer, the dimples were looking directly at me.

"Would cost you a lot more than putting gas in this old thing. A lot more—but then you could sit back and relax." His eyes swept back to Rosa, until I spoke.

"How much would you give us for the truck?" I asked curtly.

"¿Qué? What did you say?" he said, stepping back in surprise. "You in some kind of trouble?" He looked first at Rosa and then back at me.

"No, no," Rosa said. "My crazy sister is trying to be funny. Our father would kill us if we sold this old thing. He barely trusts us to drive it to visit our abuela. But she is sick, and we want to get there as soon as possible." Shooting a warning glance at me, she reached in her waistband and pulled out a small multicolored coin purse attached to a string that was fastened to her pants. Rosa was hiding money, too!

She handed him a few bills. "If you could put in as much as this will buy for now, we will manage."

He looked at the money and nodded.

We sat in the car while he pumped the gas, and when he finished, Rosa reached out the window to hand him another bill. "Gracias. Thank you so much for your help. God be with you."

Shaking his head, he backed away from the window. "No. Absolutely not. It was my pleasure," and the dimples flashed again. "Be careful, señoritas." Then he climbed into his orange truck and pulled away as Rosa started up the engine. We watched the needle move until it pointed all the way to full.

"How much did you give him?" I asked.

"I don't think that much. I'm not sure. Dios lo bendiga." She shifted into drive and stepped on the gas. "You see, la Virgen is with us!"

"Maybe so," I answered, but I wondered how generous "Dimples" would have been if Rosa had a wide nose and a few missing teeth.

How vividly I can recall that feeling of freedom and endless possibility as Rosa and I drove along that afternoon. Our gas tank was full. We each carried some money. And we were on our way to Oaxaca! I felt like an adult, grown up and in control. For me, all fear and uncertainty had disappeared, as well as any sense of regret. Only when I thought of the boys did I feel a twinge of sadness, yet I was certain we would be together again one day. At that moment, I felt a joy I hadn't known since before Papá disappeared.

After passing by Tuxtla Gutiérrez in the distance, I had settled back, closed my eyes, and dozed off for a bit. Suddenly Rosa's panicked voice woke me, "Which way do I go? I just passed a sign. I should have looked more closely!"

Ahead the road split, and it was coming upon us fast. "Stay on the one that seems straighter!" I cried. She did, and we continued on, both of us leaning forward again, peering at the road, at the fields flitting past beside us, and at the hills in the distance.

Less than an hour later, we saw the sign for Arriaga and realized our mistake. We had curved left, and now instead of crossing the Chiapas-Oaxaca border, we would be arriving in Arriaga, a city in Chiapas known mostly for La Bestia, the Beast, a deadly cargo train that desperate Central American migrants used to hitch a ride through Mexico on their way to el norte. Heavily patrolled by both police and ruthless gangs, the Beast was a dangerous free ride toward either a new beginning or a tragic end.

"Shouldn't we turn around?" I suggested, as Rosa pulled to the side of the road and rolled to a stop.

She sat for a moment and then said, "No. This might be better after all. If Tito is looking for us, if he found someone to drive him or notified police, they would be looking in Tuxtla and beyond, heading toward Oaxaca." As her own words seemed to sink in, she sighed and settled back into her seat, relaxed and relieved. Then she bowed her head, blessed herself, and said a silent prayer.

When she finally turned to me, I said, "Your Virgin?"

"Of course—nuestra Virgen," she said with a smug smile, our Virgin, then shifted into gear, scattering rocks as she pulled back onto the road.

I wanted to volley back, "Not just two stupid girls who don't have a clue as to where they are going?" but I kept it to myself, for until the tire blew out just a few minutes later, I was beginning to question my own disbelief.

Two cars stopped to help us after the truck spun in a circle and then slowly thumped and bumped backwards down an embankment, coming to a stop practically on its side. Shaken, Rosa and I awkwardly climbed out on her side with the help of two men. After assessing our few bruises, including the ones that had nothing to do with our little accident, we insisted we were fine and did not need to go to a hospital but would gladly accept a ride to a service station on the edge of Arriaga. Once there, we pretended to seek help until our ride drove away. Then exhausted, dripping with sweat, and still stunned by the turn of events, we skittered behind the building toward a low cement wall and sank onto the only patch of shade beneath a small tree. Rosa began to sob.

I kept my eyes on the hills and distant mountains that surrounded Arriaga, for even quaint Zinacantán had a beauty that was absent from this sad place. To the left of the gas station was a sagging one-story building with boarded windows and a door hanging off its hinges. To the right, there were two heaping mounds, one of dirt and one of gravel. A gray hawk, perched above us on a wire between two posts, scanned its surroundings. Clutched in my hand was a plastic water bottle given to me by someone at the scene of our accident. I unscrewed the top and took a long drink. It was warm and tasteless. I passed it to Rosa, who sniffled and then lifted it to her parched lips. I could hear the sounds of traffic and horns blaring in the distance.

"Now what?" I asked softly. "Should we find a bus station?"

Rosa sat watching the hawk and then finally spoke, almost in a whisper, "I think we are close enough to the Oaxacan border to walk. If it's 20 minutes by car, as that man said, it can't take too long on foot. We should save our money, Alma." She paused then added, "I'm not really sure what we are doing, are you?"

The hawk screeched, startling us both as it lifted off and flew behind us toward the mountains.

I turned to Rosa and waited until she met my eyes. "We need to get to Oaxaca to start," I began, "see if anyone has heard from Papá, and then, if not, on to el norte."

Rosa sighed and shook her head. "Alma, it will be enough to get to Oaxaca and find someone we can trust. Maybe Mundo. He was Papá's friend, so he might help us. Or maybe Father Estrada. He has always been kind to us."

I thought of the priest who had called authorities in an effort to find out something about Papá when he first went missing—but to no avail. I bit my lower lip to keep it from quivering. If there was still no word from Papá once we got to Oaxaca, I was determined to find a way to get to America. Something in my gut told me this was the answer. But for now, I simply nodded.

Following the sounds of ranchera music and the smells of street food, we made our way toward a clock tower in the distance. As we got closer to Arriaga's town square, our spirits lifted, and once there, to our stunned surprise, we discovered that we were standing beside train tracks. They ran straight through the heart of the city.

"Problem solved!" I joked to Rosa. "We can ride La Bestia to Oaxaca!"

But she wasn't laughing. Instead she turned to me with wide, serious eyes and said, "Alma, it's as good as a guide. We just need to follow the tracks . . . at a safe distance . . . and we will find our way. Then once we get across the state border, we can decide how best to get to Oaxaca City."

As we walked around the town square that afternoon, we noticed a sharp contrast between the locals, hurrying about in light dress, and the obvious migrants, huddled in small groups, wearing baseball caps, hooded sweatshirts, and backpacks. I took my backpack off my back and carried it on my arm like a purse, while Rosa, who wore her embroidered tote bag with its strap across her chest, reached in and pulled out the keys to Tito's truck. She let them dangle in her hand as we walked about. Whether we looked like locals or not, we certainly didn't look like Central Americans waiting for the train.

First, we headed to a small mercado, where we settled on a stack of tortillas, a covered plastic bowl of beans, extra water bottles, and then after some excited discussion, a small clay pot, matches, and masa with vanilla and cinnamon, so we could make warm atole to drink at night. The latter I tucked away in my backpack. Sitting on the grass, we each ate one tortilla and a finger scoop of beans, then packed the rest away in Rosa's tote. We took turns stretching out for a short nap; then, after refilling our water bottles, we set out walking, keeping a good distance between us and the train track, but close enough to follow its path.

Within half an hour we were out of the city, first walking past farmland and then into stretches of forest and fields of green. The first hour was exhilarating as we walked along embankments, through brush and beneath shaded trees, but soon we tired. Our pace slowed, and our feet ached. While we kept fairly close to the tracks, we had yet to see a train pass, so when we reached a steep ravine, we chose to dash across the train's bridge, our hearts pounding even though no sight nor sound of the Beast chased us. The sun had been descending for some time, and while there was still light, a cool breeze began to blow, which at first was soothing, but soon crept through our clothes, turning the day's sweat into a chilly dampness. We trudged past farmland again and could hear occasional cars on a distant road, but we had not yet encountered any living being beyond squirrels and birds and lizards. We took turns taking the lead, but a blister began to form on my left heel, and so I eased up and let Rosa pass. In a trance, I followed her for at least another hour, my eyes fixed to the ground before me.

Suddenly she stopped and I almost ran into her. Glancing up, I spotted the ruins of a building silhouetted against the deepening gray sky. She turned to me and I nodded. All I could think about was removing my heavy shoes and letting my feet breathe. Without a hint of caution, we stumbled toward it, only to be stopped by a curt, "Stop or I'll shoot!"

I was stunned. For hours we had trekked with no one else in sight. As I stood, my mouth open wide, Rosa wheeled around and pulled me into her arms, holding me tight, perhaps out of both fear and a need to protect me. She took in a breath and spoke to the shadows beneath the trees, "We are only women. We are harmless," words that should never be used in such a situation, for to tell a hungry coyote that you are a vulnerable rabbit is beyond foolish.

There was a rustle of branches, hushed whispers, then the sound of approaching footsteps, quick and firm. "You are alone?" the same voice asked.

"Yes." This time I answered, perhaps because Rosa now recognized the error of such a response, but also, I had detected a nervous, youthful quality to the voice—though it then dawned on me that in Chiapas, youth did not preclude danger.

"Step apart. One of you, come forward slowly. Muy despacio."

Rosalba loosened her grasp and took a few steps toward the voice. Suddenly three figures appeared from the brush; one held back pointing his gun toward Rosa, while the others approached. To my surprise, they were smaller than her. By Mexican standards, Rosa was a tall woman, so most men were at least her height. These men, who I soon saw were merely boys, were inches shorter. One tugged at her bag, pulling it over her head; the other searched along her hips, perhaps for money or weapons, but did not discover the coin purse in her waistband. Next it was my turn. After tossing my pack to his friend, one patted me down along my back and sides, avoiding my front. He looked no older than ten and smelled like a chicken coop.

As the gunman approached us, Rosa took my hand, lifted her chin and said to him calmly, "We are simply passing through. Please let us go on our way."

He was older and taller than the others, perhaps closer to my age. His thick mop of hair hung in his face, casting a shadow that kept his eyes hidden.

"What are you doing out here alone?" He spoke to us in Spanish, but the boy looking through Rosa's bag shouted something to him in the Indian language of my grandmother. I knew the sounds, the rhythm, but I did not comprehend the meaning. I turned to Rosa who whispered, "Our food, I think he said something about our food."

"Where are you going?" he asked again.

"To Oaxaca. Our father is waiting. He will worry if we do not hurry, so please let us go." Rosalba's voice quivered. She was squeezing my hand so tightly I thought I had screamed, but it was the boy's laugh that pierced the night.

"To Oaxaca and your father is waiting? ¿De verdad? Well, he has a bit of a wait anyway, so a few more minutes won't matter." With that he motioned us to walk ahead in the direction of the building and spoke sharply in that other language to the younger boys, who followed carrying our bags.

They wanted something certainly, something we would surely lose, but that was not the only thought that bore down on me as we entered the decaying shelter. It was the weight of what we had taken on with so little planning. Rosa, whose head was forever in the heavens, would say, "Put our faith in the Virgin of Guadalupe, and we will find our way," while I walked with feet planted firmly on the ground, believing that if so many others had made this journey, then we could as well. But certainly, those others did not just dash out the door in a fit of anger.

Trembling, we stepped through the doorway with hands tightly clasped. I saw that the shelter was missing one wall and most of a roof. A small campfire had been set up on this open end with pieces of wood neatly stacked in a pit surrounded by stones. A few herbs floated in a chipped clay pot of water nearby—apparently the beginnings of their evening meal. Rosalba and I circled to the far side of the pit. The boys followed, only to lay the packs at our feet and step back beside their companion.

I could see his face now in the firelight. His eyes were almost black and his brows thick under a disheveled horse's forelock of dark hair. A shadow of a mustache was beginning above his full lips. To our surprise, he lowered the gun to his side. "You will need protection," he was saying matter-of-factly, and nodded toward our packs. "Share your food, and we will guide and protect you on the rails."

"The rails? What are you talking about?" I asked, until I realized he assumed we were planning to take the Beast. "But we aren't taking the train! We are walking . . . and taking the bus."

As Rosa stepped forward, he instinctively raised the gun but then lowered it again. She paused, her eyes on the gun, and then spoke. "Our father is waiting for us just across the border, and then from there, we are taking a bus . . . to Oaxaca City, so we must hurry. He is waiting." Rosa caught my eye sharply.

"Yes," he acknowledged with a glint in his eye. "And I am walking to Mexico City where el presidente is waiting for me. He has planned a fiesta in my honor." He crossed his arms and waited.

After a moment of silence, both he and Rosalba began to speak at the same time. He nodded his head, indicating she should proceed. She glanced at me and then lifted her gaze to meet his.

"Where we are going is not your business," she said. "As for our food, we have very little. Please, have mercy on us and let us go on with our journey."

He sighed, slid the gun in his back pant waist, then seated himself on a wooden crate near the wall. He spoke slowly and with the weariness of an old man. "I am trying to get to el norte. My brother is working in a place called Temecula. He said when I turned fifteen, I could join him. That was over a year ago, and I have tried three times," he said, nodding his head. "I almost made it across the U.S. border without a coyote, only to be chased by la migra back across to Mexico. The other two times I was caught here in Mexico and sent back—to Guatemala. This is number four, and there will be five, six, seven: whatever it takes to get there."

He glanced at the boys who had squatted beside him. One had a runny nose; neither had bathed in quite a while.

"They have no mother or father, nadie," he said. "Their grand-mother died two months ago, and they hope to find their aunt, who lives in Texas."

He turned his gaze on me and paused. Our eyes locked, and he kept them there in silence. I felt like he could see through me, beyond the Alma I pretended to be: stubborn and defiant with my mother, cold and unyielding to Tito, bossy with my brothers. Did he hear my pounding heart?

He turned back to Rosalba, allowing me to exhale. "We are hungry. Tenemos mucha hambre," he said. "Please have mercy on *us* and share your food. We can help you get to Oaxaca or wherever you are going. Believe me, you'll need protection." I knew Rosa's answer before her lips parted to speak.

His name was Manuel, and he told us that as the second oldest of ten children, he had worked picking coffee beans at a young age to help his mother and father. But then his brother left with friends to work the fields in California and sent back more money than the family together had made in one whole year—enough to allow their mother to stay home with the youngest instead of working the fincas herself. So, Manuel had set out to join his brother.

I watched him slowly eat his tortilla, bit by bit, as he watched the boys devour theirs in two bites. He told us he'd met Chuy and Benito on his last deportation from Mexico, and though he had tried to convince them to return to their village, they had insisted on trying one more time. Apparently, they had evaded placement in an orphanage by claiming to be the sons of another man in their group. This man had gone along with their story, but when they reached the border of Guatemala, he simply told them to go home and left without a backward glance.

"It is better for me to travel alone. But what can I do?" Manuel said, nodding his head toward the two.

I could not look at his dark, piercing eyes without trembling inside, so I had taken the masa and the small clay pot from my pack and knelt at the fire. Dissolving the masa and spices in water, I busied myself with the task of preparing the atole. While Rosa and he talked softly, I watched as it boiled and thickened; then, removing the pot from the fire, I set it aside to cool.

"The trains are very dangerous, no?" Rosa was asking, as I watched the steam rise. The boys were huddled beside me, eagerly waiting for the sweet drink to cool. I stretched out my weary legs and leaned back against the wall. I desperately wanted to remove my clunky shoes, but not in Manuel's presence.

"Not if you know what you're doing. And I do," Manuel was saying with pride. "When to jump on, how to climb to the top, how to hold steady, where the tunnels are, and of course when to jump off so you don't get caught at a checkpoint. I could help you. But you have to do as I say, or yes, you could be killed—or worse, watch the train take your leg and leave the rest behind."

My eyes widened in horror as I gasped at this image, and he turned to me laughing. I felt my face flush as he reached out and grabbed my leg and yanked. "Whooosh! Like that it's gone!" I screamed, and the boys giggled.

"I'm not riding on top of any train!" I kept my eyes on Rosa, but I could still feel my leg tingling where his hand had been.

Rosa reached for the atole and tested it before scooping a bit with her fingers then passing it next to the boys. "Don't worry, Alma, we aren't riding on top of any trains," she said. She turned to Manuel. "I just wondered if there was a safer way to ride them, like sitting inside a car."

Manuel laughed and spoke to the boys in their language and soon all three were laughing at us. That's when I came to my senses. If

anyone jumped on trains, it would be me, not Rosalba. She feared
crossing the tree trunk bridge that I used daily, instead walking
clear around the arroyo to a safer path. With my head straight now, I
turned to Manuel and said, "I thought you preferred to travel alone.
Why would you want us along as well?"

He shrugged and shifted his eyes downward, allowing me to watch
his face as he answered. His nose was long and straight, his lashes
thick like his eyebrows. "I don't know. Guess I figured two girls alone
might need some help." He swept his fingers through his thick hair,
which fell back over his forehead immediately. "And I already have
these two, so what's two more?" He paused, then looked up at me and
added, "Whatever. Do what you want. I don't care. No me importa."
Then he looked away.

Suddenly, overcome with an agitation that I couldn't explain, I
heard myself say, "And you got caught every time you tried, didn't
you? Why should we stick with you?"

"Alma!" Rosa snapped.

"Well, it's true, isn't it? How can he show us the way—even to
Oaxaca—when he's been sent back each time?" All I could think of
was that we had wasted time, given up some of our food, and why . . .
so some boy from Guatemala could tell us stories and grab my leg?
¡Basta!

I struggled to my feet, wincing at the pain of my blistered heel.
"Just because you have a gun, you think you can boss people around?"
Trembling I turned to Rosa. "We need to go," I said stubbornly.

"Go where?" Rosa asked, half laughing, which only piqued my
anger. "It's dark. It's late. We need to sleep and get a fresh start at
dawn. You're being foolish. Sit down!"

I looked at the boys scooping atole into their mouths with dirty
fingers, at Manuel who glared up from under his thick brows, and at
Rosa who was patting the ground beside her. I thought of Mamá and
how she turned her back as I scurried down the mountain. I thought

of Papá and how safe I felt when he held me in his arms. I wanted to scream and run out into the darkness, but instead I stamped my foot and said, "I don't want to sleep here. I don't trust them. What if we wake and our things are gone?"

Before Rosa could answer, Manuel jumped to his feet and, reaching behind his back, pulled out the gun. In one swift movement, it lay at my feet.

"Here, es tuyo!" he hissed. "Sleep in peace." And he walked out into the night.

I have often wondered what course our lives would have taken if I had not been so difficult. But Rosa later said that the words I spoke were true, as impulsive statements often are, and that this time the Virgin had placed them on my tongue to send Manuel into the night. Virgin or not, I tend to think the words came from a darker place. But still, if we had all been sitting quietly together in that shelter, if we had fallen asleep, who knows what might have happened. Instead, no sooner had Manuel stepped out through the doorway, then we heard shouts of surprise, followed by thuds and moans that sent the boys scampering out the back and into the field like frightened rabbits. Terrified, Rosa and I had reached for our packs and were stumbling for the opening as well, when Manuel was thrust through the doorway, bleeding from his nose, with an arm around his neck and a knife at his throat.

We froze as the man that held him shouted, "Don't move or he is a dead man." An animal-like groan echoed in the distance, and in my fear, I swore I felt the ground tremble.

The smell of alcohol reached me first, then Manuel's pleadings. "No," he was saying. "I have never seen them before. They are not with me. I travel alone."

There were two men, both about Tito's age, dressed in soiled T-shirts and jeans. One with a thick mustache held a bottle, the other, slightly balding, the knife. "No?" one was saying. "Not together? Looks like someone is playing house here." Their guttural laughs and harsh sneers reminded me of the street boys who once chased me home from school in Oaxaca.

The one with the bottle approached us and, lifting it toward Rosalba, used it to stroke her chin. "Are you his hermana? His novia. Or his puta?" Rosa cringed. Sister, girlfriend, whore!

"They are not with me!" Manuel insisted. "I don't even know their names." Then he turned toward us. "Tell them. Tell them we are not traveling together!"

A tear streamed down Rosa's cheek, and it was then that I felt the cold metal in my right hand. Obstructed by my pack, pressed tightly against my breast was Manuel's gun. I had scooped it up when I'd grabbed my pack. The walls of the structure rattled slightly, and a rumbling roar echoed in the distance. I imagined a creature from the bowels of hell, heaving its way up through the earth.

I stepped back as the man beside Rosalba spit in her face, then cracked the bottle across her cheek knocking her off her feet. "Dirty Guatemalans," he hissed. "Stay home where you belong. Don't bring your filth to our blessed Chiapas."

"Chiapas? Chiapas? But we *are* from Chiapas! We are not Guatemalans!" I pleaded, at the same time realizing that Manuel had been trying to protect us. Men in Chiapas often watched for Central American immigrants who crossed the border into Mexico and then took matters into their own hands. Despite our same skin color, that simple line of division defined a hatred that I had only heard of before. I thought of my cousins who joked about throwing rocks at a group of Salvadorans.

The man laughed harshly and turned toward me. "Of course, you are from Chiapas," he said shaking his head and taking a step forward.

I moved back, shouting the name of our village, but his red-rimmed eyes seemed to glow as the devil's howl grew louder.

"Stop!" I screamed as I pulled out the gun. My hand shook as I tried to hold it steady. He lifted his chin in derisive laughter; then I saw his arm swinging upwards. I closed my eyes and squeezed the trigger.

A loud crack split the air as I was knocked back from the force of the gun and stumbled over a pile of wood. As I fell, I heard screams and groans, then the sound of dirt and rocks scattering onto the fire. I scrambled to my feet in complete darkness. Beside me, I could hear Rosa's soft moans as she struggled to stand as well. Then someone was coming toward us. I raised my pack in front of my face to ward off the blow, but an arm went around me instead, and Manuel's voice, reassuring and firm, said, "Alma, soy yo, Alma, it's me." Then, as if in flight, my feet left the ground with Manuel's arm underneath mine, lifting me, pulling me, pushing me out the back, into the field.

"Rosa!" I shouted.

"She's here, right behind us!" Manuel said, and I could hear her panting as well.

"Faster, faster," he kept saying. We ran in the darkness, stumbling over rocks, as we made our way to what I now realized was the rumbling roar of a freight train. My legs were heavy with fear, but Manuel's arm never left mine.

Then we were beside the rattling boxcars, running, panting, gasping. Sparks flew from its wheels, lighting our way. Slinging my backpack over one shoulder, I glanced back to see Rosa, with the boys on either side of her, just a few feet behind.

"Grab the metal bar, the ladder!" Manuel shouted, pointing just above waist level. We were close enough now to see the boxcar ladder on the inside corner above a set of wheels. It was within arm's reach, and though the train was slowing, it still seemed fast and frightening to me.

"Rosa!" I screamed. "Rosa!"

I could hear her shouting, "Go! Go! I'm right behind!"

Manuel was panting beside me, then a quick intake of breath and he shouted, "Up, up! ¡Ahora! Now, now, now!"

"I can't. No!" But my arm reached out anyway, my legs propelled me forward, and I flew, grabbing the metal bar and heaving myself up with a determined force. Beneath me I felt suction like the undertow of the river in Chiapas, but I thrust upward with a grunt. The strap of my pack tugged hard on my shoulder as it flung back, hitting with a thud repeatedly as I climbed the roaring monster. My hands grasped, clawed, and clung. My feet found footholds I couldn't see. I could hear movement below me, but my focus stayed on the few feet above. Suddenly I found the top and pulled myself up with a groan, but a searing pain tore through me as my leg scraped a jagged edge. Cold air stung my cheeks like dry ice. My long braid flew up with such force, I feared it would pull me backwards. I crawled forward to the center of the boxcar's roof, trembling, sobbing; then, I turned to reach for Rosa.

"Down. Just lie flat." Manuel's voice in my ear. I obeyed and collapsed, face down, eyes closed. I could hear muffled shouts behind me, but when I lifted my head, the roar blew them away.

"Rosa!" I shouted her name into the wind, then lowered my head and strained to hear an answer. "Where's Rosa?" I cried.

Manuel was beside me again, shouting in my ear. "With the boys . . . behind us. Just keep down and stay quiet. I'm not sure why the train is slowing. Might be a checkpoint." But no sooner had he spoken these words then the train began to pick up speed. I heard Manuel let out a long, deep sigh.

"Don't worry, Alma, it will be okay," he said, trying to comfort me.

"But Rosa, did you see her? Are you sure she got on?"

His face told me the answer before he could speak. "I think I heard the boys shout that they were all right, but I could go back and check." He sat up and glanced back, then let out a long whistle. He repeated this, three times. No answer. "The moon is bright tonight. I can see well enough. It would just take a few minutes. I won't be long."

My heart was pounding so hard I thought it would burst through my chest. I didn't want to be left alone, but I was desperate to know about Rosa. I wasn't going anywhere without her. What if she didn't make it? What if she was injured or stranded alone back there, or worse?

I'd jump off the damn train if I had to.

"Are you sure you can do this?" I asked, raising up on one arm and looking toward the edge.

"I've done it many times. Many, many times."

"And you'll only be gone a few minutes?"

"Prometo. I promise."

I squeezed my eyes shut. "Go! But please hurry, and be careful!"

I heard him land on the next car, but beyond that was only the roar of the wind in my ears. I opened my eyes and stared into the darkness, and waited, and waited. Minutes passed. I shouted into the darkness, but no answer returned. I shouted again and again until my voice was hoarse, but the roar of the train only tossed my words into the air and blew them away like shredded corn husks.

I curled up in a fetal position, hugging my pack to my chest, and began to sob softly as the train lurched and lumbered its way through Chiapas. The harsh rocking movement stirred memories of that horrible bus ride from Oaxaca and my life with Papá to Chiapas and Tito's stick house. How my heart had ached with each turn of the wheel away from Papá then, and now, though these wheels were turning back toward him, it meant nothing without Rosa. I prayed to her Blessed Virgin with all my might that she was with me on this train, Oaxaca bound.

Utterly exhausted, I was eventually rocked into a deep sleep, dreaming of dark winged creatures swooping high and low as they maneuvered their way through narrow canyon passes.

When I woke, I was surrounded in gray. I struggled to lift my head, but my rigid neck would not yield. I pushed up with my arms and slowly turned my head forward. As I bent my knees, a pain shot up my leg and continued to throb as I drew them up and under me. Slowly I rose up, lifted my head, and looked around.

Like our drive down the mountain, I was immersed in a fog so thick I could not see the edge of the boxcar. A cold mist soaked my face and hair like steady rain, and the wind whistled like one hundred flutes playing an ominous song. I was soaring through the heavens, my heart pounding in both terror and an unmistakable awe. Then I remembered.

"Manuel!" I gasped, reaching out beside me, my arms stretching and moving about the periphery. Nothing.

"Rosa?" I shouted. "Manuel! Rosa!"

No answer. Only the wind's foreboding howl.

3

Angels' Mist

Suddenly I heard singing. A chorus of voices rose behind me, like a throng of angels coming to my rescue. I lifted my head and strained to hear what hymn they sang or what message they might be bringing. Instead what I heard in the distance sounded more like cantina music—rough, loud, and off-key, but it comforted me, nonetheless, for it did not fade as the train jerked clumsily through the fog. Clearly it was not coming from a passing village, but somewhere on this train. I was not entirely alone.

I tried shouting out again, calling for Rosa and Manuel, but the only sound to return was this drunken chorus, very faint in the distance. Hopefully, Rosa was a few cars back, as Manuel had said. And Manuel himself? Remembering his story of the dangers of the train, I cringed at the thought of what horror might have befallen him. It was then that I remembered the red-rimmed eyes and the crack of the gun, and I sat up suddenly and shuddered. My God, had I killed that man? Had I taken a life? I had completely forgotten about that moment when I pulled the trigger. Surely, I would be punished. Perhaps, I was being punished right now, with Rosa and Manuel gone.

But as the sky began to lighten, the singing stopped, and soon after, the train began to slow. The dark shades of gray had slowly turned white until a piercing beam of light broke through the mist. The warmth caressed my cheeks as I lifted my face to greet the sun. In an instant the clouds were gone, and around me I could see stretches of pasture dotted with a few cows. I also discovered that I was smack in the middle of a rust-colored boxcar with little more than an arm's length of roof on either side and nothing protecting me from sliding right off. Before I had time to panic, however, I heard shouts. Turning, I gasped. Manuel was running along the top of the car behind me, and in one terrifying leap, he landed with a thud on the edge of my car, then crawled up beside me.

"Alma, I'm so sorry I left you alone." He struggled to catch his breath. "I went back to find the others, and then the fog came and I couldn't return. Lo siento mucho." He held onto my arm with both of his hands, as I stared back in wonder. "Are you all right?" he whispered.

"Yes," I managed. "I just can't believe my eyes. I thought you were . . . that you had . . . ." I looked to edge of the roof.

He smiled and shook his head. "Not me. I can move like a cat on these cars. ¡No hay problema!"

"And Rosa?" I trembled and held my breath.

"She's farther back than I thought and too low for you to see from here. But she's okay, just shaken up and worried about you, especially because you were alone in the fog." He turned back and, placing his fingers in his mouth, let out a long whistle. He did this again and again, until we heard a very faint one in return.

"Now Rosa knows you are okay." He sat back on his heels and ran his hands through his hair.

"Thank God," I sighed, but I couldn't stop shaking. I fought back tears. "And the singing. I heard singing, I think," I said, looking questioningly at Manuel.

He nodded and laughed. "Yes, you weren't hearing things. To keep awake, men sometimes sing. No one sleeps at night on these trains. Too dangerous."

I shuddered to think I had fallen asleep. "So, they won't fall off?" I asked.

"That, and . . ." He paused. "Well, a seemingly friendly companion could help himself to your belongings, and sometimes there are dangerous people . . . gangs that claim a particular train. They demand money for protection and permission to ride, or they don't ask at all—just take." He looked far off into the distance. His sweatshirt was torn at the shoulder and his cheek was smudged in black. "I saw a man tossed off one time. May he rest in peace, " he said softly, bowing his head. Then with a deep sigh, he continued, "I tried to get back to you, but the fog was so thick. I figured it would keep you safe from harm, as long as you didn't panic. No one moves about these trains in the fog, and I headed back as soon as it started to lift."

"No, it's okay. I'm all right. Just so relieved and thankful that you found Rosa."

My Rosa, I kept thinking, *she's okay. She's here with me, and we're on our way to Oaxaca!* I buried my face in my hands.

Then I heard him say, "Rosa said if anyone could ride on top of a train alone in the fog, it was you." When I looked up, he was leaning in toward me, and his dark eyes were shining like the eyes of a raven in the sun. I held my breath. Then glancing away, he added, "We've been lucky. Let's hope the gods stay with us."

We swayed in silence as the train eased on down the tracks.

An unsettled feeling was poking at my newfound relief, and again I remembered. "Manuel," I asked timidly. "That man . . . did I kill him? ¿Está muerto?" I looked up into his face to see his immediate response. If he tried to lie, to protect me from the truth, I would know it. But what I saw was not what I expected. First his eyes, then his face, then his whole body shaking—with laughter.

"No, pobrecita, no, you did not kill that pendejo, though you may have destroyed the hearing in his ear," he said between chuckles.

"What do you mean?" I asked, confused. I'd heard the gun. I had seen him fall.

"It was not a real gun, Alma. My uncle used it to start dog races. I took it my last time home. I knew it might serve me well—and it did. You saved us from a beating—or worse."

"You mean they might have killed us?"

"Well, I suppose it depends on how drunk they were, but I meant more . . ." He looked down at his hands. ". . . what they might have done to you and Rosa."

My heart pounded and my hands turned prickly cold.

"I'm sorry I didn't trust you, Manuel," I whispered.

He shook his head. "You have nothing to be sorry about. How could you know? I might have been a thief. You have to be careful on this journey. Don't trust anyone—especially people of authority. And anyway, if you hadn't chased me away, those two could have snuck up on us all, taken our gun, and the ending might have been much worse."

Suddenly he sat up and looked around. "The train is slowing again. It must be the checkpoint. Listen, this is the plan. I've already discussed it with the boys and Rosa." Then he proceeded to tell me that if the train did slow for a stop, he and the boys must run or they'd be caught by the Mexican authorities and sent back, once again, to Guatemala. Rosa and I were safe, of course, being Mexican citizens, and the officials might let us go; however, sometimes the authorities were not so honest. There was a chance we could be robbed or, as he put it earlier— worse, so he advised that we all stick together and run, and Rosa had agreed.

This time I chose to trust Manuel.

"Come," he was saying. "Follow me down the ladder. Hold tight and stay quiet."

"Will the boys know to leave now?"

He nodded toward the field beside us. "You'll soon see people leaping off this train like fleas off a dog. They will know."

I slung my pack onto my back and crawled behind Manuel. My thigh throbbed where I had scraped it climbing up. I could see a slight tear in my pants, encircled by a reddish stain. I took a deep breath and waited, as Manuel slid over the edge and down to the top rung. Looking down now in the bright light of day, I trembled. How had I gotten up there? The ladder ended far below the top. How had I managed to propel myself those last few feet? Perhaps Rosa's Virgin of Guadalupe was with me after all.

Manuel had climbed down a few rungs and held his hand up toward me. "Slide down, I'll help you."

I could see the ground between the cars moving swiftly past and the massive wheels of the car behind turning and spitting up gravel in its wake. There was no way I could do this. Not until the cars stopped. They'd have to go on without me.

I shook my head at Manuel. "¡No puedo! I can't. Not while it's moving."

"Hold tight to the top, and there's a foot hold here and here. You can do it." He glanced to his right around the corner of the car then back up at me. "Let it slow a bit more. Then try." Reaching up, he added, "Give me your pack."

I slid it down to him with only a moment's hesitation. The thought entered my mind that he could run with it—my few meager belongings. My little box of stars. But I knew he wouldn't. He secured it over his shoulder, then smiled up at me. "Relax. We'll give it a minute. You can do it, you'll see."

I turned around on my knees and placed my toes over the edge. The car lurched from side to side, rocking my body unsteadily. I thought of my shoes that my mother had gotten from the church. "They're from America," she had said, donated from some church in el norte. But they were not shiny or sleek, or colorful or new, like I imagined an American teenager's shoes would be. These were dull, round, and brown, with laces and a thick sole, but so far, they had served me well. I thought of Tito crying out as I stomped on his ankle, and right now, they were clearly a godsend: The sole could grip, and the shoes would not slip off.

I closed my eyes and waited for the train to ease up, but even as it slowed, the force of the rocking was still too much for me.

"Alma," Manuel's voice rose up from below, "we have to go now. If we wait, they may catch us. Please!"

Just as he spoke, I heard shouts from the ground. Glancing over my right shoulder, I saw Rosa and the boys running along a slight bank beside the car. Behind them several others were running through the field away from the train. Rosa stopped and put her hands to her face. She looked frightened for me. "Oh Alma!" she cried, scaring me even more. But the boys pulled her into the nearby bushes and out of sight of any authorities that might be ahead.

"Now, Alma!" Manuel insisted. "¡Ahora!"

I scooted back, my knees firmly on the edge. One quick jerk and I'd be down between the cars and under the wheels. I said a silent prayer, not to the Virgin but to my father: *Please help me. Dame valor, give me the courage of Dolores.* I slid back slowly, my hands grabbing the edge until my feet found the protruding ledge below. I froze; what now? Where could my hands go? I was literally hanging onto the right corner of the boxcar. I could see the green bank rolling along beside me. Perhaps I could just jump. I'd jumped out of trees, off of roofs, even off of a moving horse.

"Don't stop, Alma. Keep going—one smooth move down and I've got you."

I stretched my leg down, grimacing at the pain in my thigh, and moved one hand toward the ledge below. Suddenly the car leaned into a curve and I slipped, my feet and my hands losing contact with the boxcar. And I thought of the brown mare, how I'd sat side-saddle, then gave a push with my legs. Up and out. So I kicked, bucking like a horse, my feet slamming against the car. I propelled my body up and away, as if I was diving sideways off of the train. In an instant, I crashed onto the bank and rolled downhill, coming to rest a few meters from the track.

I lay still and struggled to catch my breath as the train rattled by. My shoulder throbbed in rhythm with my thigh, and my head and neck ached, but otherwise, I was intact. I felt strangely calm, like I was waking from a dream, feeling sleepy, yet trying to remember every detail.

I watched as Manuel leapt from the train, tumbled to a stop, then jumped to his feet and ran rapidly in my direction. Behind me I heard shouts—Rosa and the boys racing toward me. Slowly I sat up. My shoulder refused to move, so I hugged it close to my side.

Rosa flung herself at me and clung and cried. The boys, wide-eyed, just stared. And Manuel sank down beside me, panting, then reached up and stroked my hair. Despite the sharp pain in my shoulder, I smiled. No one was singing now, but I was surrounded by angels.

4

Little Box of Stars

It was almost like Christmas. Rosa had taken her treasured, multi-colored rebozo from her bag and tied it around me as a sling for my shoulder. Little Chuy retrieved from the depths of his pocket a tiny piece of chocolate half-melted into its foil wrapping, while Benito handed me a stick of gum. And Manuel, Manuel gave me his eyes—so full of concern, of remorse, of apology. Did I see what I thought I saw in those eyes? His caress, when he stroked my hair, felt so tender, like Papá's. My heart quietly danced beneath the rainbow of colors.

From the field beside us came the sound of voices and footsteps. The boys jumped to their feet and looked all around. Uniformed men strode down along the track, while others appeared from the field, herding the few they'd caught in the skirmish. Chuy and Benito whispered to each other, then looked questioningly at Manuel, but he continued to kneel, head lowered, until without a glance at them, he simply shook his head. In a flash they took off, dashing between boxcars in the opposite direction and out of sight.

Manuel lifted his eyes to mine, then to Rosalba's, and sighed. "May our nahuales guide us and the saints protect us." He rose, stood before us, and faced the approaching men.

Rosa helped me to my feet. I winced as I set my shoulders back and lifted my chin.

"But Manuel . . . you should flee!" I pleaded, though I knew it was too late anyway. He should have as soon as he hit the ground. But he hadn't because of me. "I'm so sorry," I whispered.

Manuel shook his head. "When I first met you, I thought tu nahual, your animal spirit, was a horse, a stubborn wild horse. But now I am wondering, perhaps a hawk or a falcon—something that flies?" He grinned down at me.

"No," Rosa said. "A horse with wings. That's our Alma."

"If I was," I said, trembling, "I'd spirit us all away!"

The officers motioned us toward the front of the train. As we walked, I glanced up at the weathered boxcars. They were frightening just at a standstill; I couldn't believe I'd tackled one in motion.

The man with the largest belly commanded us to sit along the bank. Two guards stood before us, hands firmly resting at their hips on their guns. There must have been at least twenty of us or more, mostly men, except for one other woman, but the officers stared blankly beyond our heads, as if we weren't even there. Then another police officer approached and motioned for the first three on the bank to follow, and they were taken around a bend beyond our view.

We sat in silence, like the train, waiting. Only the sounds of muffled voices in the distance, the wind in the brush, and the gravel crunching as our guards shifted from foot to foot. What would happen now? Where would they take us? When our turn came, we rose together.

"Hurry, hurry, vámonos," a sharp-beaked officer insisted. His voice matched his bird-like face, high-pitched and shrill. Even his outstretched arm waved us forward like a wing, though as I passed, the sharp scent of body odor hit me. No bird gave off such a potent smell.

The large man, who seemed to be in charge, stood back, arms folded and resting atop his protruding belly. Two other officers approached us, one asking, "What have you got?"

Rosa and I looked at each other, then at Manuel.

Manuel whispered, eyes cast down, "Money. They want to know what money we have."

"Wait, wait, wait." A deep voice boomed from the back as the large man stepped forward. "What are you doing, Ramírez? These are just kids. Just send them back."

He approached, looking us up and down, then turned on his heel. "Next!" he commanded to the bird-man. Then to Ramírez, "We don't have time for this. Put them in the vehicle."

I glanced toward the empty vehicle. Where had the others gone? I turned toward the field and saw in the distance figures moving rapidly away. Had they let them go?

"Wait," I said. "We have money as well." I reached in my pocket and pulled out a few bills that I'd placed there in Arriaga. I offered it first to Ramírez and then to the one in command. "Please, let us go. Our father is waiting in Oaxaca."

The large man approached me, took the money from my hand, but kept his eyes on mine. "Where are you from? Guatemala? El Salvador? Honduras?"

"No. We are from Mexico. I was born in Oaxaca, but we have lived in Chiapas since . . . for this past year." I turned to Rosa and Manuel. "This is my sister and . . . my brother."

Ramírez was laughing. "If you are from Mexico, why didn't you just take a bus?" He shook his head. "Nice try, idiots."

Manuel stepped forward. "Our cousin dared us. Said he'd give us thirty pesos if we rode it to Oaxaca."

"Thirty pesos? ¡Estúpidos!" the third officer retorted.

The officer in charge nodded. "Pretty stupid thing to do for thirty pesos. You could have been killed." He fingered the money. "What will you do in Oaxaca?" he asked.

I swallowed. "My father has found work for us."

"Why didn't your father come and get you?" Ramírez spit out the words, then turned to his boss. "They're lying. They're not Mexicans."

"Shut up, you moron. Now go get the next group. I'll deal with these." He turned back to me and stepped closer. His thick mustache curled over his fat lip. It was threaded with gray, like Tito's. "How many stars does the Mexican flag have, four or five?" he asked.

I shook my head. "It doesn't have any stars. Not the Mexican flag." I knew that Honduras's flag had stars, but I wasn't sure how many.

"What do you use to make salsa?"

What did he mean? Spices, mortar? I knitted my brow quizzically. Was it different in Central America? My grandmother used the Indian terms, but what if they were the same as Guatemalan? Then I heard Rosa say beside me, "You mean the molcajete? Forgive me. My sister hates to cook. She'd rather play with numbers on her paper."

The numbers! I thought of my little box of stars as the man paused and turned to Manuel. Grabbing his T-shirt between his fingers, he asked him, "And what do you call this?" I held my breath. He was trying to trick us or catch us in a lie. In Mexico, we usually called it camiseta. In Guatemala, perhaps something else—playera?

"My box!" I shouted. "Wait! In my box I have papers—my school grades from Oaxaca." I reached for my pack on Manuel's back, grimacing as my shoulder sent a jolt of pain. I knelt on the ground, struggling to open it, until Rosa squatted beside me and unzipped it with ease. I had wrapped the box in my red rebozo. As I opened the layers, I held my breath. How had it weathered our travels? Was it still intact? My father had given me the hand-painted box filled with stickers and stars when I was seven. Whenever he returned from el norte, I would greet him with a stack of schoolwork and my little box of stars. I loved watching his large hands open the lid, his fingers slipping through the selection until he found just the right star to reward my hard work.

As I spread open the cloth and found the box whole and undamaged, I wondered if his hands would ever touch it again. It was a deep shade of blue with one white calla lily painted on the lid, its stem arching down over the side. My eyes filled with tears as I lifted the lid and searched through my treasures. *¿Dónde estás, Papá?* His picture from the newspaper was still there, safely tucked in a corner—and at the bottom, folded in half, was my last report card from 1998. This one he had never seen.

I unfolded it slowly and blinked back my tears; then still kneeling, I held it up to the officer, who leaned forward. Squinting, he looked it over, then nodded.

"What happened to your shoulder?" he asked.

I looked sheepishly away. "I fell from the train."

"She needs a doctor," Rosa spoke beside me. "Please let us go on to Oaxaca. My father will take care of us. Please, let us go."

He didn't speak, but glanced first at the approaching men and then at the money in his hand. He signaled for the men to be seated and then turned back to us. He watched in silence as Rosa took the school report, placed it in my box, gently re-wrapped the red cloth, and placed the small bundle securely in my bag. Slowly she helped me stand.

Manuel took the bag, slung it over his shoulder, and stepped forward, "It was my fault," he said, his voice quivering. "I talked them into riding the train. And . . . well . . . it's my fault she fell. I should have taken better care . . . of my sisters." He bowed his head and mumbled, "At least let them get to Oaxaca . . . to Papá. Please."

"Well, you should be ashamed of yourself, young man!" he snapped, startling Manuel. "And you should be punished. But I'm sure your father will see to that." He tossed my money at my feet. "Now get the hell out of here. And stay away from those trains." Then he turned on his heel and strode toward the poor souls who were emptying their pockets a few feet away.

Spotting a road beyond an embankment, we scurried up and began to walk in the direction the train was facing. My shoulder and thigh throbbed with each step of my foot, as if a taut wire connected the two and tugged harshly as I plodded along. At the same time, it felt good to have my feet solidly on the ground. It still amazed me that I had scaled that train, ridden through the dead of night, and made my graceful departure while it was still in motion.

Rosa was limping along as well, and it occurred to me that she had had to leap from the moving train too, though from a lesser height. "Are you okay?" I asked, turning to her bruised face. Her cheek was swollen and discolored where the man had struck her with the bottle.

"I'm just so tired," she said, hugging my good arm and resting her head on my shoulder for a moment as we walked.

Manuel kept glancing back, and I knew he was worrying about Chuy and Benito.

"What do you think happened to them?" I asked.

He shrugged. "Hard to say. They've been through this before. They'll be okay," he said, but his face showed his doubt and concern. "Thanks for saying I was your brother," he added, his face softening.

My cheeks burned as I said, "Thanks for staying with us. You didn't have to."

Our eyes met briefly, and he looked away first. Why had he chosen to stay? Was it possible he cared for me? But how? I wasn't beautiful, like Rosa—yet he seemed to like me.

We walked a bit in silence and then, gazing at the horizon, he said, "We are definitely in Oaxaca and probably close to Ixtepec. They sometimes stop the train before it gets too close to a city. But I'm not sure how far that would be on foot."

"Do you know how far we are from Oaxaca City?" Rosa asked, but Manuel just shook his head.

On either side of the road, farmland stretched on forever, only a few small buildings in the far distance ahead to the right. As the sun rose, and with no trees for shade, we began to feel its heat.

To distract myself from the heat and the pain, I did what I often do to pass the time; I played with numbers in my head. I pictured in my mind a blank piece of paper and a freshly sharpened pencil. First,

I found the point at which we were walking and then the buildings beyond, imagining a perfect diagonal line. Then I formed a right triangle with this diagonal as my hypotenuse. So, as I trudged along between Manuel and Rosa, I created measurements and computed distances in an effort not to focus on the pulsating pain in my shoulder and leg.

If it was two kilometers north, squared, plus 2.5 kilometers east, squared, that'd be . . . 10.25. Square root of 10.25 is about . . . 3.2 kilometers. The buildings are 3.2 kilometers away. Now, if it was 2.5 kilometers north and . . .

Suddenly Rosa dropped beside me, first onto her knees and then over on her side. I sank down, screaming out both in pain and alarm. "Rosa, Rosa!" I shook her shoulders with my good hand. Her eyes rolled back and drool oozed from the corner of her lip and down her cheek. Her lips were dry and cracked.

Manuel helped me move her limp body off the hot pavement and onto the field beside the road. I reached into my pack for water, but my bottle was empty. Manuel pulled a half-filled bottle of murky water from his sack, then taking off his T-shirt, he wrapped it over the opening. Supporting Rosa's head with one hand, he tipped the bottle up. The water that dripped through the shirt, he aimed at her lips, explaining, "I got this water from a stream, but a guy told me this might make it safer to drink."

Rosa moaned and her eyes fluttered, then opened. "Alma? Alma?" she called my name, in a little girl's voice.

"I'm right here. It's okay. Estoy aquí."

"Everything is spinning. And my head is pounding."

Manuel sat back on his heels and looked toward the buildings in the distance. "I'll see if I can get help. I'll be right back." He sprinted shirtless, in the direction of the buildings.

I stretched out beside her and stroked her arm. "Just relax. It will be okay."

Tears began to stream down her cheeks. "Oh, Alma. What have we done?" she asked, squeezing my arm. "Maybe we should just go back."

"Go back? What are you saying? To Tito?"

She shook her head, "No, no of course not. I don't know what I mean," then softly, "I miss Mamá and the boys . . . and Papá." She was quiet for a moment; then a sob erupted as she said, "Maybe Mamá's right. He must be dead. Otherwise we would have heard something."

"Rosa," I said firmly, for her statement that Papá might be dead only made my will stronger. "The only way we can know anything is to go looking for ourselves, all the way to el norte, asking questions, maybe even finding Dolores Huerta." I sat up and leaned over her, feeling her warm breath on my face. "Dolores is an important woman. If we can find her, maybe she can help us; she'll know who to ask and where to look. You'll see."

Suddenly her face relaxed and she smiled. Her hand reached up and stroked my cheek. "Oh Alma, you are so like Papá. Do you know that? You remind me of him every day. Your face, your spirit, the way you talk. Just like him."

Tears filled my eyes as I curled up beside her.

"We certainly can't go back to Chiapas," she sighed, "and I'm not sure what we can do in Oaxaca. I guess I am just overwhelmed by fatigue. Everything seems so difficult when I'm tired—and right now I just want to sleep for ten days."

Relieved that she was herself again, I closed my eyes. I hugged my arm closer to my chest trying to ease the pain, and as I did my fingers instinctively began to trace a jagged line beneath my chin.

I got this scar when I was three. It was my first memory of Papá leaving for el norte. During his absence, I was inconsolable, so when he finally returned, I had flown down the path to meet him. Sobbing hysterically, unable to see through my tears, I stumbled on a stone step, landing flat on my belly and chin. With the wind knocked out of

me, I awoke in my father's arms, blood soaking both of us. I remember the pain of a needle, the tug on my chin over and over again,
while my mother's scolding voice tried to pierce through the deep,
gentle cooing of my father. "Ay niña, mi ángel . . ."

Often, even now, I run my fingers over this jagged scar and listen
for—and almost hear—those soothing sounds of comfort.

5

Simple Solutions

Manuel returned wearing a yellow T-shirt two sizes too large and dragging behind him a couple of reluctant beasts. The old, gray, slay-backed horse ambled from side to side as if it had had a bit too much tequila, while the mangy-looking burro looked like its disgruntled mate. By the time they finally reached us, both Rosa and I were worn out from laughing.

"What's so funny?" Manuel asked. "I think I look pretty hot. Huh?" He struck a pose that made us giggle even more, then asked, "You are feeling better, Rosa?"

He knelt beside us, and still holding the rope in one hand, he slid a brown sack off his shoulder to the ground. I opened it to find a plastic jug of water.

"The old woman said to bring you to the house, and she will see what she can do. I told her you were my sisters, and we were on our way to Oaxaca." He nodded to the creatures that were grazing on the few weeds beside us. "She said not to touch the other horses, to take these two. I guess she figured we couldn't get very far on these poor souls."

We eagerly took turns drinking from the water.

Manuel and I then helped Rosa get up onto the old horse. She settled her hips into the deep curve of its back and then leaned forward, resting her head on the back of its neck, her arms hugging it tightly. She sighed, then winked at me, "Beat you back! ¡Ándale!" We used to say that to each other on our way home from school in Oaxaca just as we reached a certain curve in the road.

I turned to the burro, which was smaller than the horse, but the thought of climbing on with one hand, and my tender shoulder and burning thigh, seemed a daunting task. Just as I reached up to grab the burro's mane, Manuel's arm went around me, and he whispered in my ear, "Here, turn toward me." I held my breath. How I wanted to lean into him, to let my head rest on his neck. Our cheeks brushed as I turned. Then he squatted and lifted me at the waist, high up in the air, well above the burro's back. I lifted one leg up and over, and he gently lowered me and let go. Our eyes met for a moment, then he turned and, picking up the ropes, began to lead us. My heart pounded faster than my throbbing shoulder.

There were four different houses spaced a good distance apart. The one in the center was the largest, with a brick front and tin roof, while the others, built with wood, were smaller. Beyond the houses were a dilapidated barn and a fenced-in field where two brown horses grazed. An older woman stood in the doorway of the brick house, her long gray braid hanging down over her right shoulder. She held her hand up to block the sun as she watched us approach, but when she lowered her hand, what I had thought was a squint was clearly a grimace. Once we dismounted and Manuel led the animals away, she looked us over head to toe, then after pointing toward a water pump, she disappeared inside, returned with towels and a bar of soap, and handing them to us, she asked, "One of you is ill?"

I turned toward Rosa as she answered, "I am feeling a bit dizzy. I think I need to eat something and rest, and I'll be fine. Muchas gracias. Thank you for the water."

She nodded, then turned and went back into the house, clearly latching the door behind her. A few minutes later, we heard the latch again and out she came carrying a sack and a few blankets. We could smell the food even before we opened it. She motioned toward a few oak trees beside the house. "Rest in the shade. If you wish, you can join us for dinner later when the men return."

Exhausted and starving, we eagerly spread out the blankets under the oaks, devoured the food, and then, without a word, stretched out and fell deep asleep. I woke briefly to the cries of a baby inside one of the smaller houses, but Manuel and Rosa didn't stir. Later, when a truck pulled up and male voices boomed from within the brick house, we all came fully awake. Shortly after, a stocky man, wearing a straw cowboy hat, approached and motioned us to follow him into the house.

A long table took up the length of the room and seated around it were three men, two women, one holding a baby, and three little girls with large dark eyes. A bench was pulled up for us to join them. As I settled in, I noticed the few small windows were dressed with colorful fabrics, just like Mamá used to do, bringing tears to my eyes. The old woman entered carrying a large pot, but despite the vibrant yellow apron she wore, her face remained somber.

As we sat listening to the chatter of this family, my spirits began to revive a bit, though the pain in my shoulder increased. At one point I winced, and the old woman, whose name we learned was Lupe, asked what was wrong. Rosa told her that I had stumbled and fallen in our travels. Lupe nodded her head and, turning back to her meal, curtly said, "After; we fix after."

Rosa was the one to tell them our story, and for the most part it was the truth. Our father was missing, our mother had moved to Chiapas, but we had decided to return to our hometown of Oaxaca City. She did not add that we would journey on to el norte, perhaps because it would raise too many questions, or perhaps it was not as firmly planted in her mind as it was in mine. She added one white lie, however, saying we had a cousin to stay with in Oaxaca. I suppose it sounded better, that we had a plan, a place to stay, which we didn't. Manuel kept his head down, devouring his meal, and I picked at mine, as the pain made my stomach turn. When I glanced up, Lupe was watching me.

"What is your cousin's name?" she asked, still looking at me.

Without hesitation, I answered with another white lie. "Mundo, and he is my father's cousin." Then I placed a large spoonful of beans in my mouth and forced them down.

While this house looked sad and drab on the outside, inside it was bright with color. Besides the windows dressed in multicolored fabrics, even the well-worn, brown sofa was draped along the top with a cloth of shimmering green and yellow stripes. We learned that Lupe and the other young women wove colorful fabrics and made them into all sorts of crafts: belts, purses, miniature dolls, bookmarks, headbands, place-mats, and that every other weekend they took them to sell at a relative's table at the Mercado Benito Juárez. When Rosa and I heard the news that they were driving to Oaxaca at the end of the week and we were welcome to ride along, it took our breath away. While I was anxious to get to Oaxaca City, the thought of a few days rest and a ride into town was more than convincing, especially after hearing that it would take three or four days at the very least to walk there. Even Manuel seemed relieved at the news, nodding in agreement and saying he would be happy to help care for the animals the next few days.

About an hour later, after the long table had been moved back to a far corner and as candles tossed dancing shadows on the walls, I sat beside Rosa on the bench now placed in the center of the room. The spicy smells of the meal still lingered. Everyone else had stepped outside, except for Rosa and Lupe. I could hear hushed whispers beyond the curtained windows, as Rosa stroked my back and Lupe removed the sling that had held my shoulder. If my eyes weren't open, I would have sworn I was in a tiny boat swaying gently over calm waves. My cheeks burned, and a warmth spread throughout my entire body. I felt more content than I can ever remember: I had just drunk a small glass of tequila.

Slowly Lupe extended my arm, massaging it, stroking the skin. I closed my eyes as her calloused fingers relieved the itches and the aches. But as they found their way to my shoulder, I tensed. Rosa turned my head and pressed it to her shoulder.

"Remember the time Papá took us to Papantla and we saw the men, los voladores, fly?" she whispered. "Remember the colors, the red, orange, and yellow, like large birds in the sky?"

I tried to remember, but the hands were moving firmly around my shoulder and under my arm, pressing, palpating deeper and deeper. I tried to imagine the large colorful bird men swirling far above, but suddenly the room itself was spinning and my stomach was turning as well. Then Lupe's long braid swung off her shoulder and tapped against my cheek, startling me. I pitched forward, and as I did, Lupe tugged sharply on my arm with one hand and pressed down firmly on my shoulder with the other. I heard a *pop*, but in the same instant I doubled over and emptied the entire contents of my dinner all over the freshly swept cement floor. I heaved until there was nothing left to come up. And it was then that I realized that both of my arms were wrapped around my stomach and the throbbing in my shoulder was gone. As I caught my breath, I slowly lifted my shoulder up, then down, then side to side. It ached—a deep, dull soreness—but no sharp pulsating pain.

I remember them helping me to the soft, lumpy sofa, and Lupe washing the cut on my thigh. At first it burned, until she massaged the area with something thick and cool. That night I slept deeply, though I heard the stirrings of Lupe's sons as they rose early and left for the fields. I drifted in and out, hearing their voices as they passed. I knew that two unmarried sons lived in this four-room house with Lupe. The others—two sons and their wives, a daughter and her husband, as well as a baby and three children—lived in the smaller homes. But they all ate together at Lupe's each evening. I felt such a deep peace and contentment that night, perhaps because of the tequila, but just as potent was that warm, fluid feeling of family.

That first morning when I finally awoke, I found Rosa and Lupe in a small room in the back. A wooden loom leaned against the wall beneath the open window with threads of many colors dangling and swaying in the light breeze. Along one wall, cinder blocks and pieces of wood were fashioned into a haphazard array of shelves, and stacked upon them floor to ceiling were Lupe's creations. ¡Los colores! The room was dizzy with color.

Rosa was holding a small doll with large embroidered eyes, a long thick braid of black yarn, and a bright green skirt with orange zigzag trim along the bottom. "I'm going to make her a rebozo to wrap around her and place a small basket of flowers on her arm," she said, her eyes bright with excitement. She had recovered quickly from her own ordeal and was clearly refreshed from her night's sleep. "Lupe says we can help her this week and even at the mercado if we want."

"How is your shoulder this morning?" Lupe asked, setting down a pair of large blue eyeglasses and beckoning me to stand beside her. Though I had yet to see her smile, there was a softer tone to her voice.

"It's just a little sore," I said, moving my arm in a circle as I stepped forward.

She ran her hands over my shoulder, then said, "Just a minute," and disappeared.

I scanned the shelves and ran my fingers over a stack of folded fabrics: thin stripes, thick stripes, flowers, dots, and diamond shapes in every color imaginable. I picked up a miniature drawstring purse to find a collection of worry dolls inside. Change purses, eyeglass cases, tasseled bookmarks—and then my eyes spotted on the far-right shelf, a stack of fabric-covered books.

I reached up gingerly, waiting for that jolt in my shoulder, but it didn't flinch until I gathered the books and lifted them down. Even then, its complaint was mild, a lameness that would pass in a few days.

When I opened the books and found they contained blank pages,

I was disappointed at first, but then the thought of keeping a written account of our travels began to excite me. I shuffled through the books, admiring each combination of color or intricate design. Some were covered simply in solid or striped fabrics. Others were pieced like patchwork with different fabrics and fine stitching. And still others were decorated with hand-embroidered designs. It was this last stack that I was drawn to, three in particular because they were all worked on a deep blue cloth.

The first was a sailboat gliding over a blue sea. Beneath that was one with a white seagull soaring across a blue sky. And then the third took my breath away. It was simply a white calla lily against a backdrop of blue. Just like my little box of stars. My fingers traced the curve of the white flower. Una flor delicada.

Lupe's voice startled me. "Outside. Out, out. Go see to the animals. ¡Vámonos!" I glanced up just in time to see Manuel disappear from the doorway. Had he been watching me?

Lupe entered the room shaking a brown bottle vigorously in her hand. "Take off the blouse," she commanded.

I quickly placed the books back up on the shelf, glanced self-consciously at the doorway, and slowly unbuttoned my white blouse. I blushed as she said, "Bra too," for even my mother hadn't seen me naked in a while. But Lupe's matter of fact manner left me with little choice and also strangely put me at ease, and so I obeyed, though I shyly covered my breasts with my blouse. The truth was, I was glad to take off my bra. It was so small that my breasts were bursting out the sides and top, leaving creases on my skin.

Shortly after she opened the bottle, both Rosa and I began coughing. The sharp smell permeated the room. "Sit," she said nodding toward her chair before the loom. As I did, I sheepishly looked up at Rosa, who stifled a laugh.

Then Lupe began to rub the sticky white lotion into, around, and under my shoulder. I could feel the heat penetrate deep into the injured joint. As her rough hands massaged, she said to Rosa, "Now watch closely. You will do this morning and night for one week." Rosa's eyes widened and when they met mine, I couldn't hold back my laughter.

And for the first time, Lupe smiled, saying, "Yes, you will both stink. 'Look out,' everyone will say. 'Here come those stinky sisters! ¡Cuidado!'"

The next few days, Manuel tended the animals and fetched water, while Rosa and I helped Lupe with her crafts. The stitching was all done by hand, something Rosa had enjoyed doing at home, so she was able to produce a couple of dolls in one day, while I found pride in three simple eyeglass cases. But it was soothing, sitting on the sofa or on a bench outside, slowly stitching pieces together, then turning them right side out and seeing a neat finished product. I wondered who would buy them and where they would journey. Lupe said many American tourists had bought her goods. She was a woman of few words, working quickly and quietly, never resting for a moment. Her gray braid always hung over one shoulder, and while she worked, she wore those oversized blue glasses that slid down her nose from their weight. I liked that she firmly told me what was expected, quietly corrected me if I was wrong, and then responded with a simple "Good," when I finished. Lupe was calm and reassuring, unlike my mother, who was always barking like a small dog. I wondered what it would have been like to have a mother like Lupe.

When we finished a full day's sewing, we helped Lupe with dinner. Each evening, when I heard the truck coming in, I felt an excitement similar to that I used to feel when Papá came home from el norte. I vaguely remembered Mamá preparing tamales days ahead and cleaning the house like it was up for inspection. What I didn't know— and wondered with great sadness—was how Mamá reacted when he came in the door. Was she beaming with love? Was she timid because they had been apart so long?

I didn't know because all I remembered was dashing toward the door to be the first to hug him—thinking only of myself, oblivious to the needs of others. The thought of this filled me with shame.

Those few days at Lupe's were a much-needed respite not only from what we'd been through, but for what lay ahead. Though the meals were simple, made with whatever Lupe had that day, and though her sons were worn out by their labors in the sun, there was a sense of communion that I hadn't felt since Papá left, so on our last night there, I felt both sadness and exhilaration. It had been a joy to stop there and regain our strength, but it only made me ache all the more for what was and yearn to move on to what could be.

After dinner that last evening, everyone helped pack the crafts onto the truck, which was then covered with a tarp. Then, since many of us would be rising early to head for the mercado in Oaxaca City, we called it a night. But as Rosa and I prepared our little bed on the sofa, Lupe motioned us into her bedroom, where neatly folded on her small bed were a few blouses, pants, and skirts. "See what fits you, take what you need," she said. "And Alma, see if one of these fits you better." Reaching into a drawer beside her bed, she pulled out a couple of bras. They seemed huge, with large cups and thick straps, but they would serve me better than the small piece of cloth that made me look like a four-breasted beast.

"Lupe, you have been too kind to us. Gracias," Rosa said, hugging her.

Lupe accepted her hug with a nod, then said, "There is no 'too kind.' We give what we have to those who are in need. And now you both do the same." She placed her hand first on Rosa's arm, then mine, and said gently, "I have been in your shoes before, and others have been kind to me. No one reaches my age, loses two husbands and three children, and makes it on their own strength. Nos ayudamos mutuamente. We help each other."

Then her eyes opened wide. "Oh, I almost forgot," she said, turning to the little table beside her bed. Lifting a cloth, she pulled out the little blue book with the calla lily. "This is for you," she said, handing it to me.

I caught my breath. "Oh, Lupe. For me? Oh, thank you!" My hand trembled as I reached out.

"No, not from me. From your brother?" She said the last word with a twinkle in her eye.

I blushed as I looked up at her. "Manuel?"

"Yes," she said with a smile. "He asked how much they sell for and insisted on paying the full price, though I did convince him that most customers bargain for a bit less, and he agreed."

"And he said *for me*? You're sure?" No boy had ever given me a gift before. And Manuel would certainly need every peso or quetzal he had.

Lupe only smiled and nodded her head. Then she turned to Rosa. "Someone should tell 'tu hermano' to be careful how he looks at 'su hermana' if he wants others to believe you are truly brother and sister traveling together."

I glanced at Rosa, whose eyes were bright with curious surprise. "I had no idea," she said. "Did you?"

"Did I what?"

"Did you know he cares for you?"

"I don't know anything." I suddenly felt uncomfortable and confused. "I've never said a word to him. And anyway, it's just a book! A book with no words!" I looked from one to the other, holding the book forth as if in explanation.

Lupe laughed. "Ah, those are the best kind."

Rosa shook her head. "Well, I have certainly been blind. I hadn't even noticed."

"There's nothing to notice! So, he bought me a book. So what!" Then grabbing Rosa's arm, I pleaded, "And don't you say a word to him, not a word!"

Lupe ushered us out the door. "You both need your sleep. You've a journey to prepare for." As I walked away, my cheeks burning like they did the night of the tequila, I heard her chuckle softly in her room, a light girlish laugh full of memory and delight.

But I couldn't sleep. Long after Lupe blew out the last candle, after the tossing and turning in her sons' room ceased, and after Rosa's breaths became slow and deep, I was still wide awake. I reached for the little book that was in the top of my sack and crept to a table where I remembered seeing a pencil. It was still there. Then I sank down on the floor beneath one window where the light of the moon shone down through the bottom of the curtain. Sitting cross-legged, I could see the cut on my thigh. The length of a cayenne pepper, the line of clotted blood was thick at one end and curved to a point at the other. Mi pimienta de cayena. I ran my finger over the bumpy scab and thought of Manuel. *"Go! I'm right behind you. Up. Now. Up!"*

I repositioned myself so my little book was illuminated. The calla lily glowed in the dim light. I opened to the first blank page, paused, and wrote, "The Journal of Alma Cruz." Or should it be "Journey"? I settled back to contemplate where to begin. Perhaps the day Papá disappeared? Or the day Rosa and I set out?

The year Papá left seemed important, so I neatly wrote the numbers "1997." Then I sat back, looked at them, and stopped. The numbers. So neat, so compact, so certain. I had never been one to keep a journal of words. No, whenever I sat with a blank piece of paper, I always played with numbers. So that's what I decided to do with my little book. I turned back to the title, erased, and began again. "The Math Journal of Alma Cruz."

The room was still, except for the rhythmic breathing of Rosa and the even-patterned muffled snore coming from the wall beyond. I turned the page, leaned forward, pencil point to blank paper, and smiled.

Math Problem #1.

In Chiapas, 75 people sneak onto the train. At Checkpoint One, 64 people run into the fields, 33 are caught, the rest hide and manage to re-board the train. At Checkpoint Two, half of those now on the train are stopped and asked for money. One-third of those have nothing and are taken into custody to be deported. The rest pay and are allowed to re-board. How many of the 75 make it to Oaxaca?

Yes, Papá would be so proud.

6

Oaxaca Once Again

Early the next morning, we woke to the sounds of sputtering motors that coughed and hacked, just like Tito on Sunday mornings, until one harsh eruption left a sudden silence. Once dressed, we emerged with our packs from Lupe's house to find two weathered pickups and a flat-bed truck waiting beside Lupe's truck of crafts. Several men huddled beside the trucks, some talking softly, others silent except for long deep sighs with each exhale of cigarette smoke. A few women lumbered over the uneven terrain. Wrapping their colorful rebozos tightly around them, they hugged themselves as they walked. They were returning from one of the small houses beyond, where they had dropped off their children.

I caught a quick glimpse of Manuel as he climbed onto the back of the flat-bed with one of Lupe's sons. I think he looked up at me from under those thick brows, but the shadows kept any message hidden in the dark.

Rosa and I climbed onto the back of a pickup, joining some men and women who worked the corn fields with Lupe's sons. As the trucks began to lurch forward and gain momentum, we huddled closer together against the cool morning air. A sleepy silence gradually escalated to animated conversation, so when Rosa and I were asked where we were going, this time I chose to relay our story. I added only that we were journeying on to el norte to look for our missing father. Suddenly we were bombarded with warnings and advice.

"Don't trust anyone! ¡Por Dios, ten cuidado!" one man said, which had been Manuel's constant warning to us as well.

"This is not a journey for young girls. There will be no good end." An old woman shook a scolding finger at us, but before we could answer, another voice rang out, "How do you know? You've never traveled farther than Mexico City and lived all your life in the village where you were born!"

"May la Virgen de Guadalupe protect you," whispered a man with large, sad eyes.

And finally, "Save up your money and get a good coyote. There is no other way." These words we knew to be true, but unfortunately the most we had between us was not quite 500 pesos. Even a cheap coyote was significantly more than that.

To divert this doomed conversation, I began to ask them questions to see if anyone knew of my father or even Dolores Huerta. Not a glimmer of a response followed; in fact, all conversation came to a halt. We rode in silence for several minutes, bumping along the road.

An older man, who had been sitting quietly in the far corner, leaned forward suddenly and shouted, "What was that name again?"

Everyone turned in his direction. My heart fluttered as I replied, "Juan Cruz. Juan Miguel Cruz Ochoa."

Even as I stated his full name, I realized it was unnecessary. My father was Juan Cruz to everyone. He would nod his head and in one swift exhale say, "Juan Cruz," while shaking the hand of a new acquaintance. But as I shouted those four full names loudly so the old man could hear, they rang out across the length of that truck bed like a roll call, like a simple statement of existence—Juan Miguel Cruz Ochoa.

They fell with a thud as the man shook his head. "No, no! The woman's name. What was it again?"

I waited until a passing truck roared by. "Huerta," I tried, but it got no further than Rosa beside me. He cocked an ear in my direction. "Dolores Huerta!" I offered again with a forceful grunt.

His weathered face broke into a grin as he lifted a fist in the air. "¡Huelga! ¡Huelga!" he chanted, as my father had told us the striking farm workers had done long ago. "Strike! Strike!" I crawled down the center over knees and toes and sat down beside him, rubbing my thigh and realizing that my shoulder barely hurt.

"Yes, yes, I remember her," he nodded. "I was working the grapes with some Filipinos when all that got started. What a woman. ¡Mujer increíble! The growers were afraid of her—called her 'the dragon lady.' And the workers, some of them wouldn't even speak to her. Said a woman belonged at home with her kids, not running around doing a man's work." He laughed, exposing a large chipped tooth. "But they were just afraid of her. Hell, I watched a guy try to cross the picket line. ¡Ay! She got in his face and shamed him until he turned tail and ran."

"But my father? You don't remember a Juan Cruz?"

"No, lo siento. Don't say that I do, just the dragon lady," he said with a wink.

"Have you seen her since? Do you know where she is now?" I asked.

"Oh, that was years ago. Many years. No, I wouldn't know about now." He looked up at the others as if they had an answer, then back at me. He shrugged. "No sé. Maybe she's dead?"

I bit my lip and sat back. Dolores, muerta? I hoped not.

"Why do you want to find her?" someone asked further down the row, but before I could answer I heard another voice shout, "She said she's looking for her father, and maybe that woman knows something."

A few scattered murmurs were followed by silence, until a man's voice spoke. "Muchacha, I hate to say this, but you know—maybe your father doesn't want to be found. Maybe he's got a new wife and family. It happens all the time, you know. Es verdad."

I looked down toward the voice, but three different men were looking back. I wasn't sure who had spoken, so I said to all of them, "That's not possible. My father was a man of honor. He loved us!" But even as I spoke those words, I felt a chill along my spine. Was that what I was secretly hoping? As heartbreaking as it would be to think he had abandoned us, at least he'd be alive. But no, that was not my father. Letter or no letter, there had to be some other explanation.

I glanced at Rosa who was sitting across from them, but she turned her head as a woman's voice on the end said seductively, "Honey, a man is a man—and even a man of honor can't help being a man." Everyone laughed.

I closed my eyes and leaned my head back, letting it bump repeatedly against the side. Then I heard Rosa's confident voice, "You can all laugh, but Alma and I know our father. Es un buen hombre." When I opened my eyes, she was smiling at me, her face soft with trust, her eyes full of faith. I quickly looked away.

"Don't listen to them," a motherly voice was saying. "They're a bunch of baboons. Listen to your hearts. You'll find him."

I studied my short stubby fingers and thought of my neat, block-like printing, so perfect for listing numbers. Rosa's letters were full of loops that overlapped those above and below. And my mother, well, my mother's printing was large and crude, like a child with a fat crayon. Not like that perfect script in the letter. When I glanced up, Rosa's eyes were pensive and serious. I knew she was studying me, so I lifted my chin and smiled, but she didn't smile back. She was trying to read me, to penetrate my thoughts, but I held my gaze steady. She would never discover that. Not even Papá knew I saw his secret letter.

It was a slow, bumpy six-hour ride as we wound through the mountains, past smaller cities such as Tlacolula and San Jeronimo Tlacochahuaya, and then along stretches of farmland. We stopped twice to relieve ourselves, but other than that, I was curled up like a scorpion's tail the whole way, dozing off and on as the trucks made their way northwest.

It was no mystery why I awoke as we approached Santa María del Tule, just 14 kilometers from the outskirts of Oaxaca City. My eyes filled with tears just thinking of the magnificent Árbol del Tule, a 2,000-year-old Mexican cypress tree in the center of town where Papá had taken me so many times. I remember Papá said it was more sacred a temple than the Monte Alban—the famous Zapotec ruins outside our city—because the grand ahuehuete tree had been planted by the gods themselves. Its huge gnarled trunk, the size of a house, yielded its own forest of trees reaching high into the sky. When I was very young, I asked Papá to dig it up and replant it next to our home. It would be my own private forest. I remember him laughing and swooping me up in his arms, as he asked, "Mi niñita, how about if I dig up our house and move it here? It would be much easier." For weeks I had pestered him with a shovel and even went so far as to begin digging beside our house myself.

Papá dreamed of owning his own farm in lush Zimatlán or picturesque San Sebastián de las Grutas. That's why he journeyed to the farmlands in the United States. He would never be able to buy his own land on the wages he earned on the farms of Oaxaca—though he loved working that land. Of course, once his family began to grow, this money was needed to feed and clothe us, and his dream remained just that—a dream.

As we passed Santa María del Tule and were approaching our Oaxaca City, both Rosa and I turned facing outward on our knees with our arms resting along the side of the truck bed. None of it looked familiar, but we were passing through the eastern edge and we had lived on the southwestern fringes of the city. We passed a large dilapidated building and a dirt lot with stacks of wrecked cars and trucks, then a little further down we saw a house with a red tile roof and a lush grass lawn next to a block-long nursery of plants and flowers and small trees. But very soon we were in traffic, weaving our way diagonally through the city toward the town center. When I finally glimpsed the twin bell towers of Oaxaca Cathedral, my heart pumped madly. We were home! But then the reality hit, like a quick punch to the stomach: There was no "home" to go to. No Mamá and the boys. No Papá. My heart sank.

My excitement was subdued as we passed the cathedral and then skirted around the zócalo, though I caught a glimpse of the pedestrian plaza with people strolling about and vendors selling huge, colorful balloons, roasted corn, and ice cream. How many times had Papá and I shared an ice cream right there, sitting on a wall in the shade, watching people go by? Turning at the majestic city hall Palacio de Gobierno, we approached Benito Juárez Mercado and pulled to a stop beside the brick building. Part indoor, part covered outdoor, the market stretched for two blocks and sold everything you can imagine: the freshest fruit and vegetables, poultry and fish, both modern and traditional clothing, shoes, belts, hats, piñatas, toys, souvenirs, and every craft imaginable. Papá always said that nowhere in Mexico could you find better mole, chocolate, or chapulines than in Oaxaca. The mole sauce and the chocolate I loved, but I never, ever acquired a taste for the spicy fried grasshoppers called chapulines.

I felt such a mix of emotions as I climbed out of the truck and stood waiting for the others to join us. I searched for Manuel, but his truck was nowhere in sight. Listening to the cries of the vendors and the distant threads of ranchero music coming from the zócalo, I suddenly felt a deep sadness. Somehow, I thought coming home to Oaxaca would be different.

Rosa turned to me and said, "I want to help Lupe here at the mercado tomorrow. The men are setting up camp close by. We can help unload the crafts and . . ." She paused. "Let's tell her we will join 'our cousin' after the mercado ends tomorrow. That would give us time to make a plan." She spoke rapidly with a strained look on her face, but as Lupe's truck with the wares pulled up, Rosa's eyes lit up and her face softened. I couldn't say no to that.

A few hours later, Rosa and I strolled the familiar streets around the zócalo, arm in arm, past sidewalk cafés strung with lights, past a young man playing a soulful accordion, past a group of giggling children hopping up and down the bandstand steps. We were both quiet, feeling a mixture of fatigue, relief, and sorrow. We did not speak of tomorrow or yesterday. We simply walked.

Rosa broke the silence with a whisper, "We are getting closer to Papá. I can feel it."

"Do you think so? ¿Verdad?" I heard my small childlike voice respond. To hear her say it, gave me such hope. I leaned into her as we walked. "Rosa," I said gently, "it doesn't feel like home, does it?"

"No, not at all."

We walked a few paces in silence.

I stopped and turned, facing her. "Then let's just keep going. North. Take a bus maybe as far as we can to the border. If we stay here, we will spend our money just spinning our wheels. Let's just keep moving!" My heart raced at the thought. "You just said it yourself. We are getting closer to Papá—but he's not here!"

She took a deep breath before she spoke, and when she did, her voice was firm and strong, "I have been thinking the same thing. Lo mismo."

"Are you serious? You have?"

She nodded. "We need to check in with Mundo first and see if he has heard anything. I'm not sure what Mamá told him before we left, if she said anything at all, and I'm not sure if he would have been able to reach us in Chiapas anyway."

The thought of that desolate stick house and Tito's foul belching turned my stomach. "I could kiss the ground here! Gracias a Dios, we got away, Rosa!"

She sighed, "I just wish there was a way we could talk to Mamá and the boys. Make sure they are all right."

"Mamá made her choice," I reminded her, "and the boys will be okay." Despite Tito, they seemed to thrive, running wild in their bare feet, climbing trees, catching lizards, and caring for the goats and chickens. I knew José missed his school friends, but he didn't miss school itself. As for little Ricardo, he did cry himself to sleep some nights calling out for Papá, and that made my heart heavy.

But Rosa's voice lifted my spirits as she said with conviction, "So after the mercado, we'll find Mundo, and then we will head for el norte."

A plan, I thought, as my mind turned to Manuel.

Shortly after, when we got to the trucks where they had set up camp for the night, I finally saw him. He was just beyond the fire, listening to two men duel with their guitars. His dark eyes flashed as they darted from one musician's hands to the other. The mass of hair on his forehead danced about as his head swayed to the beat. It was the first time I had gotten a chance to really look at him without worrying about his eyes meeting mine. To all appearances, I was listening to the music as well. And in a way I was, for the battling guitars seemed to be keeping pace with the fluttering in both my heart and stomach. Between the two, I could barely catch my breath. Oh, mi corazón.

It still amazed me that he had risked so much to stay with us. He could easily have been deported by the authorities at the train, yet he stayed. Why? Was it for me? I wasn't pretty like Rosa. My face was plain, my nose wide, though Rosa often told me my face lit up when I talked and my eyes danced with light. She said I was pretty in my own lively way. Once she made me try it in front of a mirror, but I ended up giggling and looked more like a wrinkled fig. I never believed her. I figured she was just trying to be nice. But was it possible that Manuel saw something? Or was it just brotherly affection after all?

We hadn't had a chance to speak since Lupe gave me the book. There were always so many people around, and I couldn't imagine bringing it up in company. It would have to wait until later, when we were on our way, whenever that would be—and if he was going with us. I supposed we would discuss all that after the mercado. Count our money, discuss our options. But I couldn't help wondering—how far would he travel with us? After all, he was looking for his brother in a place called Temecula, and we were looking for Papá or Dolores, wherever that might be. At what point would we have to say goodbye? No sooner did this thought enter my mind, then the music stopped— and it seemed, so did my heart.

Math Problem #2

Two trucks leave for Oaxaca. One breaks down in Tehuantepec, 250 km from Oaxaca at 12 noon. The first truck continues on at 50 km/hour, makes one 30-minute stop, then a second 10-minute stop. The second truck is repaired in 45 minutes, travels at 50 km/hour, makes one 40-minute stop only. What time does each truck arrive in Oaxaca?

7

Abundance

I had been to the mercado many times as a child, but I had never seen it from the perspective of the vendors. We woke early and set up Lupe's goods well before the tourists and native shoppers were about, yet the ordered confusion of the market erupted well before any bargaining began. Squawking poultry competed with squealing children as their parents hurriedly set out their goods: fruits and flowers, rugs and runners, saddles and sandals. Everywhere I looked were the colors of the rainbow, and if the same could be said of smells, well, that was true, too.

As Rosa and I helped Lupe display her crafts, I made a point of setting out my eyeglass cases right in front. *Where will these travel?* I wondered again with excitement. Then, as I touched them gently, I thought, *And where will I travel as well?*

The morning went slowly with few buyers, but as the sun rose in the sky, the aisles began to fill with all sorts of people. A tall, thin woman, with hair the color of lemons and skin so pale I could see the vessels in her cheeks, fingered my eyeglass cases and spoke to a man beside her in a harsh guttural language that I had never heard before.

He then spoke in very odd Spanish asking Lupe how much. But before Lupe could answer, the woman moved on to the end of the table where she poked and prodded several other items, then shaking her head walked on down the aisle.

Suddenly Manuel appeared munching on a piece of Mexican

sweet bread. "Want some?" he offered, holding it forth. I blushed as I heard Lupe chuckle. I shook my head and kept my eyes averted. The delicious aroma made my mouth water. I wanted some desperately, but it seemed like such an intimate gesture, and there were too many eyes around.

As if she read my mind, Lupe pressed a coin into my hand and said, "Go with Manuel and buy another—and get some chocolate, too." Chocolate was a Oaxacan specialty.

I glanced at Rosa, who nodded and continued arranging a display of rebozos.

I grabbed my bag from under the table and gently slung it over my still tender shoulder. We ambled down the aisle in silence. Manuel tore off a piece of his bread, and this time when he handed it to me, I took it. I ate it in small bites as we walked, savoring the sweetness. Turning a corner, he stopped to buy a fruit drink, then motioned to a bench beneath a tree. "Lupe's son has insisted on paying me for my help," he said, holding out a few coins.

Once seated, I cleared my throat and began. "The book . . . with the calla lily? Thank you so much. It's lovely. Thank you." I looked up quickly into his eyes, then back at my hands.

"It looked like your little box of stars," he simply said.

Silence.

Brotherly, I decided, nothing more. Of course, he didn't feel anything more for me. What was I thinking? Hurriedly I reached into my bag and took out my journal.

"Let me show you what I'm doing." As I opened to the cover page, *The Math Journal of Alma Cruz*, he stretched his arm behind me along the back of the bench, and his other hand reached over and covered mine so that we were both holding my little book. He leaned in, his fingers squeezing mine, our cheeks barely touching. His breath was moist with a light fruity fragrance from his drink. He peered into the book and began reading the first problem. It seemed to take him forever. My heart fluttered like it had the night before. I sat frozen, holding my breath while he read.

"Wow," he said after what seemed like several minutes, "it's confusing. What's the answer?" He turned toward me but made no effort to move back. I looked up, and as I did his lips swept forward and brushed mine—lightly. I gasped and drew back.

"Lo siento," he said softly, still holding my hand. "So sorry."

"It's okay," I whispered, looking up timidly into his eyes.

"Is it?" he asked leaning in. This was not brotherly.

My cheeks burned, and I wondered if my eyes were dancing with light. Manuel reached up and stroked my face with the back of his hand. I lifted my chin and, like a kitten, rubbed against it. But as I did, I could see out of the corner of my eye two uniformed men walking toward us. My heart pounded with each step of their boots as they marched closer and closer.

In an instant, I pulled Manuel's face to mine and, wrapping my arms tightly around his neck, I kissed him deeply, holding him close and tight. He moaned softly, his hands now pressing me hard against his chest, his lips parting mine, his warm tongue tickling.

I had never been kissed before. My skin tingled, a tiny moth fluttered about within my chest, my stomach bounced like a child's ball, and my legs turned to liquid. Even my fear of the authorities melted away. We continued to kiss even after the footsteps approached, paused and moved on, interrupted only by a slight reprimand grunted by one of the passing officers, "Take it to las grutas!" a reference to the caves beyond the city.

When Manuel realized what had prompted my passionate kiss, he laughed and said, "I paid them well to do that you know!"

I slapped his knee, then turned to him and earnestly pleaded, "Please be careful. I don't want you to be deported."

"Neither do I," he replied, "for many reasons now." He squeezed my hand.

"So, you are traveling with us? To el norte?" I whispered. "¿Conmigo?"

"If you want me to," he said. "Yes. I will help you find your father, and you can help me find my brother."

Together. We would travel to el norte together. I leaned my forehead against his chest, and his hand stroked the back of my neck. I had not felt so safe since I had been in Papá's arms.

Later that afternoon, as we approached Lupe's stall, I tried to pull my hand from his, but he held it tight. I took a deep breath and relented, squeezing his back. We exchanged a smile. So, when I saw Rosa's serious face, I thought she disapproved of this intimate gesture, but I soon discovered that she was focused on something else entirely.

"Alma, Alma, hurry. Look who's here!"

Standing beside her was a round face that I thought I'd never see again, my favorite teacher Señorita Garcia from my primary school. I flew into her open arms. "¡Maestra! Teacher!"

"And to think I almost didn't come to market today!" she exclaimed as she gave me a bear hug. "But look at you, a young woman now. Una mujer bella. I can barely see traces of my little math whiz!" Her dark hair was pulled back tightly into a long ponytail that hung down her back. Dressed in a loose white embroidered blouse and long skirt, Señorita Garcia was short and plump, but her matronly figure always left my mind the minute she started teaching. She was deliberate and precise, as she'd flit back and forth animatedly at the chalkboard, underlining with a flourish. Like me, she loved math and knew how to make it fun by using our names or our surroundings to make up math problems. In fact, she was one of the reasons I wanted to be a teacher. I couldn't wait to tell her about my math journal.

As soon as she released me, she stepped back and, after glancing briefly at Manuel, she took both my hands and said, "Rosa tells me that your mother has moved to Chiapas and your father has been missing for three years! Oh Alma, I am so sorry. I remember him well."

"You do? You remember my father?"

"Oh yes. Your father was so supportive of your schooling. We spoke a few times, about your grades, your potential, even about the cost of high school and university. He had such hopes for you, Alma."

My heart swelled at the thought of him talking with her. I knew few fathers were as supportive of their daughter's education as he was, for while it was mandatory in Mexico for all children to attend school through the secundaria, which was seventh through ninth grade, there was little follow-through on those who did not. Consequently, many girls in Oaxaca stopped after the sixth grade, usually at their parents' request. They were needed at home or in the fields, and many set out for the cities in Mexico or el norte to find work. Rosa had stopped after secundaria. But I had intended to finish and go on to preparatoria, the equivalent of high school, and perhaps even university. While my father had always agreed, I didn't know he had even spoken to Señorita Garcia about this.

"I remember him well, Alma," she said of my father, "so earnest and polite. I can see him still with his hat in his hands, nervously twisting the brim as we talked. He was so proud of you."

"I tried to find you the year Papá disappeared, but they said you were taking some time off?" I remember how disappointed I'd been when I sought her out back then. I had wanted her to talk to Mamá about keeping me in school.

Her smile drooped into a frown. "Yes," she said softly, "after my mother passed away. My father had some issues with his health as well, so I took a leave . . ." She paused and then with a heavy sigh, "I've been working a couple days a week for the past year, and I tutor as well. But what a joy to see you again! Here I imagined you sailing into preparatoria and soaring through advanced math classes!" She squeezed my arm. "You have younger brothers as well, no? I did not know them. Are they with your mother?"

I nodded. "Yes, in Chiapas." Then, as she looked again at Manuel, I introduced her. "This is our friend Manuel. He is traveling with us."

She had reached out her hand toward him but stopped abruptly. "Traveling? Traveling where?"

I hesitated and looked to Rosa, unsure what she had said and what I should reveal. "Well, we just came up from Chiapas . . . after visiting our mother . . . and now we are thinking of going on to el norte . . . to see what we can learn about our father." I paused as Rosa's eyes shifted away from mine.

"To el norte? And how are you planning to get there?" She looked first at Rosa, then me and then Manuel. No one spoke.

"Well?" she asked firmly, but there was a softness in her eyes.

Manuel started to fidget beside me. Finally, Rosa spoke up. "Maestra, we have just arrived from Chiapas. We are helping our friends here at the mercado, and then . . . well . . . we aren't exactly sure what we are doing next."

Leave it to Rosa to speak the simple truth.

"Have you someplace to stay?" Maestra was in teacher mode; her eyes focused, her mind working.

Rosa and I exchanged an awkward glance, which was answer enough.

"Are you in some kind of trouble?" she asked gently. "¿Hay algún problema?"

"No! Not at all," Rosa quickly answered. "We left Chiapas and hadn't quite figured out what was next."

I bit my lip and took a breath, "The truth is Maestra, it wasn't good for us in Chiapas . . . for many reasons. You see, my mother's boyfriend is . . ." I wasn't sure what to say, so what came out was, ". . . not a good man."

Her eyes darted from Rosa to me. "Did he hurt you?"

Neither of us answered at first. Rosa lowered her head. Manuel looked at me with wide questioning eyes.

"Almost," I said gently, looking at Rosa. "But we got away."

"Oh my," Maestra said, but before she could speak, I added, "And then we met Manuel on our way to Oaxaca, and he has helped us in so many ways. He is going to Temecula, California, to work with his brother."

Señorita Garcia took a deep breath and looked at all three of us. Then in her matter of fact tone she said, "You will come home with me then. We will have dinner with my father, and from there, we will see what we can do." She paused, then turned to Manuel, "You are most welcome to come as well."

Manuel shook his head. "You are very kind, but I don't think so," he said, and my heart sank, though I understood his concern. He did not know her, and after all she was a teacher, a figure of authority. He had told us repeatedly to be careful. Not to trust anyone.

Before I could reassure him, Maestra had placed her hand on my arm and said, "Listen. I believe everything happens for a reason. I am here today because you needed an old friend. There have been times when I needed the help of others. Now it is my turn to help you, and one day, you will do the same. It is the way of the world." As Señorita Garcia nodded her head, her large hoop earrings brushed her shoulders. "So, it is settled. Let me finish my shopping and add three more for dinner tonight. I will meet you back here shortly." As she walked away, I watched her long dark ponytail sway back and forth against her flowing white blouse.

Manuel stood beside me, still as nervous as a cornered cat. I reached for his hand and said, "Por favor. Just for dinner. And then we will see." I looked up into his eyes, pleading. If he wouldn't go, I knew I couldn't. He squeezed my hand in response and nodded, but his face looked unconvinced.

When I turned to Rosa, she had tears in her eyes, "I lit a candle in la Catedral while you were gone," was all she said. For her, la Virgen was fast at work, but for me, I felt in my soul that it was Papá who was guiding us each step of the way.

Saying goodbye to Lupe was difficult for Rosa—how she had blossomed in those few days working with her. While I needed explanation and guidance, Rosa moved in an effortless rhythm right alongside Lupe. Even here at the mercado, Rosa looked radiant explaining the many uses of a rebozo to a young American tourist. First, she had wrapped it to hold a sleeping baby, then to carry school books, and finally with an uncharacteristic batting of her eyelashes, she demonstrated how a young girl used it coyly to flirt. Her giggle had warmed my heart. As we said our goodbyes, I wondered if Rosa might be happier staying right there, but I never said a word. If she was thinking the same, she didn't mention it either. So, it was a tearful goodbye with Lupe with promises of meeting again someday.

I thought of my cruel parting from Mamá and my tears of anger. As for promises, what could I have pledged? That I'd find Papá? If he was alive, what could that mean for Mamá but a pain just as deep as that she already felt—or worse? Is abandonment in life more painful than abandonment by death? Or does hope sneak in, with thoughts of regret and return, to ease the pain and keep you half-listening for the door?

No matter what, I knew I'd always be listening.

Señorita Garcia lived with her father just outside of Oaxaca City. Her father had been a professor and her mother, a school teacher. That this was the home of three teachers was immediately evident upon entering their house. Where books didn't line the walls on shelves, they were stacked haphazardly about. While this was the type of house in Oaxaca that usually had all the modern conveniences, one thing their home did not contain was a television. Her father, she said, lived in a world of poetry and ancient history. Newspapers and journals were his only link to the modern world. She, however, was planning to buy herself a computer.

I had never been inside such a house before. Mamá had friends who cleaned similar homes and told her of gleaming bathrooms with flushing toilets and tiled showers, separate bedrooms, a phone, and sometimes more than one television. This home, though cluttered with books and newspapers, was as beautiful as any hotel might be. It was literally built around a tree with large red flowers. From almost every room, you could enter, or at least see, the lovely garden where her father sat beneath the tree in a large wicker chair with thick red cushions. He was leaning forward so immersed in his book, he could just as well have fallen into it. Like his daughter, he was short and round, with thinning gray hair that encircled a shiny bald spot on top of his head. He wore his glasses half-way down his nose, just like Lupe. I watched as Señorita Garcia walked into the garden and spoke quietly to her father. He glanced toward the house and started to rise, but she shook her head and he sank back into the cushions. I watched him lean into his book again as Señorita Garcia headed back to us. What a life, I thought, to sit and read and read.

"Papá keeps a very disciplined schedule. I told him to wait until dinner to meet you," she said, closing the door behind her. "He writes in the mornings and reads in the afternoons, and in the evenings, he eats and argues with me." With a deep sigh, she turned to us and said, "You must be exhausted, so perhaps a bath and a siesta before dinner?"

With that she ushered Rosa and I down a hallway, telling Manuel over her shoulder to sit for a moment and she'd be right with him. I saw him look helplessly around and finally perch on the edge of a wooden bench.

After soaking in a warm tub of lavender suds, Rosa and I sat on a bed in a room with a door that closed. I had just finished brushing and braiding Rosa's hair, and she had begun to brush mine. I gazed at a painting on the wall of sunflowers in a basket, feeling like I was in a dream.

"Everyone has been so kind," Rosa was saying. "It's like the world is helping us along the way, day by day—like it was meant to be." She stopped for a moment and touched my arm, so I turned. Her eyes were shining as she said, "Maybe we will get to el norte. Maybe we will find Papá."

I hugged her tightly and clung to her words as well. But something about this kindness frightened me, though I wouldn't speak of it to Rosa. I knew there was not an endless supply of goodness in this world, and it worried me when things went too well. I found myself wishing that bad things were happening, so I could look forward to the good. Instead, I felt a gnawing anxiety of what might be lurking around our next corner. I immediately pushed these dark thoughts from my mind and turned to focus on the sunflowers. As I shifted on the bed, a sharp pain radiated down my arm from my healing shoulder. It would always plague me, I knew, but was it proof that I'd paid my dues or a reminder that in life there would always be pain?

Tired of my own thoughts, I reached for my journal while Rosa continued to brush my hair.

Math Problem #3

Señor Garcia, who is 68 years old, has read, on the average, 8 books every month for the last 47 years. If he continues this pace, how many more years must he live to reach his goal of 10,000 books? If this is not possible, how many books must he read each month to achieve this goal by the age of 90?

8

The Length of Mexico

Professor Garcia studied his daughter quietly while she laid out our story of a missing father, a mother and her dubious boyfriend in Chiapas, and finally, of our hope to try to learn something of our papá, who may or may not be in el norte. When she finished speaking, he kept his gaze on her for a few moments, then, clearing his throat, he turned and spoke directly to Rosa and me.

"I sense my daughter is skirting the real issue here. You are thinking of going to el norte?" Before we could answer, he continued. "You know this is a very dangerous idea. Thousands have died in the deserts alone, not to mention the criminals smuggling drugs across the border or preying on innocent victims like two young women. You've heard of Ciudad Juárez?"

"¡Papá!" Señorita Garcia interrupted, but her father placed a hand in the air to stop her.

"I'm just laying out the facts," he said, still addressing us. "I'm sure you've heard all of this before."

Ciudad Juárez was spoken of even as far south as Chiapas. Everyone knew of the hundreds of women found dead in that god-forsaken border town and the lack of evidence—and effort—to solve their murders.

Sitting around a table in the garden, we had just finished eating while listening to the birds flitting above and inhaling the scent of some sweet blossom that perfumed the air. Rosa was dressed in a pale blue blouse that Lupe had given her, and I had been thinking how lovely she looked and how she should be married to a professor and living in a house just like this. Thoughts of Ciudad Juárez shattered that vision until Rosa placed her hand on Señorita Garcia's to calm her and turned soft eyes toward the professor.

"You are quite right," she said, "so please, tell us, what do you suggest?" How I wished I had her composure and grace.

He smiled, "You mean beyond not going at all?"

She nodded.

He sighed and, removing his glasses, rubbed his eyes. "If I were your father, I would not want you to risk your lives. ¡Absolutamente no!"

At this I could not keep still. "We are not risking our lives! Thousands of people cross the border with no problem. You make it sound so doomed."

"Yes, doomed and very dangerous, and Elena," he said, now turning to his daughter, "I hope you have no intention of aiding this plan beyond your sympathies, an excellent dinner, and a good night's rest, for if you are once again going to champion another grand cause, may I say that I am not pleased that my daughter wishes to become an expert in human smuggling. This is illegal, you are aware?" He turned to each one of us. "¿Ilegal, entiendes?"

"You are impossible! I knew I shouldn't have included you in this," said Señorita Garcia as she sat back in disgust. "'Championing another grand cause'? 'Expert in human smuggling'? I don't know what I was thinking." Her black eyes flared as she crossed her arms tightly across her chest.

"Were you thinking that I would be obnoxiously pedantic and didactic, but ultimately obliging and fiercely supportive?" Her father pushed back his chair.

I wasn't entirely sure what he was saying, but I was fascinated by the fireworks between father and daughter—and I couldn't help but wonder what Papá and I would sound like at that age.

Rosa, however, was more focused on the message. "Illegal?" she kept saying. "Illegal? I hadn't thought of that."

"¡Dios mío! Illegal in whose eyes!" Maestra was standing now. "You're trying to find your father! If you feel following his path might give you information . . . even some closure . . . well, who under God's blue sky could forbid this?" Her lower lip began to quiver, but she lifted her chin as she spoke to her father, "Don't you think I'd do the same for you! I'd go to the ends of the earth if you were missing!" With that she stormed into the house.

The ends of the earth! She understood! More than anyone else, she understood how I felt. I turned to Manuel, whose head was lowered.

"I'm so sorry," Rosa was saying. "This is all our fault. We had no right to impose on your hospitality and disrupt your evening in such a manner."

My mouth dropped open. What did we have to be sorry for?

But when Professor Garcia finally turned his eyes to Rosa, they were brimming with tears. "No, no, my dear. Not at all," he said, his voice breaking. "You must forgive me. I have hardened in my old age, and I often forget my own manners. You, like my daughter," he paused and glanced toward the door, "have been through a great deal of suffering, and I am forgetting myself . . . forgetting the man I aspire to be. Perdóname por favor." He rose slowly from his chair. "Please sit and enjoy the birds. They will soon be bedding down for the night. They are most vocal at this hour. It's a delight to behold." With that, he ambled to the door, then turned and added, "Just relax, and we will be right with you."

As soon as the door closed, Manuel said, "I think we should leave."

I looked from Manuel to Rosa.

"We all need a good night's sleep," Rosa said, then added, "We will talk in the morning. What else can we do?"

"She's right," I said to an anxious Manuel. "Please give it the night," then softly I added, "You are in no danger. Está bien. They are good people."

Though clearly not convinced, he did help us clear the table and move into the kitchen. Since there was just room for Rosa and me, Manuel hung back and watched as we carefully washed and dried each dish, gingerly placing them on open oak shelves that lined a wall beside a small table and chairs. The kitchen walls were covered in red and yellow tiles, and above the sparkling white sink that had running hot water was a shelf with a large vase filled with red and yellow calla lilies. I touched them to see if they were real. They were! We then finished up with the other items: pots, bowls, glasses, and utensils. Mesmerized, I gently opened and closed each cupboard and drawer, my fingers gliding over the treasures inside, until I found where each item belonged. I could not imagine living like this every day.

The sun was beginning to set as we wiped the garden table and straightened the chairs. Manuel spoke of taking a walk when the door opened and both Professor and Señorita Garcia stood in the doorway. "Please come in and let's talk."

Whatever had transpired between father and daughter, there was now a tenderness as they each apologized and put us at ease. Then her father spoke, "As with any dispute, we have reached a compromise. One that I believe will be of some help to you." He paused, and then turning to his daughter seated on the sofa beside him, he simply nodded his head. With some effort, he rose and slowly made his way into an adjoining room, leaving the door partway opened.

Señorita Garcia cleared her throat and, clasping her hands together, leaned forward. "My brother, Orlando," she glanced at the partly opened door and lowered her voice slightly. "Orlando drives a bus." She said these words gingerly, giving each word equal weight. They hung in the air like thick fog. She exhaled with the effort, then continued, "I will call him tonight and see what we can arrange. We believe we can get you close to the border of Arizona or California, but beyond that we can do no more."

"Close to the border!" I gasped. "That's at least three thousand kilometers or more!" I turned to Rosa, whose face looked more puzzled than overjoyed. "Rosa! You are right. It is meant to be! Don't you see?" She swallowed hard, but her eyes softened, as I said, "Maybe he is alive, Rosa. Maybe he is waiting for us to find him somewhere."

Without a word, she nodded and folded me in a tight embrace. Over her shoulder, I saw Manuel's face, his eyes wide with fear.

"A bus the length of Mexico? ¿Estás loca?" Manuel exclaimed, once we were out the door and walking in the cool night air. "They might ask for papers, for identification perhaps, as we cross state lines!"

"Maestra will ask her brother about that. We will be careful. Let's wait and see what he says." I pushed his hair back so I could see his eyes, but as always it stubbornly fell forward. "Please stay with me until we know more. Please don't leave."

He stroked my face and then took it between his hands and kissed me. We stood by the side of the road for several minutes, my face pressed against his chest. I wished we could stay like that forever.

When we returned to the house, Maestra, perhaps sensing Manuel's concern, asked to speak to him alone in the garden. She gave me an encouraging smile as she closed the door. I stood there for a moment, then walked toward the hallway to find Rosa. As I approached the room that Professor Garcia had entered, I noticed it was brightly lit. Peeking in, I saw an office, lined with books, of course, with a large desk on one side and two upholstered chairs on the other, where Professor Garcia sat reading. He lifted his head and said simply, "¿Sí?"

He sounded annoyed, so I stammered, "I'm sorry . . . I'm disturbing you."

"Well, that depends. If you were going to ask me to lift a heavy object or drive into the city, yes, I'd be disturbed. But something tells me that you have a question and are merely seeking my knowledge or opinion—and that is something I am always pleased to extend." He set down his book and motioned to the other grand chair beside him. "Por favor, siéntate."

As I sank onto the soft cushion, I noticed on the table beside his chair a black and white photograph of a beautiful young woman. Professor Garcia must have noticed my gaze, for he said softly, "My Rita. Wasn't she lovely? She was my student at the university. Three years later, my wife. May you be as fortunate in love." He bowed his head, and I blushed at the thought of Manuel. "What can I do for you?" he asked, folding his hands in his lap and giving me his full attention.

Looking around at all of his books, I took a deep breath. "I wondered if you had any books on a woman named Dolores Huerta?"

He wrinkled his brow, "Dolores Huerta—that name sounds familiar, but I can't place it. Was she a revolutionary? A poet? Where have I heard that name before?"

"My father spoke of her many times. When he was very young, my age in fact, he worked the fields in America and met Dolores and Cesar Chavez."

With that, his eyes brightened. "Ah, yes, now I remember! In the 1960s—the farm workers' strike. Of course! They were so effective with their boycott that even workers at the docks of England refused to unload shipments of grapes." He sat up straight. "Your father witnessed quite an important part of American history."

The thought of my father as a young man in the midst of something important set my heart at a gallop. "Yes, he spoke of a march up through the state of California—many kilometers. He said they began with a few hundred people, and by the time they reached the capital city, there were thousands!" My eyes filled with tears as I pictured my father telling this story, and he had so many times. He'd been just sixteen and already a weathered farm worker himself. I'd seen an old photo of him bare-chested, grinning, his arms around his compañeros in a field somewhere in California.

"Yes, that I remember. The march from a small farming town to the big capital city. I even remember the number: 300 became 10,000. And your father was there?" His eyes widened.

I nodded, thrilled that he, too, remembered important numbers, and that he was impressed with my father's past.

"Wonderful! ¡Magnífico! Yes, no wonder he spoke of this often. A monumental moment in American history. Now, what of this woman, Dolores?"

I took a deep breath. "Well, she was an important part of his stories. She helped organize with Cesar Chavez. He said she was unlike any woman he had ever met. Very determined and not afraid of any man—white or brown." I grinned at the next thought, "He used to tell me I had her spunk . . . that they should have named me Dolores."

He laughed, and I relaxed a bit. Then leaning forward, I looked him squarely in the eye. "But I think she is still living . . . somewhere in California. So, Rosa and I thought that if we could find her . . . maybe she might help us . . . she might know how we can find out about Papá." My voice trailed off, for saying it aloud to such a wise man made it sound like a stretch. But what else did we have?

"I see," he responded, then studied me quietly for a few moments. When he spoke again, his tone was serious, like a doctor giving a diagnosis. "I know nothing of this woman's activities today, but let me call a few colleagues. I am told one can find all sorts of information in an instant with the use of computers. I'm afraid I am still immersed in scrolls and ancient manuscripts, and I write with the use of a legal pad, but let me see what others can discover with the use of modern technology." He reached out and squeezed my arm. This simple touch released a flood of tears that I struggled to hold back. "You clearly love him very much. How pleased he will be to see how passionately his daughters are striving to find him. I wish you the very best. Sí, de verdad," he said gently.

"Gracias. Thank you so much, for everything," I said in a faltering whisper, then rose to flee before I embarrassed myself. But at the door I couldn't help but stop and ask, "So, do you think . . . is it foolish to hope that . . ."

He immediately interrupted my halting question with a firm, "Hope is *never* foolish. Nunca."

After Maestra said goodnight at our closed door, I slipped out to find Manuel sitting on the sofa with blankets and a pillow on his lap.

"I'd be more comfortable under a tree or in their garden," he said quietly.

"Nonsense," I replied. "Here, let me help you." Together we covered the sofa with one soft blanket. I set the pillow at one end and fan-folded the other blanket toward the bottom. "Now take off your shoes."

As he pulled off each athletic shoe, I noticed he was wearing two pairs of socks, and the shoes were a tad too big. He grinned. "A gift from Rafael." So, Lupe's son-in-law had been as generous as Lupe.

I sat on the edge of the coffee table. "What did Maestra say?" I asked timidly.

His eyes shifted away from mine, but his dimple appeared for a moment, and then he spoke. "She said her father will not allow her to go along with this venture unless I pledge to accompany you both for the entire journey, whatever that may be." He lifted his eyes to mine. "She told me to sleep on it and give her an answer tomorrow."

I held my breath.

"No es necesario. There's no need to sleep on it, Alma. He is right. It is my duty to protect you, both of you. No matter what." He took both of my trembling hands in his. "I feel responsible in many ways. Stopping you on your journey, frightening you both, forcing you to share your food, and then not protecting you from the men." He shook his head and scoffed, "Then leading you to the Beast and your fall," he paused, "I could have done better."

"No! No!" I exclaimed. "You have been responsible! You stayed with us when you could have been deported. You helped me with Rosa when she collapsed. You have been wonderful!" I held his face between my hands, but he pulled away and lowered his head again.

"My father says this often, that I could do better, at picking the beans, at finding ways to bring in some money, at getting across the border to my brother. Soy un fracaso. So many times, I failed. I must do better. And now, I must do better for you." He looked up with such sadness, then took my face in his hands and kissed me softly on the forehead, holding his lips there for a moment. "For many reasons, I must do better for you, my little unicorn. And that's what I told Maestra."

Long after Rosa fell asleep, I tossed and turned, overwhelmed by conflicting emotions. I was overjoyed that Manuel had pledged to stay with me, but my heart ached at his feelings of inadequacy. Tomorrow we would seek out Mundo to see if he had any news about Papá, a trip that filled me with both hope and fear. The only thought that I could focus on to calm me was my time with Professor Garcia. Like Papá, he had listened. Like Papá, he had made me feel like what I thought and said was important. He was going to see what he could learn about Dolores, and that made my heart sing.

Restless, I reached for my journal of numbers. As I traced the lovely white flower on the cover lightly with my fingers, I felt certain that one day Papá might touch it as well.

Math Problem #4

Three hundred people set out from Delano, California, heading for the state capital of Sacramento. By the time they reach their destination, they have grown to ten thousand strong. Consider the numbers 300 and 10,000. What are their common factors?

*A common factor is a whole number that will divide exactly into two or more given numbers without leaving a remainder.

Señorita Garcia had offered to drive us to Mundo's, but Rosa refused, insisting we would take the bus and be back by day's end. Meanwhile Señorita would make final plans with her brother, and Professor would make some calls about Dolores. With so much to hope for, my heart felt as light as the hummingbird flitting about in the garden.

When we finally arrived at Mundo's house the next day, a woman who cared for his elderly mother answered the door and said she wasn't sure what street he was working that day. As we walked away, Rosa and I both paused to glance at our old shed behind the house. A young woman, with a baby bound to her chest, was hanging clothes on the line that we had put up when we first moved in. A lump formed in my throat as I thought of José and Ricardo . . . and Mamá. Rosa took a deep breath and approached the woman. I hung back with Manuel, squeezing his hand.

Rosa shook her head as she returned. "She has no idea where he is. Her aunt left early this morning with Mundo, but she does not know where they went to set up the cart."

With a sigh, we set out to search all the areas we had covered in our months with Mundo. We found his weathered stainless-steel cart at the third spot we looked, its dark green vinyl roof cover flapping in the slight breeze. One wheel was bent slightly, tilting the cart toward the street. It was parked in front of an abandoned storefront, whose metal doors had been rolled down and locked as long as I could remember. Beside Mundo's cart was a smaller one offering fruit and drinks packed in ice. It wasn't a busy spot, but he set up here from time to time because he had no competition. While there wasn't a lot of foot traffic, cars and trucks made quick stops throughout the day.

Mundo lifted his head as we approached and paused, perhaps waiting to see if we were potential customers, but suddenly a huge grin lit up his whole face and he threw his arms open wide. "¡Mis muchachas! You are back from Chiapas?" He was a big man, tall and wide, so when he gathered us both up at once, we were crushed together in one swoop, laughing and catching our breath. He glanced at and then beyond Manuel, who hung back a few steps behind us. "And your mother? Is she back as well? I didn't think things would go well with that man." His smiling eyes suddenly became serious, "But if you are looking for work, I am afraid I have nothing to offer right now."

"Oh no, no," Rosa began and then went on to explain our story. She did not mention Tito beyond saying our mother was still with him, but when she got to the part about Papá, I knew his answer before he spoke. Everything about him drooped: his head sagged forward, his full lips turned down, his shoulders caved slightly, and even his large belly seemed to sink.

"No, I have heard nothing at all. I am so sorry to say."

We stood in silence, until I heard my own broken voice speak. "Do you have any idea where we might look for him . . . in el norte?"

"In el norte? Oh, my dear girl, I can't imagine where he is," he faltered. Then in one exhale, he said gently, "I'm afraid Juan may have come to a sad end. You would have heard something by now if he was . . ." He stopped.

"You mentioned a detention center once. Where is this place? Perhaps we can find him there?" My voice was stronger now.

He looked at me a long while before he spoke. "It has been too long for that, I'm afraid. He would have been released by now, deported back to Mexico, and he certainly would have been able to contact us."

"He could be ill or injured," I paused. "Or there could be some other reason?" I watched his eyes closely, but all I saw was sadness.

Before we left him, he offered us tacos, and then reaching into his tin box, gathered up some bills and pressed them into Rosa's hand. "God be with you," he whispered. "Please let me know if you learn anything about Juan."

We rode the bus back in silence.

This I remember vividly. As we passed familiar sights, it felt different to me, empty, cheerless, forlorn. Oaxaca was not home. Nor was I Papá's little girl, the giggly yet serious student, anymore. I wasn't sure who I was or where I belonged. I glanced at Manuel who had taken the seat in front of us so we sad sisters could sit together. I leaned against the window and closed my eyes. Something was pulling me north, away from Chiapas and Mamá, away from Oaxaca, pulling me north with Manuel toward whatever I could learn about Papá. But Rosa? I reached for Rosa's hand. She responded by grasping mine in both of hers. "What now, Rosa?" I asked softly. "Where do *you* want to be? What feels right to you? With Mamá? With Lupe? Here in Oaxaca with Mundo or Señorita Garcia? ¿Dónde?"

I remind myself often that I asked her this, and that when she turned her face to mine, her eyes were bright with tears as she answered firmly, "Wherever you are is my home. Contigo. Let's go look for Papá."

Two days later, Señorita Garcia drove us to Mexico City to meet her brother. In all it took about six hours, plus one stop to eat our packed lunch. Rosa sat in front, so I was able to sit in back with Manuel, holding his hand the whole way. I loved how he played with my fingers and sometimes tickled my thigh. I took his hand and placed the tips of his fingers on my pimienta de cayena scar, running them back and forth and thinking how one day I would show him. A couple of times, I leaned my head on his shoulder and dozed off for a while. There was something special about this quiet time where we couldn't really talk privately, yet the touch of our hands spoke volumes.

Shortly after we had first settled into the car and were on our way, Señorita Garcia told us about her brother, which explained some of the awkwardness we'd felt whenever she spoke his name around her father. Apparently, Orlando, unlike the rest of his family, had detested school, finished reluctantly with poor grades, and then left home at sixteen, refusing to go to university. His passion was soccer, a sport he had tried to pursue until an injury ended his chances. He now drove a bus for a living. While he had kept in touch with his sister and his mother, he and his father had not spoken in years. Señorita Garcia had tried many times to get them to reconcile, but both were too stubborn.

"Even at our mother's funeral," Señorita Garcia said sadly. "It would have broken her heart to see how they avoided each other. Tan triste."

I was thinking how tragic this was when Manuel suddenly spoke up, "What would it accomplish? It wouldn't change anything. Your father will always be disappointed in him, and your brother will always carry that with him."

The car was quiet for a while. No one spoke. Each of us following our own train of thought with this last statement. My heart ached for Manuel, trying desperately to join his brother and make his family—his father—proud. I hoped I wasn't holding him back or slowing him down, although this latest turn of events, that was taking us the length of Mexico, was certainly a stroke of good luck. I squeezed his arm, and he gave me a half smile.

Señorita Garcia's thoughts apparently led from Orlando to me, for she glanced up at me in the rearview mirror and said, "Alma, wherever you end up, go back to school, and especially if you get to el norte. If you settle there, take advantage of their adult school. Learn English as soon as you can—it is free. And pick up your math again. You must." She moved her eyes from the road to me repeatedly. "Promise me, wherever you end up, you will go back to school. ¿Sí?" Her eyes were waiting for my answer. I had shown her my math journal the day before, and she had been beyond thrilled, immediately checking and confirming my answers.

"Sí," I promised, though the thought of going to a school in America terrified me. I hadn't been to school here in two years. Would I be able to catch up anywhere after falling so far behind? I met her eyes in the mirror and managed a smile. "And I will continue my math journal, too," I reassured her.

She nodded. "Good. You can always come back here, you know. When your journey is finished, you can always come back." When she spoke those words, I had an inkling even then that I might never return to Oaxaca.

We approached Mexico City by late afternoon. At first, we were stunned by the tall imposing buildings in the distance, but as we got closer, it was the endlessness of the city that took our breath away. No matter which direction we looked, homes and buildings stretched beyond the horizon, until they looked like little ants marching up to the base of mountains in the far distance. Señorita Garcia grasped the steering wheel tightly as we wound our way into a maze of traffic. Rosa read off the directions for her, and we all craned our necks to check as she changed lanes nervously. Too many cars and trucks. Too many people. We all agreed that we would never want to live here.

Orlando's apartment was on the third floor above a store front, a 7-Eleven in fact. Señorita Garcia said that after driving a bus, Orlando wanted to live where he could walk to shops and restaurants, and 7-Eleven provided him with pretty much everything he needed. It was a narrow street lined with shops—a barber shop next door, a restaurant with a red canopy directly across. It could have been charming except for the electrical poles that lined the street and their maze of wires that stretched above and across in a crazy crisscross fashion.

Orlando lived alone in a small one-bedroom apartment. Not one book was visible, only a large television in one corner and a few soccer magazines on the coffee table in front of the blue sofa. He seemed so unlike his sister and father. Slender, a mass of thick black hair, no balding at the top, he was soft spoken with kind eyes. Perhaps he took after his mother.

Señorita Garcia hugged him fiercely until he pulled away laughing. "Mi hermano! My baby brother," she said. "I've always been like a second mother to him. I was twelve when he was born. He was a bit of a surprise for my parents," she added with a chuckle. He shook his head and rolled his eyes upward.

After offering us each an ice-cold bottle of fruit-flavored soda and discussing his plan for dinner from a local take-out restaurant, he explained that we would be leaving very early in the morning, so it was wise to get a good night's sleep. He asked Manuel to accompany him to the restaurant, and when they returned, there was an ease between them that made me smile. Over dinner, brother and sister argued about sleeping arrangements, for Señorita insisted she would take the sofa and Orlando his own bed because he needed his sleep for the long drive ahead. That's when we learned about the bus's separate compartment near the luggage that relief drivers use to sleep. On a long haul, two drivers took turns, one drove, one slept below. There would be no second driver tomorrow, so this was where he planned to put Manuel, dressed in a bus driver's uniform—in case of checkpoints, just to be safe.

"They don't happen often, and when they do, they generally check the passengers only," he reassured us. "But if you are caught, which I don't expect—again I've never had a problem—but if you are, I know nothing about it. ¡Nada! You stole the shirt and hid away there, okay?"

Manuel nodded with wide eyes.

As we prepared to turn in for the night, we said our real goodbyes to Señorita Garcia, for we would be getting up before light, and she would be heading back to Oaxaca shortly after we left. Both Rosa and I once again thanked her repeatedly for all she had done. But this time, instead of her usual response of "It's nothing," she paused, and what followed revealed a side of her quite different from the Maestra I knew. Even Orlando, who was standing in the doorway on the way to his room, turned at the tone of her voice. It was low and sad.

"I do hope I am doing the right thing here," she began. "My father was right in laying out all the dangers, if you do decide to try to cross the border, but there was a time in my life that I wish I had taken a risk. Something I wanted to do . . . someone . . ." Her voice trailed off.

Orlando leaned in as if straining to hear her thoughts.

"What happened?" I was surprised to hear Rosa's voice behind me.

Señorita lifted her chin. "He was right," she turned toward Orlando, "Papá tenía razón. The worst happened, and . . . Raul . . . lost his life." I watched as a single tear dripped down her cheek.

"Raul?" Orlando asked. Clearly, he knew nothing of this.

"Another teacher I worked with long ago, when I first started. He was helping a group in western Oaxaca, an indigenous tribe, the Triqui, helping them organize. I wanted to go with him that summer, but . . ."

"Papá wouldn't let you." Orlando said, matter of fact.

She shrugged. "There was an ambush, police or paramilitary, doesn't matter. So . . . he was right."

"Was he?"

They looked at each other across the room in silence. Finally, she spoke, almost in a whisper, "I do wonder. If I had been there, it might have ended differently. Tal vez. I might have sensed something or persuaded him to do something else. Who knows?" Her voice broke, "I might have saved him . . . or died with him. ¿Quién sabe?"

Orlando crossed the room and gathered her into his arms. "I'm so sorry, Elena."

He held her while she sobbed, and then, taking a deep breath, she sat back and wiped her tears with the back of her hand. "It was a long time ago," she said.

"I must have been away at soccer camp? Wait, was that the year you went to stay with tia Irene?" Orlando asked.

"Yes," she answered, "although I spent some time with Raul's parents first. We were secretly engaged, you see. Mamá and Papá knew nothing, but his mother knew. She understood the depths of my grief."

"Not even Mamá?"

"No," she looked up with a frown, "you know how she was. Papá always came first. She would have insisted on telling him, and he would have put an end to it."

Orlando grunted. "Did Papá ever know the whole story?"

She laughed sarcastically. "Actually, yes. After Mamá died, when he told me I could never understand his feelings, because I had never loved a man. Oh, I was so angry!"

Orlando's mouth dropped open. "You're kidding? He learned the most painful part of your life in the heat of an argument?"

She nodded.

Shaking his head incredulously, he said, "Well, that's the only way I've ever communicated with him. Thought it was just me."

"It made a difference, I think. He has been gentler with me. In fact, since Mamá died and he had his heart problems, he has softened. You should give him a chance, before he dies. You may never forgive yourself. Piénsalo."

"Oh no, no. I don't need to think about anything concerning him," he said, literally backing away from her. "Don't start that again. Don't worry. I will have no regrets, believe me."

With that, he said goodnight and closed his door.

Señorita Garcia then turned to us and said, "Just be careful out there, whatever you choose to do, be careful. But not too careful. Have no regrets."

No regrets. I now know that no matter what path you take, there will always be regrets. Siempre. For what you did, what you didn't do, for what you should have done. There's no escaping that fact. It's how you live with the regrets that determines your life.

Waking before the sun, we gathered our things and barely had time to kiss a groggy Señorita Garcia goodbye. "Stay in touch. Let me know where you go. Send me math problems! No me olvides." She was still talking as we closed the door.

It was dark as we rode through Mexico City to the bus terminal, but even in the dim light I was overwhelmed by the immensity of the city. Silhouetted against the sky were buildings as tall as mountains and beyond that the remaining blanket of a city stretching out as far as the eye could see.

Despite the early hour, the terminal was teeming with travelers, though most were sleepy and silent. Orlando handed Rosa and me two tickets and instructed us where to board the bus. Rosa reached into her handbag and he waved her off. "No, no, it's all taken care of." Then he motioned Manuel to follow him, and abruptly we were separated.

"Wait!" I shouted, and they both turned. "You're sure he'll be all right?" I asked plaintively. Orlando shot me a quick, hard look, reminding me to be more discreet, but fear for Manuel's safety was more than I could bear.

Manuel stepped forward and wrapped his arms around me. "No te preocupes. I'll be fine, don't worry."

I buried my nose in his chest and inhaled his scent. He lifted my face to his and kissed my forehead. Then he turned and, following Orlando, was swallowed up by the crowd.

Rosa took my arm, "Come on, mi hermanita, let's begin our journey." As she hurried me to our bus, she whispered, "We're on our way!
Can you believe it?" It was the first time I'd seen her excited about
anything in a long time. In fact, I couldn't remember a time when
she'd seemed almost childlike with excitement. It was definitely con-
tagious, but I couldn't let go of my image of Manuel in some small,
confined space.

Our first destination was Guadalajara, another six-hour trip. We
were seated just a few rows behind the driver's seat, so when Orlando
finally took his seat and started up the bus, I kept my eyes on the
back of his head, waiting for some sort of signal—a nod, eye contact,
anything—to tell me that Manuel was on board and okay. But he
simply watched the road ahead.

"Relax," Rosa kept saying, squeezing my hand. "Everything is fine,
I'm sure."

While I had faith in Orlando—he was after all a Garcia—I could
not rest easy. Even the videos on the hanging monitors added to my
anxiety, for they were filled with men kicking, and screaming, and
fighting. I fidgeted in my seat, flip-flopping just like the ninjas on the
screen, until the woman in front of me leaned over her seat back and
hissed, "¡Basta! Will you please sit still!"

Rosa spoke up immediately, "Please forgive her; she is very
nervous."

"I don't care what her problem is, she is driving me crazy."

An old woman sitting beside Rosa asked, "¿Por qué? Why is she
nervous? Where is she going?"

Rosa and I exchanged a glance, and what I heard Rosa say almost
made my eyes bulge out of their sockets. With a face as serious as a
nun's, Rosa said to each of the women in a whisper, "Mamá is sending her to become the wife of an old man in Guadalajara."

All anger disappeared. Their eyes and voices softened at once. "Oh
pobrecita, you poor thing," they murmured.

The woman in front sat down, then turned again, and through the crack between the seats said, "May la Virgen bless you with a kind man."

"Perhaps he'll be too old to bother you," the woman by the window mused. "Perhaps he'll die and leave you some money while you're still young."

Rosa squeezed my hand tight, but I couldn't hold back the giggle—and neither could she. We snorted and sniffled. I rubbed the tears from my eyes and tried to keep my lips turned down in a frown. After that, I felt a bit better.

In Guadalajara, we were to switch to another bus that would take us the longest distance, through Mazatlán to Hermosillo—only three hours from the border city of Nogales. Orlando had arranged to drive that bus as well.

We waited by the first bus until it was empty, then watched as Orlando disappeared toward the back. A few moments later, Manuel appeared, face flushed, hair soaked, carrying a blue shirt in his hand.

Orlando walked behind him. "Put that away for now," he said pointing to the shirt. "Put it back on once you get inside again." Then handing me some money, he said, "Take this. Get him something to drink—and get yourselves something as well. I'll meet you right here in thirty minutes."

"No hay problema. I'm all right," Manuel said even before we could ask. "From time to time it gets hot back there. But at least I had it to myself. The last time I did this, they crammed five guys in a space that fits three."

"You did this before?" I asked.

"Sort of. We snuck in with the luggage. This is a bit nicer. It's a separate compartment, and there's actually a mat and pillow to lie on."

"But the next ride will be much longer!" I said. "Manuel, what if you can't breathe?"

"I can breathe. Don't worry. It's a nice little coffin—relax," he teased.

But I could tell he was not feeling well. And this was after only six hours. "Maybe there is some way Orlando can let you sit on the bus," I tried. But I knew the answer.

"I don't want to take that chance. We've been lucky so far, no checkpoints. But let's stick to the plan. I'll be fine."

Orlando put me somewhat at ease when he met us with two large jugs of water—I hoped for Manuel. As before, he told us where to board the bus and led Manuel away. Once we were settled in our seats, Orlando appeared carrying only one jug. This time he spoke to a few passengers near the front, then leaned toward us and said, "How's everything, ladies?" Then in a whisper, "I made sure your friend was quite comfortable."

Some hours later, I fell asleep only to be awakened when we stopped for a time in the Mazatlán terminal. I saw Orlando step off the bus with his jug of water and return with a large cup of coffee. As he glanced at us, my sleepy eyes widened; he gave a quick nod. Relieved, I fell back asleep.

Though we rode along the coast through the night, I saw nothing of the ocean, but I did relax in the cool night air. As the breeze blew in through the open windows, I was relieved to think that at least Manuel would not be roasting.

When we finally arrived in the city of Hermosillo on a bright sunny morning, I felt such excitement. "Rosa, Rosa—we're just hours from the border! ¿Puedes creerlo? And no checkpoints at all! We made it! Can you believe it?"

"Yes, I can," she said, shushing me and trying to stand and straighten her back. "I feel like I've been riding forever."

We hobbled with the rest of the passengers toward the front of the bus and then waited while they unloaded the luggage. Once finished, Orlando nodded and went around toward the back to get Manuel. A few minutes passed.

"Should we go in the back and see?" I asked.

"No, he said to wait here." So, we waited, but still no Orlando—or Manuel.

"Something's wrong. Lo sé."

Loosening Rosa's grasp, I pulled away from her and ran toward the back of the bus. Just as I reached the rear tires, Orlando came around the corner, and I stopped dead in my tracks. His face was contorted, his eyes wild.

"I can't . . . I can't wake him up," he gasped, and my knees buckled beneath me.

9

Nogales

"Water—get some cold water and ice," I heard Orlando say, as he grabbed my elbow. Leaning into him, I looked back and saw Rosa running toward the terminal.

"I have a water bottle in my pack," I said, steadying myself.

He nodded, and we hurried around the rear of the bus.

Manuel, bare chested, was slumped inside the compartment, his legs dangling over the edge. Orlando's blue uniform shirt sat in a heap beside him. His head was tipped back with his eyes closed and his mouth open; water dripped down his chin where Orlando may have tried to get him to drink. The half-full jug of water sat open beside him.

I climbed in and placed my hands on either side of his face. His skin was hot to touch, and his breaths short and rapid.

"Manuel, Manuel!" I pleaded, "Por favor, open your eyes. Talk to me. Manuel! ¡Háblame, cariño!"

He stirred and moaned.

"He needs fresh air and some cool water," Orlando said.

He leaned in and lifted Manuel's limp arm up and placed it around his neck. "Straighten his legs," he instructed me.

As I bent and reached for his legs, the sharp odor of urine stung my nose. His jeans were soaked. Once we had his legs before him, I sat on the edge beside him and put his other arm around my neck.

"Let's see how far we can get walking him like this," Orlando said.

"If we can just get him to a bench inside where it's cooler, we can tend to him. We'll say he's drunk, if anyone asks. And if he's doesn't improve—we'll get him some help and deal with the consequences. Okay?"

I nodded.

"Ready? ¿Estás lista?" he asked. He slowly stood, securing his other arm around Manuel's waist and hoisting him up.

I moved with them, supporting Manuel on my side as best as I could. Together we limped along. I could feel the heat from Manuel's body against mine. His legs staggered between us, but he began to breathe deeper with occasional coughs in between. Orlando strained with each step.

"Don't look at anyone," he grunted. "Just keep walking until I find a spot to set him down. Stay calm. We can't afford to draw attention."

We made it into the terminal and headed for the first bench. Suddenly, a man, wearing the same uniform shirt as Orlando, approached from the right, motioning me aside, and scooped an arm under Manuel, helping Orlando set him down.

"A stowaway?" he asked with a hint of disgust in his voice.

Orlando groaned. "I wish." He shook his head. "My nephew—who apparently 'stowed away' some tequila. Got drunk in the back of my bus. Kids, nothing but trouble. That's why I never had any of my own. ¡No gracias!"

"Ah," the man nodded knowingly. "Need some clean up on the bus?"

"Already notified," Orlando said smoothly, "but thanks for your help. We've got it from here."

Rosa cautiously approached once the man turned away. She was carrying two cups, one with ice and one full of cold water. I scooped a few cubes of ice into my hand and rubbed them over Manuel's forehead and temples, through his hair, and along the back of his neck. He murmured something I couldn't make out. Steadying his head, we poured a small amount of water between his lips. He gasped a bit but managed to swallow. His eyes fluttered, then opened and focused on me. "Alma, mi amor," he said.

Orlando let out a long sigh. "I'll be back in a minute. Got to get you something to drink with lots of sugar. If anyone bothers you, just mention my name and stay put." Orlando looked exhausted. A shadow of a beard was coming in, his eyes were rimmed in red, and sweat soaked the underarms of his shirt.

I looked up at him and heard myself say in a voice that sounded like Rosa's, "You are the kindest man. Muchas gracias."

His weary face softened into a smile.

Manuel awoke with such a bad headache that he could barely keep his eyes open in the light. Otherwise he seemed okay—quiet and queasy, but okay. I squeezed his hand and rubbed another ice cube along the back of his neck.

He kept whispering my name, "Alma, Alma." It sounded so pretty, like feathers falling.

Orlando returned carrying Manuel's pack and a soda the size of a bucket. "Here, drink this," he said, helping Manuel sit up straight, then to all of us, "We will rest today. I have a motel room I stay at between hauls, nothing much to look at, but very clean, good beds, and it looks like you can all use some sleep. Later this evening," he turned to Manuel, "if you are well enough, a man is coming to drive you all to Nogales."

Manuel nodded with his eyes squeezed shut.

Orlando reached into his shirt pocket, then shaking his head, turned and disappeared again, only to return minutes later with a pair of sunglasses, the price tag hanging off the side. Handing them to Manuel, he said, "Looks like you can use these. I left mine on the damn bus." He sat down beside us. "You sure you're okay?" he asked Manuel.

Manuel slipped the sunglasses on and looked up. "Yes, I'm fine now. I don't know what happened. Just all of a sudden, I felt dizzy, and I don't remember anything else. Nada."

"I should have made more stops to check, but I didn't want to draw attention. Sometimes the damn fan doesn't work well in there and the air gets too warm. Have to do something about that." Orlando bit his lower lip. "Okay, let's get to the men's room so you can clean up and get out of those pants. Then we'll have some breakfast."

Later in Orlando's motel room, we took turns showering while he went out to take care of some business. Then one by one, we stretched out on top of the beds. I curled up with Manuel on one and Rosa took the other. Manuel drifted off to sleep immediately, and though I closed my eyes, I couldn't sleep, partly with worry for Manuel and partly because of our unknown future. What would we do in Nogales once we got there? How would we find our way across the border? Suddenly, the adventure felt scary.

I wondered how Papá had managed to cross and if he ever had gone through Nogales. I knew it had been an easier journey when he was younger, before they erected fences further east and made them taller and more complicated. I still found it strange that while they put up walls, they also put people to work as soon as they got over them. We heard many times that jobs were easy to find in el norte for both men and women, farm work and construction, house cleaning and child care. I wondered how hard it would be to cross now, and if we did make it, what jobs we would find. Maybe Rosa and I could take care of children while Manuel worked with his brother.

I hadn't asked Rosa yet, but I was hoping we could help Manuel find his brother first, and then maybe we could try contacting Papá's son Diego and his aunt Berta. Rosa had shown me their telephone number that she carried in her bag. She worried about losing it, but I reassured her after looking at the numbers once that I had committed it to memory. We had no idea how they felt about us or how they'd react if we ever knocked on their door. Diego was our half-brother, yet we had never met. Papá talked about him from time to time, and Diego knew about us, but we lived in separate worlds. Mamá was jealous of that part of Papá's life, so any discussion had led to tension. But still, Rosa and I had discussed the possibility of contacting them if we actually made it to el norte. They were a connection to Papá.

And then there was Dolores. My heart sank at the thought of Professor Garcia's news. He was not sure how I could contact her, for one of the things he had learned was that she was traveling all over the country for a women's group to encourage Latinas in America to run for political office. Where her home was, he didn't know. But I could always contact a United Farmworkers office and see if they could help. His sources also told him of a serious injury Dolores had received at the hands of a police officer—broken ribs and a ruptured spleen. She had been protesting on a picket line for some injustice, but that had been more than ten years before. I wondered if my father had ever heard about that. Apparently, Dolores had recovered, for there she was, back out on the road, encouraging other women to be leaders.

Professor Garcia had been quite impressed with her accomplishments, for he had also learned that she had been given an award by the president of the United States. It was called the Eleanor Roosevelt Human Rights Award. The professor wanted me to remember that because Eleanor Roosevelt was another great woman who I should learn about and admire. So, while it was encouraging to know that Dolores was still alive and quite active across the country, I still wasn't certain how to find her. The best advice he could offer was to keep an eye on the news and find someone with a computer.

One step at a time, I told myself, just like solving a complicated math problem. Turning on my side, I could hear Rosa's breaths soft and easy. I closed my eyes again and summoned my Dolores spunk. ¡Sí, se puede! I could do this. I just needed a few hours of sleep.

It was late afternoon when Orlando returned to our room looking dog-tired and disheveled. He pulled up a chair, plopped down, and leaned forward, his elbows resting on his knees and his hands clasped between them. "Okay," he said, taking a deep breath. "I've got some important news for you."

Rosa and I exchanged a glance as we sat side by side on the edge of the bed. Manuel straightened up, resting his back against the headboard.

Orlando's eyes brightened as he began, "First of all, my sister is to know nothing about these details. Okay? She believes, as agreed to by our father, that we are helping you get settled in Nogales, close enough to the border to take other matters into your own hands. She wanted me to help you find a place to stay and some work to get by for now. For this, she gave me a certain amount of money. She promised our father she would do nothing more, although I know she wishes she could." He sat back, stretched out his legs, and crossed his arms against his chest. "Well, I promise my father *nothing!* I can help you get across the border—or at least I know someone. Now don't get me wrong, this is not an area I am experienced in. I just know people who are, and this guy, well, I have done him a few favors, and he owes me. So because of that and this money, he has agreed to get the three of you across." He paused, "What do you think?"

We all spoke at once, a jumble of excited responses. "Are you serious?" "But how?" "Is this really possible?"

Manuel moved down to the end of the bed. "He's a coyote?"

Orlando nodded. "A journey across the border is always uncertain, no matter whose hands you are in. It may be smooth—Señor José is a good man, a good businessman—then again, you never know. It all

depends on the patrols. Anything can happen. I want you to understand that. Now, I can give you the details, unless you want to use the
money to take some time in Nogales and find your way on your own.
Your ride should be here shortly."

By noon the next day, we were sitting in an empty house in northern
Nogales, Mexico, with ten other men, women, and children, waiting
for Señor José's instructions. The house was fairly isolated, situated at
the end of a dirt road and surrounded by trees and brush. Rosa and
I hadn't had a chance to really talk beyond our rapid-fire decision
in Orlando's presence. Our ride to Nogales the night before had not
arrived until two in the morning, so our sleep had been in restless
spurts and our goodbye to Orlando hurried and brief. Rosa and I
both felt we had not been able to adequately thank the Garcias but
decided we would send a long letter when we were settled somewhere
with good news to share. We would show the same kindness to someone else in need one day.

We had been dropped off at the house earlier, just as the sun was
rising. A woman with tired eyes met us at the door and instructed us
to be quiet. Glancing around the unfurnished house, we saw people
stretched out on the floor sleeping. We were given water bottles and
blankets and told to drink water to get hydrated and try to sleep—for
we would be traveling that night. We found a corner, laid out our
blankets, and settled in. Rosa and I whispered about our fears and
excitement that we would actually be crossing that night, but even
our whispers filled the quiet room. So we lay back, closed our eyes,
and as exhausted as we were, we managed to doze off a bit.

A few hours later, we were awakened and told to gather in the
front room as Señor José had arrived. We all took turns looking out
the front window to see the man who would be leading us to our new
lives. Manuel said Señor José looked like a boxer: small, but muscular,

and quick on his feet. I could see him hopping over boulders and scurrying through canyons. He carried a small phone that fit in his hand. I watched as he pushed buttons with his thumbs, then paced back and forth beside his truck as he talked, his hand to his ear. His voice rose and fell smoothly in melodic Spanish one minute, then cut to the harsh, choppy sounds of English.

Just as we were told by Orlando, a young woman who was unpacking food and water bottles said that we were in good hands. "If you do as he says, and God is with you, you will make it with little trouble. But if you stray from his advice," she paused, and then shaking a finger at us, she said in a voice like a croaking frog, "you will rot in the sun."

She then went on to tell us about two men who had grown impatient waiting for a group to assemble and had left on their own for the border, only to return a few days later. They'd been caught by the Border Patrol minutes after scaling the huge fence. "Fools!" she jeered. "You have to know la migra's habits and how to make their tricks work in your favor. José will know the best way, the best time. ¡Pendejos!"

About this time, a woman and her two small sons entered, looking weary and frightened, certainly unfit for a difficult journey. Distracted by their arrival, we were startled when Señor José suddenly strode into the room and called us together. He wore a black tight-fitting T-shirt, jeans, and black athletic shoes. He was clean shaven, no mustache, and his dark hair was slicked back perfectly, not a hair out of place. His phone was now fastened in a case on his belt.

Just like during his phone call, he paced back and forth as he spoke. "Think of this journey in three stages. The first is getting across the border. Many of you have seen the steel fence," he glanced around at each one of us. "Getting over or under or around it is not the problem. Not at all. It is the other barriers we need to fear—the underground sensors, the high-tech lights, and of course the Border Patrol itself.

They are everywhere on the land and in the air. But if you do as I say, you have a very good chance of evading them. Once we make it across the border, the next stage is the trip from the border to the road where our vehicle will be waiting, and this will involve la migra possibly hiding like lizards behind every rock or flying like vultures above us. If we succeed there and make it to the vehicle, the final stage is transporting you to Phoenix, a big city where you can easily disappear and begin your new life."

He stopped pacing and scanned the room again. "Okay, are we ready for instructions? Escuchen con atención."

I doubt if any of us present could have listened more carefully than we already were. Even the smallest of children sat with eyes and mouths wide open.

"Wear dark clothing, black, brown, or dark blue—but not red. Wear two pair of pants—this will save your legs from cactus spines or scorpion stings—and of course wear only comfortable, sturdy shoes—not huaraches!"

I thought of Dolores dressed in red and of my precious brown shoes.

"If possible, carry at least two gallons of water, some canned food, and salted peanuts to help hold off dehydration. Now my first plan will not take us through that much of the desert, but if you get caught, if we have to abandon my first plan, I want you all prepared for the longer desert walk. This can be very dangerous if you are not careful. ¡Muy peligroso! The heat can be deadly."

"What is the first plan?" an anxious voice asked.

"I do not like to give you too much detail up front. I never know where this information will end up. So, I will tell you each step along the way. However, if we are stopped by la migra, scatter. ¡Corran! Run in different directions. Do not all follow me! We cannot all hide behind the same bush.

"Next, be patient. Learn from nature. Sit tight, wait—out-wait la migra—and you just might make it. Now, if you are caught . . . remember you are all Mexican. Pick a state, a city. Know its fiestas, its patron saint, its local heroes, its soccer team. ¡Todo!"

Manuel glanced at me. We had already taught him everything about Oaxaca that we could think of, so he could pass as our brother.

Señor José paused and cleared his throat. "But chances are they will just drop you back here in Nogales. That's the easiest and cheapest thing they can do. Then, we will begin again. It isn't over. We try a different route. ¿Está claro? ¿Sí? Okay?"

Everyone nodded.

Then he added, "Now I don't need to tell you how important it is to keep my name and this house confidential. There are not that many honest guides out there these days."

The young woman who had just arrived spoke up. "Disculpe. When will I be able to speak with my husband in California?" Her youngest boy was sleeping in her arms; the other stared up at her with dazed eyes.

"When you get to the safe house in Phoenix. There you will all contact your families in the States and make final plans to join them."

Rosa and I exchanged a glance.

"Well," Señor José said with his hands on his hips, "be ready to go right at 10:00 p.m."

I saw Rosa bless herself from the corner of my eye. Even Manuel seemed to bow his head in prayer. I sighed and squeezed my eyes shut. The first thing I saw was Papá's face—and that was enough.

Math Problem #5

The temperature in the Arizona desert climbed to 47° Celsius. Convert this to Fahrenheit.

The ground temperature is reported to be 140° Fahrenheit. Convert this to Celsius.

10

Border of Crosses, Desert of Bones

Señor José pulled up in a van shortly after 10:00 p.m. When he swung open the side door, I was surprised to find that the back and middle seats had been removed. "Squeeze in the best you can," he repeated as two or three squirmed in at a time.

We ended up sitting with our legs drawn up tight, four across, about four-deep with the children leaning on their mothers. We were jostled about for maybe an hour. The pungent smell of body odor left me nauseous and light-headed. Several people kept murmuring prayers, which may have comforted them, but only added a sense of foreboding for me. I wanted to scream for them to stop. I lowered my head between my knees but couldn't breathe. I lifted my head and gulped some air. I turned to Rosa, whose eyes were comforting. We clasped hands.

The van began to slow and took a sharp turn at an upward angle. Those in the back began to moan as the rest of us slipped back, crushing them. It bumped and scraped, then leveled out and finally came to a stop. "Not a sound!" Señor José said as he turned off the motor and just sat. Everyone seemed to hold their breath as we waited for the door to open.

"What are we waiting for?" I mouthed to Manuel, who shrugged and shook his head.

A child whined, and his mother shushed him. Suddenly a tap came on our door, and it slowly opened. A man motioned us to follow while silencing us with his other finger to his lips.

Within a matter of minutes, we all exited the van, slipped through a hole in a chain-link, barbed wire fence, and began walking hurriedly up hills and through ravines. I thought I heard a car start and a motor fade away. Señor José? Someone else was leading us ahead, so perhaps Señor José was not making the journey with us. He was, after all, the boss, not the mule. Perhaps he would be waiting for us on the other side?

After about thirty minutes, someone asked, "¿Dónde estamos? Where are we? When will we get to the fence?"

A man behind me laughed. "What fence? We crossed already. The gringos' steel wall is not complete yet. José knows where the holes are."

"But where *is* la migra? Aren't they watching the holes?"

"They can't watch every hole every minute. But don't relax yet. We have a long way to go."

"Shut up you, pendejos!" a voice hissed. "You are inviting la migra to hike with us!"

Manuel walked in front, offering his hand to both Rosa and me when needed. While our eyes adjusted to the darkness somewhat, it was still difficult to make out the path before us. I stumbled over rocks, falling twice. We walked single file most of the way, though occasionally Rosa and I leaned on each other or Manuel held my hand.

I desperately wanted to talk to Rosa. What was she thinking? Everything had happened so quickly, we hadn't had a chance to really open our hearts. Plus Manuel was always there, and I wondered how she felt about that. Things were a little different between us ever since Manuel and I had become close. I reached for Rosa's hand, and she grabbed mine tightly. I thought of the car ride to Mexico City and how Manuel and I had managed to speak through touch. I squeezed hers back and hoped she could feel how much I loved her.

We seemed to walk forever. One hour. Two. Three. Maybe more. I couldn't say. I wondered how far ahead the road was with the vehicle that would take us to Phoenix. Would we be safe then, or would the police check cars along the way as well? As we walked through the night, I felt conspicuous. Where was the Border Patrol? Were they watching us somewhere, waiting for us around the bend? Señor José had spoken of cameras. I imagined I was being watched on a screen somewhere as I was heading toward a trap. As we continued to walk, a few lagged behind. I could hear a child's soft cry. Rosa and I glanced back. If we waited or went back to help, we would lose the others. Looking around, I thought how easy it would be to get lost. I looked up at the stars, trying to find a constellation or some touchstone to use as a guide.

Suddenly ahead, there were whispers followed by a rustle of bushes. Those in front turned to us and said, "We are near the road. Find a bush and hide. Pass it on."

Manuel turned to those behind us and relayed the information. The three of us scurried to an area of large brush and squatted down.

"What do we do now? What are we waiting for?" someone said from the bushes beside us. "Shhhhh!" came a hiss from beyond.

We waited. Sitting still let the chill of the night creep in. Without movement, our bodies cooled, and we began to shiver. We huddled together for warmth. Manuel's lips brushed against my hair, and as tired as I was, I felt revived. I hugged Rosa, whose head was bowed. She looked up and forced a smile.

"We're almost there," I whispered, then closed my eyes and waited.

Thirty minutes, maybe an hour, passed until the faint sound of a motor grew louder. Car lights appeared, the car drove slowly, then stopped. A door slid open and a voice pierced the night, "Hurry, hurry!" Groans and grunts filled the air as we all strained to get ourselves up and moving and into the waiting van. Like the other, there were no seats, but we knew the routine and quickly filed in. I checked the driver. It was not Señor José.

"Any others out there?" the driver spoke to the darkness.

A man's voice answered. "Yes. Give me ten minutes." It was our guide.

"I'll give you five."

The guide stepped back and headed into the darkness. Our door closed and the van slowly pulled off the road. Lights and motor off. We sat in the dark in silence. No one spoke.

Suddenly a tap and the driver jumped, "¡Mierda! Mother of God!" The guide was at the door with a man, the woman and two children. Someone else had stayed behind to help her. Bless his soul, I thought.

Once everyone was in, the guide shut the door and stepped back into the darkness. Like a coyote, he scurried into the brush, heading the way we came.

We all settled in with a collective sigh. I didn't care how long this drive was or how crowded we were. We were on way to a city with the name of a bird that stood for rebirth. I smiled at the thought of the Alma who had learned that in school long ago. I leaned against Manuel, and he kissed my temple.

Suddenly a shout from the front vibrated through me like an electric current. "¡La migra!" Ahead there were two sets of lights blocking the road. The van swerved to the left, then jolted into reverse, only to skid backwards into a small ditch. The driver gunned the motor, but the wheels just spun. The front door swung open, and the cursing driver took off into the darkness, leaving us in a heap in the back of the van.

Two men struggled with the side door, finally jerking it open. The first out were the last in—the man, the woman and two children. Along with the men at the door, they fled into the darkness. Just as the rest of us clambered on hands and knees toward the door, a patrol car pulled up right beside it and a blinding light swept through the interior. "Do *not* try to run. Come on out, one at a time."

Startled, I sat up; it was a woman's voice, speaking first in Spanish, then in English. Trembling, I held my hand up to block the light.

In the dim shadow stood a figure in uniform, hair swept up in a bun, same Indian features as mine. As I slid out of the van, I saw her name pin: Rodriguez. She stood with both feet planted firmly on the ground and with an air of authority and power that I had never witnessed in a woman before. I wondered if this was what my father had seen in Dolores.

Her white male partner with a thick mustache bound our wrists with strips of plastic and instructed us to sit along the road. I thought of our similar experience after we had jumped off the Beast, only then we had been in our own country with only Manuel at stake. According to Señor José, they would probably send us back to Nogales, Mexico, and we would try again, a different route. But what if they sent us all the way back to Oaxaca—and Manuel back to Guatemala? I turned to Manuel, whose eyes looked defeated.

"You'll do fine," I tried to encourage him. "You have Oaxaca in your blood now—mi hermano." I squeezed his bound hands with both of mine. But as headlights approached in the distance, and a van with Border Patrol on the side pulled up, I started to shake. Rosa and I locked eyes.

As frightened as we were, processing at the Border Patrol station was clearly a matter of routine for the officers. Despite their uniforms and imposing gun belts, they were not harsh or mean, but rather businesslike and indifferent. We were asked our names and where we were from. Manuel's answers as our brother seemed convincing. One person asked if we had ever crossed before. We all stressed that this was our first time. We were moved to a holding cell that was already packed with other weary souls stretched out on the cement floor or slouched on a long cement bench that lined the wall. After fretting and sweating for hours, we were placed on a bus and driven back across the border to Nogales, Manuel still safely with us.

The bus drove along the tall steel fence that seemed to stretch for miles. As we curved around to the Mexican side, the sun came up, revealing the most breathtaking sight: White crosses with wreaths of flowers lining the fence. When I asked what it was, the answer made my heart stop. A tribute to those who had died crossing.

We rode in silence until the bus stopped and we solemnly filed out.

Once outside, Rosa turned to me and said, "Remember what Señor José said? This time we will walk the desert." Her eyes searched mine, for what? Encouragement? A change of heart?

I answered, "You said yourself, we will make it. It's meant to be." I know my voice sounded as spiritless as I felt, so I added, "So what do you want to do?"

She paused, then shook her head. "I guess we must try again. What else can we do? The money has been paid."

I leaned into Manuel and closed my eyes.

One member of our group, who had been through this before with Señor José, told us that, unlike most coyotes, José did not abandon his chickens, so to stay together and wait. As soon as the bus had driven off, sure enough, a man approached our group and said he was there for Señor José. I turned to Rosa who stood alone beside us. I reached out toward her, but she set her shoulders back and lifted her chin. "We will make it this time," she said, and began to follow the others.

We never actually saw Señor José again. That evening a guide loaded us once again into the van, telling us not to worry, that we would be taking the safest route. When we pointed out that Señor José had said the other route was the safest, he simply shook his head. Exhausted, I fell asleep, my head on Manuel's shoulder. For how long I don't know, but when we came to a stop, I woke suddenly, my heart racing. Stiff and aching, I eased myself out of the van. We made our way through brush up a slope until we came to a stop. Ahead some distance, I could make out in the moonlight what appeared to be a tall, solid wall. Would they be able to make a hole in this one? But instead of waving us on toward the wall, our guide motioned us to follow him along a parallel trail.

When he finally stopped ahead, those beside him began to raise their voices in alarm. He scolded them to be silent. Once we caught up and gathered round, we saw what caused the concern. The dim light of his flashlight revealed a hole in the embankment barely large enough for one person to squeeze through. Rosa and I clung to each other as we listened to him say that it got larger as we descended, the length was no more than fifteen meters, that we were to pull our shirt up over our nose and mouth, and most importantly, remain silent and move quickly.

"Go, go, vámonos!" he commanded to two men beside him. Then he turned to the rest of us and said, "Follow me or you are on your own," and he scurried into the hole.

Rosa and I held back as others hesitantly squatted and crawled. Finally, Manuel pulled us along and said, "I'll go first."

I watched as he disappeared into the hole, his feet kicking up dirt behind him. Rosa went next, and I crept close behind her. Dirt was crumbling around as, belly flat, I dragged myself in until it leveled out and I was able, first, to crawl and then to walk hunched down. I moved quickly to stay as close to Rosa as possible and to avoid being trampled by whoever was clambering behind me. The complete darkness, the rank smell of damp earth, the airless, claustrophobic oppression, the muffled sobs and suppressed grunts seemed to last forever, but finally I felt fresh air on my face. Once through, I was pulled to my feet by Manuel and Rosa. We quietly hugged, brushed each other off, and waited for the others to emerge. Once all were through and accounted for, we began to walk.

Once again, we had made it over, or should I say under, the border. Now, if only we could get to our transport vehicle safely, and then to Phoenix. Despite a sleepless night and a few cat naps, we were now surging with energy, determined to make it this time. We kept a quick pace, close on the heels of our guide. But a few hours into the walk, we began to slow down, letting others pass.

"Maybe we should have waited a day or two," Rosa panted. "Maybe we should have gotten our full strength back."

"I don't remember being given a choice," Manuel pointed out, then added, "but don't worry. We'll make it this time. Estoy seguro."

We walked like zombies through the night and morning. My legs throbbed. My feet and hands were numb, I thought at first from the night's cool air, but as the sun flared up in the horizon and began its blazing ascent, I realized it had more to do with a lack of circulation. With the sun directly above us, the guide finally told us to take a break. As we stretched out on the hot desert floor, I wiggled my toes and flexed my fingers in an effort to bring them back to life. Little red bugs scurried about, and as a prickly sensation returned to my extremities, it felt like the bugs were biting me everywhere.

Lightheaded and nauseous, I forced myself to take a swig of water from my jug, but it was warm and left me even thirstier. My lips were cracked and my mouth so dry, when I tried to swallow, my tongue stuck to the back of my throat. Beside me, Rosa was pulling thorns out of her pant leg, and Manuel had his head down between his knees.

Our guide instructed us to take a break and rest for a while because there was still a long walk ahead, but he kept insisting this was a safer route. As we scanned the horizon, we had to agree. As far as the eye could see was every type of cactus imaginable—mighty saguaros reaching for the sky, clumps of prickly pear and cholla— with occasional rocks and more rugged terrain in the far distance, but no sign of the Border Patrol.

Desperately, we tried to find some comfort there in the midst of the blistering heat. We curled into a circle, so our heads could rest on one another rather than the hot ground. Two men took turns watching for snakes. Arranging our rebozos, Rosa and I tried to

shade our faces, but the heat seared through nonetheless. I immediately dozed off. How long I have no idea, but it was all I could do
to force myself to get up. With the scorching sun directly before
us, we slogged on. My legs felt heavy, my head light. Each step
took enormous energy; each step felt like my last. With my rebozo
now covering my face, I peeked out periodically to watch the path
of the ball of fire. Surely it was close to sunset. Hour after hour, I
held up my finger to measure the distance from sun to horizon, but
each time I looked, the orange ball was the same distance, as if it
had stopped in its descent.

Perhaps I had already died and this was hell after all.

Just like my hands and feet had gone numb, my mind seemed to
do the same. I would suddenly come to and realize that I was walking
along, yet a moment before I had no sense of consciousness at all.
Startled, I looked around to see Manuel ahead a few feet and Rosa
behind, both oblivious as well.

To keep focused and clear, I tried to create a math problem, one
involving angles and the sun, but a fuzziness erased the picture
before me that I sketched on a chalkboard in my mind. Everything
kept going blank, but I kept trying. In the midst of one of these
attempts, a commotion ahead woke me completely. Several people
had stopped and formed a semi-circle. A few bent over and lifted
something from the ground. As I came nearer, I saw a pile of belongings. Backpacks, jackets, shoes, empty jugs, even a doll and a stuffed
tiger. Some group had decided to lighten their load. As we trudged
forward, I felt strangely comforted; others had passed through this
same spot before us. Just as I reasoned: It had been done; therefore, it
could be done.

We moved on into the descending night in silence, each struggling
with what little energy we had left. We did not cling or complain, but
stayed separate unto ourselves, pushing on. It seemed the least we
could do for each other. To just keep moving. We stopped once more

for a short rest and then chose to make as much progress as we could walking in the cooler air.

Shortly after sunrise, as the heat began to claim us once again, there was a sharp cry up ahead, not so much of warning, but disturbing in its animal-like moan. I wondered if someone had come across a deadly snake or even a scorpion. Gathering strength, we hobbled quickly forward. One man before me sank to his knees, while a woman turned away, clutching her stomach, then bent forward with dry heaves.

Manuel arrived first and, with his arm, pushed me behind him in a fiercely protective manner. I peeked around his shoulder, preparing myself for a coiled beast, but instead what I saw beneath a bush were the decayed remains of the few who had come before us. Clothing and bones were intertwined. Clumps of long black hair clung to the brush, refusing to be swept away in the warm desert winds. One of the skulls glared at the sky; the other was turned away.

"Looks like two women and two children," a man beside them said, bowing his head.

"We should bury them," said another.

"No, we haven't the time or the strength," a woman said, leaving us all in silence. No one refuted her statement.

"Es verdad. Pray for their souls and let's move on," our guide said.

Rosa was sobbing as I numbly took her arm and moved her forward. Manuel took her other arm. But within a matter of minutes, we were walking single file again, each in our own personal struggle. Then just a few kilometers ahead, another body. A full skeleton splayed out face down, faded blue baseball cap intact, arms stretched before him. I wondered if he had set out to find help for the ones behind. If so, they must have died hoping that help was on the way, while he died knowing it wasn't.

Maybe Professor Garcia was right. He'd been right the summer Señorita Garcia's novio died. I tried to remind myself of the many who made it, but the image of the others was too fresh to lighten my heavy heart.

As the sun peaked in the sky, our group began to struggle and stumble, some as muscle cramps began to plague them (something we had been warned about if we didn't drink enough water), while others, like me, were weighed down by the sight that had sapped our already waning spirits. A few insisted they needed to stop and rest, while others feared we would never awaken. Too exhausted to care, I collapsed onto the ground, my head on my pack. Instantly, I fell deep asleep. No dreams, no restlessness, just a painless blank—until my head began to throb, throb, throb. Suddenly, Manuel was tugging me awake. I refused to respond and nestled deeper into my cocoon. To my surprise, he twisted my arms until they hurt. He had never been so rough before.

"All right!" I said, trying to push myself up, but my hands were useless. Suddenly, with a jerk, I was pulled to my feet. As I came to my senses, I saw that it was not Manuel who was tugging on me, but a Border Patrol agent.

"You cabrones are lucky we found you," he was saying. "Do you know how many have died in this hellhole?"

Rosa stumbled toward me. Her eyelids were slightly swollen, so I couldn't read her face. We leaned into each other. Manuel stood beside us, his head hanging down. As disappointed as I was, I was also relieved. We wouldn't die in the desert after all, but would we begin again? I'd heard others speak of their fourth, fifth, sixth crossing. I couldn't even think on that level; it was too much.

As we climbed into their vehicle, I thought of Papá. Had he gone through this type of journey as well? I had always pictured him riding in a truck like he did on his way to work the fields in Oaxaca. But now I realized that his crossings were just as perilous. I couldn't imagine him dying in the desert, though; he was too smart for that. He'd made the trip so many times; he'd know the best place to cross.

But we were not so savvy, and I wasn't so sure of Señor José and his safest routes either. Glancing at Rosa, whose head was in her clasped hands, I knew we were foolish to attempt this again. This thought became even clearer as we bumped endlessly through the desert in the Border Patrol vehicles, coming finally to an isolated two-lane highway where a van was waiting to transport us to headquarters. I doubt we would have made it on foot; certainly, some of us would have perished.

"How did they find us out there?" I heard a woman ask as we were transferring to the van.

"El pájaro grande. The big bird in the sky," was the reply. "Didn't you hear the helicopter pass over?"

They did not tie our hands this time, for none of us had the strength to fight or the foolishness to run. We eagerly accepted the water bottles and gulped them down despite instructions to take it slow.

As I settled into a seat beside Rosa, she turned to me and through cracked lips said, "No more. We are not crossing again."

Looking back at the endless stretch of desert, I thought now of our journey south. To what? Certainly not Chiapas. Oaxaca? Señorita Garcia would help us there. But Oaxaca for me was Papá. And Papá wasn't in Oaxaca. Papá was, possibly, I hoped, *I felt*, in el norte. And then there was Manuel. Surely, he would not turn back, and I could not imagine my life without him now. So, where did that leave me? I could never part from Rosa, yet I could not see myself going back. I closed my eyes and leaned my head against the seat. The vision of the skeleton stretched out in the desert floated vividly before me, as if he was riding on waves of sand. In his dying moments, he had not turned back toward his home. No, he had faced north, his arms reaching out toward his dream, even to the end.

Math Problem #6

*Chart on wall of Border Patrol waiting room from Mexico's
Foreign Relations Office:*

*Deaths along the Mexico/California border: 1995: 61; 1996: 87;
1997: 149; 1998: 329; 1999: 358.*
*Written at the bottom: 2000, to date mid-August, 401—crossed
out and replaced with 411.*

What is the average number of deaths per year?
*Consider just the more recent three years, 1998–2000. What is
the average number of deaths each day?*

I realized, as I wrote and then computed my answer, that this
wouldn't include the bodies we saw in the desert or all those unaccounted for throughout the years.

11

Night of the Blinding Stars

This time no one met us at the drop off point at the bus station in Nogales. No Señor José. No van without seats. Not that any of us would place our trust in him again. I wondered what his success rate was percentage-wise: 50%, 30%? Hit and miss? I would never want Orlando to know of our fate; better he thought we were safely in el norte, and that his plan to defy his father had been a success.

Rosa had been silent since her declaration that she would not attempt to cross again. Curled up into herself, she slept through most of the deportation ordeal or simply nodded yes or no to the few questions I asked, so I left her alone. Manuel, who had developed a cough, had been exhausted as well. When I asked him what he thought we should do next, he pulled me to him and whispered "Let's talk about it later. Más tarde, mi amor," and then fell asleep with his head on my shoulder. So, I had let it all go, figuring our destiny would take its own path no matter how hard I tried to plan ahead.

Once at the bus station, however, a decision had to be made. Starving, we took inventory of our remaining money, bought a few burritos and iced water bottles from a vendor, sat down on a bench outside of the terminal, and ate in silence. We licked our fingers and gulped from the bottles. I savored the cool liquid easing down my throat, thinking how desperate I had been for this simple need. Could I go through that again?

As if answering my thoughts, Rosa cleared her throat and spoke.

"We should call the Garcias and arrange to go back. They will be worried about us."

Manuel kept his head down, eyes averted. I waited a few moments, then said, "Rosa, I'm just not sure."

"Sure of what? We would have died out there." There was a mark on her left cheek, a burn or scrape. I wanted to reach out and touch it.

"Sí, lo sé. I agree. But I'm not sure, absolutely sure, that giving up is the answer. I think we need to rest and think things through. Consider our options. Make a decision when we are more clearheaded."

"More clearheaded? ¡Eso es ridículo! I'm beginning to wonder if we are capable of being clearheaded," she said, grabbing her water bottle and taking a long drink.

"What if we rest and then try one more time, but not in the desert. The first route could have worked. La migra isn't always there. Look at all the people who do make it."

"You saw the numbers on that wall," she said sharply. "I saw you writing them down in your little book." So, she hadn't been sleeping after all.

"But those numbers are nothing compared to those who make it—hundreds, thousands!"

She looked at me with weary eyes. "No puedo. I can't do it again. I just can't," then softly, "You go ahead. You and Manuel."

My heart sank. "Rosa! I'm not going anywhere without you!" I shouted. A man walking by turned to look at us. I reached for her hand. "Rosa, we planned this together. Please. We can't give up. What about Papá?"

Her shoulders slowly sank. Finally, she said, "You saw the bones in the desert. You know now how dangerous it is to cross."

"But Papá has done this for years! He knew where to cross!" I cried.

She paused, then lifted her eyes to mine. "But the fences went up and the dangers increased in those last years before he disappeared. You saw the numbers in 1997. They almost doubled!"

I was stunned that she had noticed that, too. "So that's it? We just give up and assume that he's dead?"

I thought her silence was her final answer, but her eyes slowly welled up with tears as she took a breath and haltingly said, "Alma, we've been through this . . . if he isn't dead . . . if he's living somewhere in el norte . . . he would get a message to us."

"He could be ill," I said, though this was not what was eating at my soul.

"It's been three years. If he recovered, he'd contact us or those caring for him would. And if he's in a coma or something, with no identification, well, how would we ever find him? Search every institution in America?" She had moved closer to me and placed her hand on my leg.

I knew what I had to say, what I had to let out of the deep recesses of my mind, but it frightened me. Before, when I allowed even a glimpse of this possibility, it was incomprehensible . . . until now. Now I was beginning to understand.

I turned to Manuel, who had been silent. He was biting his lower lip and nervously squeezing the empty bottle. "Manuel, tell me now. What have you been thinking?" The torment on his face was the answer I expected, for it was what I felt myself.

"Alma, I don't want us to part, but I can't let my family down either," he rubbed his forehead. "No sé. I don't know what to do, and I certainly can't make your decision for you. But mi hermano, mi familia, they are waiting . . . yet, Alma," he stroked my cheek with his thumb, "I feel my life belongs with you, too."

I buried my face in his chest and sobbed while he rocked me.

When I sat up, Rosa was wiping tears as well. "You go with Manuel, Alma. I'll be all right. Believe me, I will."

But I shook my head. "No, Rosa, that's not my point. It's Papá. I think . . . I feel . . . he could be alive."

I thought of the letter in his wallet, his secret that I had held close to my heart. It wasn't meant for my eyes, so it wasn't meant for Rosa's ears either. I would not share that, but the idea, the possibility was enough . . . that he had found love . . . chose love . . . somewhere else. It had seemed impossible before. Papá would never abandon us—he wouldn't. But wasn't it possible that love could twist your heart up so tight, you made choices that were difficult to understand? Yet how to explain that to Rosa?

"Rosa," I began, "what if Papá made a choice, one that he was ashamed of now?"

Rosa's eyes were wide in disbelief.

"I know, I know," I continued, "I couldn't imagine him doing that either, but . . . what if, just what if, he is there somewhere? Don't you think he would want us to find him anyway . . . to forgive him and to love him anyway? Our Papá?"

Rosa shook her head. "No, I can't imagine that, not for a minute. Papá was not that kind of man." She paused and looked at me from the corner of her eye. "Do you really believe he would do that?" she asked.

Manuel's arm was still around me, his hand gently squeezing my shoulder. I sighed so deeply I felt like all air had left my lungs. "When I think about it, no, I can't imagine that. Not when I picture his face at the door returning from those long months away. ¡Tanto amor! But then, sometimes it's not about being 'that kind of man.'" I stopped to collect my thoughts. "Rosa, I'm not saying I think he deliberately chose to leave us. No. I'm saying that . . . well . . . it *is* another possibility . . . a possibility that considers him alive, not dead." Reaching out, I took both of her hands in mine. "I just want to know . . . whatever the answer is. I want to see for myself or at least know that I tried. ¿Entiendes?"

She closed her eyes but didn't let go of my hands. In a voice so weak I had to lean in to hear, she said, "I can't imagine going through the desert again."

I jumped in. "We can try somewhere closer to the city. We'll take our chances and hope la migra misses us this time."

I turned to Manuel as well to see his reaction. He was watching Rosa's face closely. He glanced at me and added, "If we try alone, sólo nosotros, without a large group, maybe we won't be spotted. Maybe just the three of us could sneak in under their noses."

Rosa's eyes opened, and I saw a window of hope.

"We can ask around near the border," I said, "or watch for ourselves and see where people cross." I was on my knees now, excited at the prospect of taking this into our own hands. "It wouldn't hurt to go there and talk to people and *then* decide what to do."

Rosa seemed to be considering my idea. Impatient, I squeezed her hands. "Well? What do you think?" Her eyebrows lifted and with them her lips turned up slightly. I knew this was a good sign.

That night we set up in one of many empty shacks, clearly assembled piecemeal with drywall, cardboard, an old door, cinder blocks, and miscellaneous slats of lumber; home to anyone passing through, we had been told by a family with young children who currently occupied another. "Just keep an eye out for las ratas," the father said to Manuel with a wink, "the big ones and the little furry ones." Puzzled, I turned to Manuel, who said he meant vagabond kids who lived hand to mouth, as well as real rats. Both were trouble.

Manuel had spent the afternoon quietly asking around about good spots to attempt a border crossing and their levels of success. He now knew of a couple. The unanswerable question was what to do once we got across. There was no safe house in Phoenix in this plan.

We were sitting in the darkened shack as the sun went down. It smelled of earth and urine, and I began to feel anxious. Children's voices in the neighboring shack took the edge off a bit, but I was glad Rosa could not see my face clearly.

I heard her say, "As long as there's no desert. And I don't want to feel so helpless again, like sheep, being herded places, having no control. If we can get across close to a city, I guess we can take our chances."

Manuel stretched out beside me. "If we're lucky, once we cross, we can just blend in. That's what they tell me. Hopefully, we make it to a bus station and buy a ticket for California."

"Do you suppose we have enough money for bus tickets?" I asked, touching the dwindling bundle strapped to my chest. "And will la migra be checking each bus?"

"No sé. I don't know," was his answer. "We will learn as we go. Find work, make some money. Maybe I can get in touch with my brother." He rolled away and curled up on his side, his back to me. "Enough for tonight," he said, stifling a cough.

"¡Sí, basta!" Rosa echoed, lying down on my other side. She too turned away and let out a long sigh.

I lay back between them staring at the darkness above. Rosa fell into a deep sleep almost immediately. I tried counting her rhythmic snores like sheep, but they didn't help. I tossed and turned. Though my body ached with fatigue, my mind was racing with thoughts of the days to come. Where would we be one week from now? One month? One year? And Manuel, would we be together?

Watching the rise and fall of his shoulders as he lay beside me, I thought of the words he'd spoken: *"I feel my life belongs with you, too."* He felt the same in his heart as I did! I reached out and softly stroked the back of his neck. He stirred, then immediately turned and took me in his arms, kissing me deeply. I clutched him fiercely, devouring his tongue. One week? One month? One year? What would tomorrow bring? Would I lose him like Papá? A strange hunger possessed me. I kissed and kissed and kissed him, but it wasn't enough. When Manuel's hands moved over my body, I yearned for more. I listened for Rosa; her breaths stayed even and deep. I sighed and lay back, letting him touch me in places that made me gasp.

Moments later, when he entered me gently, I felt a jolt of pain, but as we rocked lightly, making as little noise as possible, I began to feel a pleasure that warmed me from within, confirming the source of a mystery I had only imagined.

When we woke, Rosa was already up and anxious to leave the shack. What she thought of our tangled bodies was impossible to know, but as she stepped out the door, she kept her eyes averted and simply said, "Come on, vámonos. If we're going to do this, let's get going!"

Manuel and I got ourselves together without a word, but when our eyes met, I felt a burst of joy and tenderness that he seemed to feel as well. When he reached out and touched my cheek, I turned and kissed his hand.

Joining Rosa, we walked in silence in the direction of the border fence. She kept a few paces ahead, so I couldn't read her face at all. The set of her shoulders implied business, and soon I settled into the same rhythm until all thoughts of the night before were floating somewhere beyond—yet within reach.

We checked out a spot where a wooden ladder had been nailed to the fence's mid-section. While this area was watched closely, we were told that many families with children had managed to scale the wall and elude officials. It was all a matter of luck and timing.

Some distance away, we noticed a group of young boys gathered around a fire in a metal trash can. One boy held a plastic bag to his face and then passed it to the boy beside him.

Manuel, startled, watched them for a minute and then said, "Wait here," as he turned and approached the group. Two boys immediately came up to him, their palms turned up. Manuel shook his head. He spoke to them for a few minutes and then moved on toward the can, covering his nose with his hand. The two boys followed close behind him, making me nervous. I took a few steps in their direction.

A putrid smell hit my nose immediately, making me gag. I turned back toward Rosa. "Oh my God, what is that smell?"

"I don't know, but I don't like this," Rosa said, her eyes on Manuel who was surrounded now by the boys. But to our relief, he simply pushed his way through them and headed back.

Soon they were immersed in watching the flames again.

I ran up to Manuel, braving the stench. "What is that smell? What are they burning?" I asked.

"You don't want to know," he answered, glancing back. "Just a few pathetic drogos inhaling glue. I thought for a minute that one of them was . . . little Chuy." His frown tugged at my heart. He had spoken of Chuy and Benito throughout our travels, wondering and worrying.

Rosa touched his arm and said, "Maybe they made it this time. Or maybe they just went back home to Guatemala."

"There was no home for them there," he sighed.

A howl went up from the group of boys as one of them flung something in the air. Rigid and charred, the object smoked as it fell to the ground with a thud.

"What was it?" I whispered.

Manuel paused and then said, "Un gato. A cat."

"Let's get out of here," Rosa said, and turning her back on the boys, she walked quickly toward the wall. "Where's the next spot?"

We headed a couple kilometers further to a stretch of wall with horizontal slats that could be scaled with some care. Because of this, a second wall was being built to replace it, but not all sections had been completed yet. This seemed to us a better bet than the one with the ladder, where Border Patrol kept a closer eye. Once over, it would be maybe half a day's walk to civilization—nothing like our previous nightmare.

We walked along it for several minutes, running our hands over the slats and gazing up at its height. It was imposing, but doable. Maybe twice my size.

"You're sure they said it's been done during the day?" I asked.

Manuel shrugged, "They said day or night, es lo mismo. The same. Some make it, some don't. There are advantages and disadvantages to both."

Rosa turned and actually grinned at me. "At least we can see the snakes during the day!" But her eyes were not smiling.

We debated if we should wait until twilight, but Rosa seemed anxious to get this final attempt behind us. I wondered if a part of her was hoping to be caught and done with it. At least she was willing to try. I agreed, and we turned to the wall.

Manuel smoothly climbed to the top, glanced over the side and around, then lifting his leg over, he straddled it like a tree limb and motioned to us.

"You go first," Rosa whispered. "Tengo miedo. I'll see how you do it."

"Don't be afraid. You'll be fine. It's like climbing the trees back home. I'll spot you here, help you if you slide back," I said. Truth was, I feared she might not follow.

She swallowed hard, took a deep breath, and slowly placed her toes into each slat and began to scale the wall. I stood below, my arms stretched up, ready to catch her if she lost her footing. Manuel reached out his hand and helped her straddle the top as well.

I took a deep breath and began my ascent. Not only was this not a moving train, but the daylight made it an easier climb. Once I reached the top, Manuel slid over the side, took a few steps down, and then jumped. I glanced around. No Border Patrol in sight. I couldn't see the city in the distance, but Manuel reassured us it was there. What I could see were pockets of trees and brush for protection, and that gave me hope.

"You go next," Rosa said, biting her lower lip. I hesitated. "Hurry!" she said, glancing around.

I tossed my pack down, eased myself over, and slat by slat descended until I jumped and Manuel broke my fall.

Gazing up at Rosa, I saw her pause, glance behind and then ahead. I held my breath. Was she planning on turning back? Was that in her mind all along?

"Rosa, please, please! ¡Mi hermana, por favor!" I cried.

"Rosa," Manuel said, as he climbed a few slats up, "I'll help you. Hurry!"

To my relief, she tossed her bag and eased down to Manuel, who helped her step by step. When her feet were planted firmly on the ground, I looked into her eyes and knew she could have gone either way. I hugged her tightly.

"Okay, let's go," she said, in a trembling voice. "This time we make it."

We had been told that alarms under the ground might alert the Border Patrol to our presence, so we ran as fast as we could. Every now and then, we stopped behind bushes, checking for snakes and then scanning the horizon and skies for movement. We moved on, stopping frequently where there was cover. We were making good progress when suddenly we heard the distant sound of an engine, so we headed quickly to our right up a hill then down a ravine.

"Over there," Manuel panted, sprinting toward a patch of oak trees surrounded by creosote bushes.

Together we huddled beneath the thickest of branches, holding our breath. A knocking sound became louder and louder, pounding its way through the air. It was the Border Patrol helicopter, circling and zigzagging, but never quite finding its way directly above us. Its persistence amazed me. Like a horse fly, swatted away by the fierce whip of a tail only to return again and again, this mighty machine would not give up its search. Were *we* so important?

We waited until long after the sound faded in the distance to stretch and breathe deeply again, but just as we were discussing our next move, the beat became audible, then louder, sending us back to the thicket.

It buzzed us off and on most of the afternoon. But even after it finally disappeared for more than an hour, we decided to stay put until well after dark.

The three of us had stretched out side by side watching the sky. The stars blinked back at us, bright with hope. I squeezed Rosa's hand.

"It's perfect," Manuel was saying, "just a quarter moon, so it is not too light out there, yet the stars are all the more brilliant, tan brillante, better to lead our way."

We had changed into warmer clothes, doubled our pants again in case of snakes or spikes or scorpions, and drank a bottle of water for hydration. We each agreed that we had become quite proficient. Cautiously we edged out of our sanctuary and moved forward in the darkness.

Manuel pointed out a brightness in the distance. "Las luces," he whispered.

"The lights of the city?" I asked, my heart pounding. Manuel nodded.

We walked for a couple of hours at a quick but easy pace. I was just beginning to feel excited and hopeful, when we heard a crackling of branches to our right. Manuel whispered, "Maybe a lizard or bobcat?" We paused, then continued walking toward the faint light, Manuel in the lead, Rosa and I close behind.

Another rustle of branches, only this time it was followed by the undeniable sound of footsteps that made us freeze. Border Patrol? We turned. Relieved, I could see a white shirt, not the dark uniform of la migra.

"Buenas noches, good evening," a voice said. Was there a hint of mocking in his tone?

A man stepped forward, then another and another, until we were surrounded—four that I could see, plus movement behind us. Though they appeared to be Mexican, their menacing grins were not friendly. In the seconds of tense silence that followed, I knew we were in great danger. I thought of those heartless gangs Manuel spoke of on the train. My hands turned to ice.

Manuel quickly moved in closer to us, but in that instant, two men pulled out knives.

"What have we here? Two chickens and one rooster? Making your way to el norte?"

I wanted to run, but the knives were pointed at Manuel.

"Por favor, leave them alone," Manuel said. "Let them go. I'll give you whatever I have."

"Whatever you have?" he mocked. The men laughed deep in their throats, and I knew no words would change what was about to happen—though Manuel tried. He cried out that we were his sisters and didn't they have sisters? He begged them to please leave us alone, to let us go, and we would give them all of our money. But it was clear they intended to take whatever they wanted.

Rosa and I clung to each other, trembling. The men behind came in closer. One ran his hands along Rosa's back and hips and began to undo her braid. I heard her make a sound like a frightened child, just as I felt the hands of the second man reach around and clasp my breasts hard. I tried to escape, but he clamped his arms tight and jerked me back against him. Manuel leapt forward, but was kicked to the ground and held down by two men. He struggled and screamed, his face in the dirt.

Within seconds, Rosa and I were pulled to the ground. Hands ripped at my clothes. The large white bra that Lupe gave me was wrenched so hard I felt my shoulder pop as a sharp pain shot down my arm. My pesos were cast aside with my pants and my brown shoes. Beside me, I could hear Rosa screaming and cursing in a way I'd never heard before, calling them animals, monsters, and cowards. One man, whose wretched stench I will never forget, forced himself inside me, and I howled as my own unyielding flesh tore. It felt like a knife heated over coals was scraping away inside me. Another man above pulled at my hair, forcing my face toward his sweaty flesh. I gagged and choked, but he continued until I vomited. A sharp slap stung my cheek. Gasping for air, I gazed up at those stars that Rosa and I, just minutes before, had looked to with such hope. Then suddenly a throaty laughter above from someone who pushed Manuel on top of me.

"Come on big brother. Let's see how much your little sister loves you." Then they lifted him up, pulled down his pants, and shoved him onto the ground. Yanking me by the hair, someone shoved my face into Manuel's groin. I could hear them jeering and chanting as they forced my face against his flesh.

But beneath that harsh cacophony was a softer sound, a tender, hopeless moaning as Manuel sobbed. Then I felt his touch, Manuel's gentle fingers stroking my arm and my shoulder, while the cruel hand clutching at my hair slammed my head up and down. I heard Manuel whispering, "Te quiero, Alma. God help us. I love you." Words that I clung to as Manuel was wrenched aside and kicked repeatedly, while two others rolled me onto my stomach, pulled me up from behind, and pounded away. My knees and hands were torn and bleeding; my jaw and shoulder throbbed with each rapid-fire beat of my heart.

But inside . . . in my mind . . . I felt numb. There was nothing left to fear. I closed my eyes and waited for the end. I came to when someone kicked me, and I rolled toward Rosa. I could hear her soft, gurgling moans beside me. Rapid footsteps receded in the distance, and then silence. I listened hard for sounds of Manuel. Feebly I tried to call out his name, but my mouth wouldn't move, so I groaned as loud as I could. A deep, dark inhuman growl moved down my throat and reverberated in my chest. Again, I listened. Nothing. With great effort, I turned toward Rosa. Her face was swollen, her head tilted at a strange angle, and her chest was covered in blood, but she forced her eyes open and stretched out her arm until our fingers touched. My hysterical sob sounded more like a grunt.

Forgive me, I pleaded with my eyes. Squeezing my hand tightly, she whispered something. I strained to make out her words. But it was her eyes that saved me. They burned as bright as the stars that night. I focused on that light, let it wash over me and fill me with warmth, and then I let myself go.

12
Woman with the Eyes of a Saint

Rosa was milking the goat much too fast. I opened my mouth to tell her to slow down, like Mamá showed us, to squeeze slowly and rhythmically like a horse's heartbeat, but my jaw wouldn't budge. I strained, but it held tight as if frozen closed. Then from somewhere deep in my chest, a moan rattled up and vibrated in my ears. I tried to open my eyes, but even they seemed wedged tight. I tried again. Then a sliver of light.

I turned to the outline of a woman close by my side. Only a dark silhouette. The pain of light. I closed my eyes.

She was touching my hand. The rapid-fire squishing sound continued as tightness squeezed my arm, then a long hiss and the pressure was gone.

Where was Rosa? And what was the goat doing in the house?

I heard a woman's voice speaking . . . in English? Then, in Spanish, "Squeeze my hand twice if you understand me," the woman whispered in my ear.

What silly game was this? I pried my eyes open and strained to focus. She had a round dark face, kind eyes, like la Virgen. I squeezed twice.

"Ah, bien. Very good. So, you speak Spanish." She leaned in. "You're in the hospital in Nogales . . . Arizona." My eyes widened. ¿El norte? I was in el norte? I tried to push myself up, but every inch of my body pulsed with pain. I tried to speak again.

"Your jaw is wired. You can't speak, but when you are stronger, you can write messages on this board. Aquí." I heard her pick up something beside me, then set it down. "For now, just rest." She paused, and then a deep sadness carried the next words to my ears. "And try not to worry. Está bien ahora. You're safe now."

It was the sadness that brought me back, though not with great clarity. Something unbearable had come to pass, of that I was certain. I could feel it in the depth of my bowels, though I couldn't name it—and I was responsible. That I knew. Try as I might, nothing crystallized before me, no specific cause for shame, but lurking beneath the surface was a deep-souled feeling that I had been thoughtless and self-centered once again.

Always the first to fly into Papá's arms. Did Rosa, Mamá, and the boys watch with resentment? What an enormous burden, what ponderous grief, Mamá must have carried after Papá disappeared—and how I must have added to that weight when I should have relieved her. Instead, thinking only of myself. Always charging ahead without a glance at those around me.

Rosa. Something about Rosa. I struggled to remember.

Fleeting images came first. Rosa limping along the road to Oaxaca. Rosa making dolls with Lupe. Rosa laughing beside a camp fire . . . in Nogales? Yes, and with Manuel! I remembered Manuel! His dark eyes like coals warming my heart. Where was my Manuel?

Then I saw the border fence imposing and high. Beyond that, no images. Nothing more.

But I could *feel* something dark. Something as ominous as the thick fog and the whistling wind atop the box car. Like dry ice, a chilling flame bore into my stomach, then spread down my legs. I shivered. Wedged teeth chattered like mice feet on a dirt floor. Closing my eyes tight, I willed myself back into the void.

A small man, dressed in a gray suit with a black shirt and striped tie, sat beside my bed. His dark hair was slicked back neatly; silver framed glasses rested halfway down a thin nose. Everything about him was perfect. Even the way he sat, with his back arched and his head held high. He too spoke in Spanish. His voice sounded far away, even though he sat right beside me. Like the woman with the eyes of a saint, he spoke of safety. He told me I had nothing to fear, yet in saying that he was telling me that there *had been* something to fear—and that terrified me. I think I made a noise, for he sat forward suddenly, and holding forth a pad of paper and a pen, he asked me if I had any questions for him. Our eyes connected for a moment; then I turned away. He sighed and sat back in his chair.

I closed my eyes and tried desperately to push the sound of his voice even further away. But I heard him just the same. He said he was a doctor, that he wanted to help ease my pain, my emotional pain. Did I have any family? Someone they could call? I kept my head turned and my eyes closed. Silence. One minute, two. Then I heard the leather of his shoes creak as he leaned forward. But when his cold fingers touched my arm, I screamed with such force that something burst in my mouth. A team of doctors and nurses spent the next hour fastening it back together again.

Whenever I moaned in pain, the nurses brought medicine that kept me shrouded in fog. I'd curl up inside the tent of white sheets and let the mists of oblivion wash over me.

The kind woman with the round face sat beside me again, coaxing a straw between my lips and urging me to drink. I found comfort in her eyes. They were full of sad wisdom. They were forgiving. I watched as she placed the straw in the glass and, keeping her finger over the tip, lifted a straw full of juice to my parted lips. As she released it, I felt most of the cool liquid drip down my chin, but a hint of sweetness managed to slip through.

I woke to the sounds of men arguing in the harsh tones of English. One voice sounded familiar.

When it slipped into Spanish, I recognized my perfect little doctor. "No, no está lista!" She is not ready, he was saying in between his anguished attempts in English to deter the other man, who strode firmly into my room like a stubborn rooster. Not ready for what?

He was a tall, thin white man with tan pants and a blue jacket. His white shirt was wrinkled; he wore no tie. My doctor stood beside him, tight-lipped, arms crossed, in an immaculate black suit.

The tall man's face softened into a smile as he spoke to me in English. My doctor said in Spanish, "This gentleman is an official from the police, and he wants to ask you a few questions." As I looked into the dark eyes behind the silver frames, I knew that this was one time he hoped I'd remain silent.

They each pulled up a chair and sat beside my bed. With my doctor translating in soft hushed tones, I was asked once again, "What is your name? Where are you from?" And then, "Can you tell us what happened?" He held up a white board and held forth a pen.

I kept my breathing slow and even. I looked past both men into the gray sky beyond the window and tried not to hear their voices. I could see the top of a palm tree in the distance.

"Take your time. Any information at all is fine."

I conjured the sound of the train's rhythmic roar over the tracks. I even began to sway to the rhythm. *Raataataat. Raataataat. Raataataat.* Their voices became muffled. *Raataataat. Raataataat.* Fainter and fainter.

But the next question seemed to anger my doctor, for his voice rose above the rattling of my train, so I paused and listened.

"No," he was saying, refusing to translate.

The thin man turned directly to me and said two words in English. Words that I knew well, for my father had said them to me before after making lists of numbers to add. In Spanish and then in English, he would say, "¿Cuántos? How many?"

"How many?" this man asked again softly. "How many . . . men?" He held up his hand, one finger, two fingers, then three. My doctor pushed back his chair and rose in anger.

"¡Basta! Enough!" he shouted.

But it was too late. Those simple words . . . *how many . . . men . . .* pierced through my walls and tore open my thoughts. I saw Rosa's swollen face. I smelled the rancid breath of a man laughing above me.

"Rosa!" I screamed through clenched jaw. I writhed in agony feeling strong hands upon my body, holding me down, until the nurses came with the needle that made it all go away.

I responded to no one except the woman with the eyes of a saint. Her name was Ana. Ana Lopez. I answered her because she asked so little. "Juice or milk? Is this light too bright? Curtain open or closed?" Only once, she asked gently, "Quién es Rosa?" and when she saw my eyes and heard my groan, she let it be.

Of her, I asked three questions on the white board. "Where am I?" "How did I get here?" and "Was I alone?" She said that I was found lying by the entrance of the emergency room here in Nogales, Arizona—alone.

No one else in a similar state was brought in at that time. No young woman, no young man. Only me. Alone.

When she asked me where I was from—the United States, Mexico, Central America—I realized they knew nothing about me. In fact, I was referred to as Jane Doe. I didn't answer, and she didn't ask again.

It was the doctor, the perfect one, Dr. Ramírez, who would not let it rest, for he wanted to contact someone, anyone, who could bring me comfort, he said.

But I deserved no such thing.

I stopped moaning for the medicine so that I could feel the pain. In fact, I worked at making it worse—tightening my jaw repeatedly or jerking my shoulder back and forth—when no one was there, of course. And I made myself remember everything . . . vividly . . . so I would endure it again and again. This I deserved. For it was all my fault.

Ana watched me quietly. She was not a nurse, I discovered, but an aide, and so could not bring me medicine. But she tried to ease my pain in other ways, even when I said no. A soft pillow under my shoulder, a gentle massage at the base of my neck. Once I saw her add some herbs to a drink that she then coaxed between my lips. Yet I noticed that when doctors or nurses entered the room, she seemed to disappear into the surroundings. If spoken to, she would cast her eyes downward and draw into herself, then nod and hurry off to get whatever was demanded.

One evening she entered my room with an uncharacteristic air of nervousness. Pulling up a chair, she actually sat down and whispered that she'd overheard the nurses talking. They said that it was believed I had been attacked while crossing the border. Apparently, my sun-burned face, cactus scratches on my arms and legs, blisters on my feet, as well as a degree of dehydration, gave it away. They also said that a similar attack had happened weeks before.

"They are planning to move you." Ana spoke so quickly I had to focus on her Spanish, as her dialect was slightly different. "They are sending you to an immigrant detention center soon, where it's hoped you will recover from your injuries and co-operate with authorities. If you don't, you could be kept indefinitely at the center, and, mi niña, it is like a prison there."

As I listened, I pushed aside my rising fears and decided this was the punishment I deserved. Imprisonment would be an apt penance.

But Ana had another plan. She said she could sneak me out of the hospital and take me somewhere where I could get strong. When I shook my head, she wisely whispered, "Once you're strong, you will be better able to find out about . . . Rosa."

I turned anguished eyes to hers and mumbled slowly through my lips, "I know about Rosa. Ya sé de ella."

My stomach churned as I imagined her abandoned body decaying just like those we had come upon together. And all because of me. *I* had insisted we cross again. *I* had convinced her—pushed her—to try just one more time. And *I* had led her to an end far worse than the one she had feared in the desert. In the desert, we might have kept the hope of imminent rescue alive. In the desert, we might have had time for a coming to peace. But the end she met was one of despair and terror. I might as well have stripped off her clothes for them.

I turned away from Ana and curled up into a tight ball. My shoulder throbbed; I yanked it over harder still.

But she persisted. "You don't know. You don't know anything for certain. Ahora escúchame. Perhaps someone found her, and they're caring for her." Ana leaned in closer, "Someone who would *not* go to authorities."

I knew she was onto me. I knew she was trying to save me from myself, but she had a point. What if Rosa was alive? What if she needed me? If I had survived, perhaps Rosa had, too, and Manuel. Oh, my sweet Manuel. What fate had he met at their cruel hands? I remembered the chilling silence when I shouted for him near the end. He'd have been better off riding the trains with the boys from Guatemala. But he'd chosen to stay with me.

I turned to Ana and for the first time looked into her eyes without turning quickly away. The pain reflected there was overwhelming. I grasped her hand.

Tears flowed as she spoke haltingly, "My father and brother died in the hands of heartless men in Guatemala during the war," she paused and drew in her breath, "so I do understand . . . a little." She stroked my face the way my father used to do when I would carry on the night before his departure. "So, you must get strong . . . for Rosa."

I closed my eyes and saw Rosa's face, the swan-like curve of her neck, and Manuel's tender eyes beneath his tangled mass of hair; this time, I let my tears fall. First in gentle trickles and then in torrents. I hiccupped and sobbed, gasped and choked. Ana sat with me until, exhausted, I fell into a deep sleep.

The next day around noon, Ana walked into my room and pulled the stained white curtain around my bed. Tugging at her own clothes, she removed her blue nurse's smock and pants, revealing a second set underneath.

"Let's get these on quickly," she whispered, helping me out of my patient gown and into her uniform. Then she placed the patient gown back over the smock. In a flash, she disappeared into the hall, returning with a wheelchair. After helping me into the chair, she slipped blue shoe covers over my bare feet, then covered me from the waist down with a blanket. I could hear the woman in the bed beside me snoring deeply, while the TV blared with religious music and a man's voice ranted rhythmically. Whisking back the curtain, Ana wheeled me casually down the hall. We turned right twice, ending up in a short, deserted hallway. Ana helped me to my feet, removed the blanket and gown, and folded up the wheelchair.

Placing it to one side, she turned to me and said, "Let's see if you can make it down one short flight of stairs and out the side door.

My car isn't far. If we pass anyone, just act like we're on our way out for lunch. Be casual and relaxed. Keep your head down. Don't look anyone in the eye. Todo saldrá bien."

We walked around a corner and headed toward a door marked "Stairs." My legs felt weak, but my heart pounded with such fervor, I felt I could fly. One step at a time, I descended down the metal staircase. No one passed us. No one saw us step out the door. Once in the parking lot, we walked toward a small white car—two nurse's aides on their lunch break. Once settled in the front seat, I glanced up and saw a tall, slender tree, graceful as my Rosa, swaying gently beneath a vivid blue sky. I closed my eyes, and for a very brief moment, I let myself hope.

13

Not Knowing

My "escape" resulted in momentary chaos, a review of security policy, several reprimands, and a wide range of gossip. None of it touched Ana, for as she had expected, no one even noticed her presence that Sunday afternoon. And since it had not been her usual shift, she was not even questioned that evening when she appeared for work.

"I am hardly noticed when I'm there anyway," she had told me quietly, a fact that clearly brought her pain, but worked to our advantage this time.

Ultimately, they concluded that whoever dropped me off at the emergency entrance had picked me up. Ana said Dr. Ramírez was quite upset and feared my life was in danger. Some official told him they'd let him know if I turned up on a coroner's table.

Ana lived with her mother in a small, sparse apartment not far from railroad tracks, so as I lay on the sofa, I could feel the walls tremble and hear that familiar sound each time a train passed by. Strangely, it brought a comforting ache to my heart, just like the little shrine her mother had set up on the floor in one corner of their living room. In Guatemala, just as in Oaxaca, their shrine was arranged on the floor. Each evening, her mother, a tiny frail woman, would kneel on a small cushion before it, light the candles, and lift the rosary that lay in the painted dish in the center. She prayed for the souls of her husband and son who had been killed during the civil war in her country years before, and now she prayed for me as well.

Since they shared the only bedroom, I spent my days and nights on their dark green sofa wrapped up in a colorful afghan that one of them had crocheted. They left me to myself, let me sleep through the day, never questioned when I sat in the dark, and never lectured if I didn't finish the food they offered. Neither did they object when I began to watch television from early morning, sometimes through the night. They seemed to know the necessities of this passage.

And bless their souls, they never panicked when my spine-chilling screams pierced the silent night. Dark dreams of snakes slithering around my limbs, tightening their grasp and pulling me down beneath sinking desert sands, or of large powerful hands bursting through the ground as I walked, grabbing my ankles, then my calves, and yanking me down, down, down through the earth. It became my ritual to wrap myself tightly in the afghan, my arms and feet safely cocooned inside and unexposed to the whim of any beast that might happen by in the night. Ana and her mother remained calm and patient during these outbursts. They would wake me from my terror gently, and then, while her mother would prepare warm atole, Ana would rub my back, switch on the television, and search until she found some light diversion.

One such night I saw an ad on TV for free legal aid for immigrants. Silently, I memorized the number and recited it to myself like a prayer. 1 520 629-8327. 1 520 6AYUDAR. Numbers always brought me comfort. As I chanted it softly to myself over and over, another number suddenly materialized in my mind: 1 818 555-7475. It was Berta and Diego's phone number in Los Angeles. I thought of the tiny white paper that Rosa had carried in her bag and how she feared she'd lose it. I thought of my little box of stars and of my calla lily journal that Manuel had given me. Were they weathering beside

Rosa and Manuel's blessed bones? Or had they been trampled and scattered to pieces like my soul?

I imagined a pencil in my mind and tried to erase the numbers imprinted there, but they wouldn't fade. I turned back to the tele-novela I had been watching and turned up the volume.

Ana had spoken with her priest, who worked with the refugees and immigrants in the community, and he offered to make inquiries with border officials, as well as with church members, regarding any young women or men who might have been found injured or worse in the past month. She also insisted that I contact family or friends back home to let them know I was alive and to see if they had any word of Rosa. But I refused. I didn't want anyone, especially Mamá and the Garcias, to know about our fate. Like Papá, let our where-abouts remain a mystery.

Exasperated, Ana said, "But think of the pain they are going through. The unknown can be the cruelest form of suffering. You should know that better than anyone else, no?"

I coldly replied through my wire-clenched teeth, "Knowing the truth—imagining each detail over and over again—that would be cruel. No saber, not knowing, is a gift."

Ana sat with her hands in her lap and her head bowed as if in prayer, but I sensed her mind was not with God. And I was right, for she lifted moist eyes to mine and said, "Perhaps you are right. There are some things I wish I had never been told." I knew she was thinking of the torture that preceded her father and brother's deaths in Guatemala. She had told me their tragic story late one night after I'd angrily implied that she couldn't understand my suffering. Now shaking her head, she said, "But you forget. *You* are alive. They need to know that."

"No," I answered, my heart rising to my throat. "I don't want anyone to know the truth. ¡Nadie! I've done enough damage, ruined enough lives. To learn that I've survived is no joy in the face of what happened—of what I caused. It's best they never know the truth. Nunca."

Taking my hands, she pleaded, "Oh Alma, no, you must not think that way. You didn't bring that evil upon yourself or Rosa. You are not to blame. Tú eres inocente."

But I knew she couldn't understand, so I simply pulled my hands away.

As for word of Rosa making it home, I knew in my heart that wasn't so. No contact to Chiapas was needed to verify that fact. I prayed that the Garcias would never learn our fate. I couldn't bear to lay that burden on their generous souls. The way I saw it, I'd spent years not knowing about Papá. Only now could I appreciate this gift he had given us, for he would always be alive for me somewhere. Waiting.

Six weeks from the date of my hospitalization, no unidentified bodies meeting Rosa or Manuel's description had been found. A man's wife died of dehydration in his arms. An older woman and two children were found dead beneath a bush with a half bottle of water beside them. Four young men were rescued by la migra just in time, though two were hospitalized. But no one had found a young woman or man. Not dead. Not alive.

I knew there was no hope left. I wanted to die. But that seemed too kind an escape.

Ana woke me late one morning and handed me a skirt and blouse. "Get dressed," she said. "Today is the day we will set your jaw free." The church had found a doctor who would treat me with no questions asked, and the time had come for my wires to be cut.

I had spent the past weeks in Ana's blue uniform curled up on the sofa day and night. I'd lost considerable weight, not only because I was limited to liquids and some soft foods, but I had absolutely no appetite. In fact, the smell of food made me ill. So, when I put on her clothes, they hung on me like a child playing dress-up.

Looking in the mirror, I saw a stranger—a skeleton of the girl I used to be. My hair was matted; my eyes sunken into a thin face accented by dark circles that reminded me of my grandmother in Chiapas. Gone were my fleshy breasts and hips. Instead a bony, child-like body strangely contrasted with an old woman's weathered face that looked dully back at me.

"We need to get you some new clothes, Alma," Ana spoke behind me as she secured the waistband of the skirt with a safety pin.

I shrugged.

Her mother sat me in a chair and began gently brushing the tangles from my hair. "Are you nervous?" she asked.

"She probably can't wait to get those wires off. Imagine how awful not to be able to eat or to really talk," Ana answered for me.

"But it will probably hurt. She must be worried a bit. ¿Estás preocupada, mi niña?" Señora Lopez asked, stroking my arm.

"Doesn't matter," I mumbled. And I didn't care, about feeling pain, eating food, talking, getting caught and deported. Nothing mattered. Nada.

I slumped in the front seat of Ana's car and closed my eyes, opening them only when we arrived at the white rectangular building. The endless wait in the small sitting room made me restless for the simple reason that it lacked a TV. I longed for the monotonous voices that filled the silence. Finally, they called me in. The baldheaded doctor with scaly spots on his scalp drew blood from my arm, checked my heart and lungs, and asked for a urine specimen. The procedure itself to remove the wires was unpleasant, and as expected, my jaw was sore and stiff. None of this touched me in the least. I just wanted to curl up on a sofa and watch TV or sleep.

As I sat on the examining table, Ana spoke with the doctor beyond the closed door. When it opened, both entered with worried looks on their faces. My first thought was that the X-ray pictures were not good, and perhaps the wires needed to be replaced. I didn't mind; in fact, I preferred to be muzzled like a dog.

So, when Ana took my hand and said, "Alma, there's something you need to know," I was ready, but what she said took my breath away, "You are pregnant, embarazada." She waited and let the words linger. Then she continued, "The doctors knew this before we left the hospital, but Dr. Ramírez felt you were not ready to know yourself." Ana took a deep breath and squeezed my hand. "They were going to tell you . . . they were going to talk to you about an abortion, if you wanted, and then, afterwards, send you to the detention center." She looked up at me with tears in her eyes. "I knew this and didn't tell you. Lo siento. Forgive me. I felt you needed to get stronger first. I feared what this would have done to you . . . at the time."

My mind swirled. Pregnant? I placed my hand on my stomach. "A baby?" I asked in disbelief.

Both nodded.

The doctor stepped forward. "You are about seven weeks along. You can easily abort at this point. Best before the end of the first trimester, which gives you four or five more weeks to decide." He paused. "Or if you choose to carry it, you must begin to care for yourself—eat well, take vitamins, exercise, seek regular medical care."

I turned to Ana, my lower lip quivering. "Un bebé?"

"You don't need to make a decision right now—unless you are certain. No hurry. You can think about it. We'll talk later. Okay?"

I couldn't speak. It was as if my jaw was still clamped tight.

The doctor's voice floated above me, "Do you have any questions? Can I help you in any way right now?"

I sat stunned and silent.

He turned to Ana and said, "Well, take her to the women's clinic when she decides, and they will help her . . . either way."

In a trance, I was helped down from the table and out the door. We rode in silence. As soon as we climbed the stairs and entered Ana's apartment, I collapsed onto the sofa, curled up in a ball, my hand pressed firmly against my stomach. I couldn't believe there was a life within me, a life created in the midst of the most horrifying experience imaginable.

What was God thinking? Or was it, perhaps, the devil, desperate to keep his seed alive? And I was his instrument. A bitter bile rose in my throat.

Then I gasped. Or was the baby Manuel's? Could it possibly be his? ¡Dios mío!

Ana had turned on the television, thinking, perhaps, that it might bring the comfort of distraction, but derisive laughter burst from the screen—a cruel response to my desperate hopes. I wept until no tears could form.

The next morning Ana woke me from a deep sleep and led me to the bathroom where she had prepared a bath. I thought of the lavender soaps that Rosa and I had used at Señorita Garcia's, and fresh tears began to drip down my cheeks. Ana and her mother bathed me as if I were a newborn child; soothing hands glided over my skin, then dug in deeper to massage my scalp and scrub my hair. When finished, they dressed me in a sleeveless, loose-fitting dress and led me to the kitchen.

"Now that you can eat, you must eat well, por favor," Ana's mother insisted as she began to prepare a breakfast of fresh eggs.

I watched a small hummingbird just beyond the window, its wings fluttering faster than my eye could see. I wondered, was this the size of the baby inside me, or was it even smaller? Watching it flit from one blossom to another, I suddenly remembered my mother and a friend whispering about a woman who had taken a mixture of herbs to get rid of her baby without ever telling her husband. Their disapproval had been profound.

The smell of peppers and onions filled the air, and though my mouth watered, my stomach began to revolt. As if reading my mind, Señora Lopez said, "Just a little today. We'll take it slowly."

For two weeks, they bathed and dressed me daily, took me for short walks, and fed me small amounts of food throughout the day. Numbly, I went along, thankful more than anything that they respected my silence. No questions asked. No decisions to be made. For the truth was, I did not want to confront this reality.

One evening, shortly before Día de los Muertos, Señora Lopez was describing all of the ingredients that she put in her fiambre, a special Guatemalan dish prepared for this day. The list was endless: sausage, cold cuts, pickled baby corn, pacaya flower, olives . . . I was half-listening and half-dozing before the television, when a name was spoken that resounded off the walls like a crack of thunder: "Dolores Huerta." I snapped my head up and leaned on an elbow.

An anchorman with empty eyes was mouthing words I understood, such as *hospitalized* and *critical condition*, as well as words I did not know, like *aortic aneurysm*. The screen flashed familiar images of a young Dolores with Cesar Chavez leading the farmworkers, but it also showed a photograph of an older woman, tiny and frail, but with the same jet-black hair and lively eyes. This Dolores was in grave danger, and if so, my fate was sealed. That link to Papá would no longer be possible. If Dolores was close to death, then God had sent me a clear message. All doors closed—and locked.

A sadness descended, pulling me down even further than I already was. I felt like I was sinking into icy waters, deep and dark. A chill swept through me so cold that my frigid fingers ached. Burying my face in the sofa, I pulled at my hair and sobbed inconsolably.

"No! No!" I wailed, thinking of Rosa, of the many times we had

dreamed and argued, wondered and worried, planning our journey, searching for Dolores and Papá. And now it was gone. All of it
gone. Rosa. Manuel. Papá. Dolores. The weight of my pent-up grief
descended, and I wept with abandon.

Rosa had always been the one I turned to, and I wanted her so
badly now, I couldn't bear it. But she was gone—and all because of
me.

"Oh Rosa," I cried, "please forgive me! I'm sorry! Lo siento!"

Suddenly a warm hand grasped mine and pried my fingers from
my hair. A gentle voice, soft as feathers, cooed, "Está bien. It's okay.
It's okay. It's okay. It's not your fault. It's not your fault at all. It's okay."

Startled, I opened my eyes. "Rosa? Is it you, Rosa?" The loving
eyes that gazed back were as warm as the hand that held mine, so
warm I could feel the heat flow through me, easing the chill away,
soothing the pain, erasing the fear and guilt.

And I remembered.

Rosa. Those last moments. There on the ground, when I had
turned toward her, she had answered my pleas for forgiveness. She
had touched my hand and told me, no, no, I was not to blame. And
her eyes had filled me with light. The light of the blinding stars.
Light that brought warmth and peace. Peace that flowed through me,
bringing forgiveness and love. I remembered. And I let myself think
of Manuel. His aching words of comfort and love in the midst of the
horror. His tender hands on my shoulder. His tears on my cheek.

Lying back, I closed my eyes and let their love flow through me.
I felt the beat of my heart slow down gradually from a gallop to an
even pace. My breathing deepened. I opened my eyes.

It was Ana who was holding my hand and stroking my forehead.
Ana, whose eyes held all of the world's kindness, and, trembling
beside her, her mother. Both so worried, so concerned—about me. It
was as if I was seeing them for the first time.

Taking a deep breath, I gazed up and smiled. I could still feel the light of Rosa's love and the tenderness of Manuel's touch; it warmed my chest and made my cheeks glow.

Whispering so as not to disturb the little life within me, I said to the two startled women hovering above, "I want to have this baby, mi bebé. I want to because it was conceived at a moment that I was most loved."

They nodded with open mouths.

Though I yearned for it to be Manuel's, if it wasn't, if it was created amidst that horror, it was also at the instant that I experienced the most sacred love I would ever know.

"And I want to name her Luz. Luz de Rosalba. Rosa's light." For I knew, just as I knew Rosa had not made it back to Chiapas, that the life within me was a girl.

14

¡Sí, Se Puede!

For the next few days, Ana, Señora Lopez, and I crowded together on their tiny sagging sofa to catch the latest news. The minute Dolores's picture flashed on the screen, we would silence each other and listen. Her children spoke of her resilience. Yes, she was seriously ill and doctors considered her condition delicate, but family recalled for reporter after reporter how Dolores had suffered a ruptured spleen at the hands of police during a demonstration years before, yet she had recovered quickly and returned to her work. Though she was in her seventies now, everyone was confident that she would still pull through with the same determination.

"¡Sí, se puede!" a daughter proudly exclaimed, repeating her mother's famous words. "My mother said this morning, 'God has a plan for me, my work is not done.' She'll be back on her feet and in the face of injustice within a year!" Only time would tell if this proved to be true, for it was also reported that Dolores's condition had left her so debilitated that she was learning how to feed herself and walk again.

Occasionally these news stories included clips of Dolores alongside Cesar Chavez during the United Farm Workers strike. I would hold my breath and scan the faces in the crowd, hoping to catch a glimpse of a young Juan Cruz. But, like life itself, the film was blurry and ran for but an instant.

Just as the umbilical cord attached my baby to me, I felt fiercely connected to Dolores. She was the first thing on my mind each morning as the sun rose and filled the small room with light. I would think of her starting her day, so I would rise and run my own bath, dress myself, and help prepare the meals with Señora Lopez. As I lifted each forkful of food to my mouth, I pictured Dolores doing the same. As I placed one foot in front of the other during my morning walks, I knew she was making just such an effort.

If she could regain her strength to fight again, so could I. If God had a plan for her, perhaps He had one for me as well, and my work was not yet done.

And so, I began to consider my future. I could not bring myself to even contemplate a return to Oaxaca, and certainly not Chiapas, at least not yet. Should I stay with Ana in Nogales? They had opened their arms to me and offered to help me make a new life. Should I contact Diego and Berta in Los Angeles? They were, after all, a connection to Papá.

What, I wondered, would Dolores do? The answer was simple; she would continue to move forward, to pursue the cause she believed in. But what was my cause? To care for this baby, certainly, but still try to find Papá? To learn the truth about his disappearance? My stomach churned at this thought for so much had been lost in this pursuit. Was it still the right thing to do?

On the eve of Día de los Muertos, All Souls Day, with Ana at work, I knelt with Señora Lopez before her shrine as she prayed for her husband and son, and for my Rosa and Manuel, wherever their souls might be. I was at a loss for words myself, uncertain who was listening or whether I deserved to be listened to in the first place. I gazed at the statue of La Virgen de Guadalupe, whose closed eyes and slight smile gave her an air of gentleness and peace. I found a subtle comfort there, but my heart still ached. I bowed my head and sighed heavily.

Señora Lopez paused in her prayers and placed her wrinkled hand, sparkling with green rosary beads, over mine. "His will be done," she whispered. When I looked at her with pain and confusion in my eyes, she asked, "What? What is it?"

I tried to explain what was a jumble in my mind. "His will? But how could . . . what happened . . . be a part of God's will?" This was the best that I could do, though it didn't touch an ounce of what I felt.

She shook her head and sat in silence. Just when I thought she had no response to give, she squeezed my hand and said in a voice that I had to strain to hear, "My Ana doesn't know all of what happened the night the soldiers took our men and boys." She looked up into my eyes, her lower lip quivering. "Entiendo. I know your terror," she said slowly, "I know your pain." She paused and lifted the rosary to her lips and kissed them. Then closing her eyes, she continued, "It was part of our men's torture to have to watch their wives and mothers," she opened her eyes and nodded, "and then, when the soldiers were finished with us, it was our turn to watch the murder of our husbands and sons." Her tears glistened in the candlelight, which flickered a moment as if in homage, then burned full and bright. Suddenly she sat up and, leaning toward me, said firmly, "Ana knows none of this, nada, not even of my presence at their murders. She was a child, sent ahead to el norte with my cousin."

I nodded. "I'll never say a word," I reassured her. "Prometo."

"And Alma, my dear, *that* was not God's will," she said, her voice now gaining strength, "that's not what I meant. I meant the rest of my life, after that, I placed in God's hands."

I thought for a moment and then asked, "But how did you know? What His will was, I mean? How did you know what He wanted you to do?"

"Ah, that part is the blessing. La bendición. I simply didn't seek anymore. It all just came to me . . . like you did." With both hands, she took mine, and, winding the rosary beads around my fingers, she finished by placing the crucifix in the palm of my hand and folded my fingers over it one by one. I wasn't sure what I thought about God's will, but I had to admit, it brought some degree of comfort.

One week later, Ana returned from a church meeting to announce that a group of college students from Los Angeles, associated with an organization in Tucson called BorderLinks, had visited to inquire about the plight of migrants. They had toured parts of Nogales, Mexico, the border, and now Nogales, Arizona, interviewing citizens from both sides, as well as Border Patrol agents, migrants, and aid workers. She wondered if I'd be willing to talk to them about the children who ride the trains.

"You don't have to talk about anything you don't want to. They don't know anything else about you, Alma. I simply said I knew someone who had ridden the rails," she said gently.

"They're from Los Angeles?" I whispered.

Behind Ana, Señora Lopez's eyes met mine.

Though the students were older than I was, I felt like the wise elder, and not just because they sat cross-legged on Ana's floor while I was seated on the sofa above them. I felt decades older in body and soul. In fact, I wasn't the least bit nervous about facing this group of college-educated Americans. Ana had arranged the meeting at her apartment, hoping to ease any anxiety I might feel, and perhaps this played a role in my comfort level. But once they entered and each shook my hand, I felt a calm that surprised me.

There were four girls—all with long hair pulled back in straight pony-tails that hung down their backs. One had brown skin, the rest, white. And with them, two boys as well, one dark-skinned and one white. All were dressed in jeans and T-shirts and carried back-packs, which they opened once they settled themselves on the floor. Taking out notebooks and pens, they looked up expectantly. It was the dark-skinned boy who spoke in perfect Spanish, asking me questions and then translating in English to his friends. When I told of my fall from the boxcar, they looked blankly at me while I spoke, finally reacting with wide eyes and gasps as he relayed the details moments later. It was surreal watching his animated face as he translated and then theirs as they reacted. That my life became this delayed story, repeated in a foreign language and listened to with expectation, made it seem less real—like it was, in fact, just a story. And so, as they asked questions that could have touched on sacred ground, I began to weave an elaborate tale, part real, mostly fiction, that could take me gently into the future. For so many reasons, I could not speak the truth.

I told them that I had been on my way to Los Angeles, where my half-brother lived. There was a job waiting for me, I said. I had been traveling with my sister and her boyfriend, but they decided to return home after our third deportation. I continued on, however, determined to make it to Los Angeles, but just as I crossed the border at Nogales, I told them that my coyote took the last of my money and abandoned me. I had fainted along a roadside, where a friend of Ana's had found me and brought me to her, knowing she had some medical training.

The students were horrified to think a man could be so cruel as to rob and abandon such a young girl. Their eyes flashed with indignation and righteousness. Yes, I agreed: Man can be so heartless.

The girl with the brown skin sat up on her knees and in heavily accented Spanish asked, "Do you still want to go to Los Angeles?"

I could barely speak as a plan began to form that I might travel with them to Los Angeles.

"So, do you think this is God's will for me?" I asked Señora Lopez later that evening.

"Only you can answer that. Does it feel right?" She was washing dishes in the sink and had lifted her hands from the sudsy water as she turned to study my face.

"Well, it's like you described, something that came to me. I did not seek it out."

She nodded, "¡Bueno! You will know better as you take each new step."

"Is that how you felt when you came here to Arizona?" I asked.

She glanced toward the living room where Ana was watching TV and lowered her voice. "I was supposed to travel with Ana earlier. My husband had arranged for both of us to join his sister here in Arizona, but I refused to leave him. I sent Ana with my cousins." She sighed deeply. "I remember his eyes the morning that the soldiers came to our village. They spoke louder than his words. 'Get to Ana! ¡Ahora!' I tried to run, but his screams drew me back." She paused and shook her head. "I often think how much easier it would have been for him if I'd left with Ana. At least some of his suffering would have been avoided. Or if he could have known that I would eventually make it here, that I'd find Ana, that kind people would help us every step of the way. I pray that somewhere he does know that now."

I watched her hands as they dipped into the water again and thought how much she had endured.

"Do you miss your country, your home?" I asked as an afterthought, realizing that I didn't miss mine—certainly not Chiapas, not even Oaxaca anymore. It was Papá, and Rosa, and Manuel that I ached for.

"Mi hogar es con Ana," she said, echoing my thoughts.

I rubbed my hand over the slight bulge in my stomach. "I'm not sure where our home will be."

"You'll know when you get there—wherever it feels like family."

As she turned and smiled, I saw that woman again, the woman I'd seen in Ana's face, the woman with the eyes of a saint. If she could feel such kindness again, despite all she'd been through, then perhaps so could I.

The students were scheduled to return to Los Angeles in two days, so I had to act quickly, which meant I had to call Berta and Diego, to see if a visit was even welcome. I had no idea how they might respond. Did they feel resentment like Mamá? Since it had always been Rosa who spoke with Berta, would she even know who I was? And what would I say about Rosa?

"Help me, Ana," I asked as she laid out some of her clothes for me. "What can I say about Rosa?" My voice quavered with emotion. "I just can't tell her the truth."

Ana continued neatly folding a light blue T-shirt with a daisy on its pocket. "I suppose the only possible story would involve love." She lowered her eyes as she said this, and I knew she was thinking of the young man who often picked her up for church meetings. Though their relationship seemed limited to parish functions, I noticed how she hurried to the door when he came and how his eyes followed her as she reached for her bag or bent to kiss her mother. Something was just beginning to blossom there. "You already told the students something about a boyfriend, a novio, didn't you?" she added.

I nodded. "So . . . she fell in love and traveled on with him? But Rosa would never leave me like that," I said, remembering how I had refused to leave with Manuel. Yet if I had, and she had returned safely to Oaxaca . . . my eyes brimmed with tears.

Ana continued, "She would if she thought you were happy as well, perhaps with . . . Manuel." She said his name softly, knowing the sound would pierce my heart like a surgeon's blade. "You could say . . . well . . . you could say that she is with her novio, and that Manuel, your novio, has gone on to Temecula with his brother to make some money, so you can marry." She smoothed out the clothes and stepped back. Our eyes met for an instant, both of us holding back our emotions.

"Gracias," I said, hugging her tightly. "Then that will be my story."

Trembling, I reached for the phone and sank into the cocoon of my sofa. The number appeared clearly in my mind. I took a deep breath and began to push the numbers. My heart raced like a galloping horse. The voice that answered on the fourth ring sounded sleepy.

"Lo siento, so sorry to bother you," I began, speaking slowly in Spanish, "but my name is Alma Cruz. I am Juan Cruz's daughter. I wish to speak to Berta. Es Berta?" The pause was so long, I thought I had lost the connection or that perhaps she didn't speak Spanish very well. "Hello? Hello?"

"Yes," a woman's raspy voice responded. "Sí, sí, *I'm* sorry. Did you say this is Juan's daughter, Alma?"

Hearing my father's name spoken so familiarly brought tears to my eyes and stirred embers of hope.

"Yes! His daughter. And you are . . . ?"

She hesitated, "Berta. Yes, I'm sorry, yes, this is Berta."

"And Diego, is he there?" Suddenly I felt uncomfortable. Diego was my father's son, but he didn't feel like my brother exactly.

"No, he no longer lives here," she answered slowly. "He has his own place now; shares a house with a couple of his buddies."

I bit my lower lip; perhaps this was not meant to be after all.

But Berta continued, her voice perking up as she spoke. "Perdóname. I'm so sorry. He moved out just a few weeks ago, and I'm still not used to saying he's not here. Not an easy thing to get used to, sorry," then a slight laugh, "Forgive me, I was napping. I work crazy hours. What can I do for you, honey?"

I took a deep breath. "I am planning to come to Los Angeles. I'm in Arizona, and I have transportation with a group of college students. In fact, they are leaving in two days. I was thinking I would like to meet you . . . and Diego, if it wasn't any trouble."

"In Arizona. ¡Qué bueno! And Rosa? Is she with you as well?"

"No," I answered, trying to keep my voice light. "Rosa is traveling with her boyfriend. It is just me."

I had always pictured Berta and young Diego. I hadn't considered that he was a grown man with a life—a place—of his own. And Berta wasn't exactly family. She was the sister of my father's first wife. What obligation was there on her part? Suddenly I felt foolish for calling.

"You need a place to stay?" I heard her say without a moment's hesitation.

"I'm sorry," I began, "I don't want to be any trouble. I just wanted to meet you and Diego, and talk with you about . . . my father? I wondered . . ."

She interrupted, "¡Alma, qué maravilla! I'd be happy to have you! This place has been so empty since Diego left. It'd be nice to have some company. Juan's daughter! How I've wanted to meet you girls. I've heard so much about you. You're the good student, aren't you? By all means, come. I've spoken with Rosa a few times. I so look forward to meeting you." She sighed, then added, "Honey, you just made my day. ¡Muchas gracias!"

Stunned, I wrote down her address and promised to call when I had more specifics.

As I hung up the phone, Ana was looking at me with raised eyebrows. "She knew my name!" I cried. "Papá told her about me, that I was a good student!" Tears, this time of joy, dripped down my cheeks. "It's all set. She said she'd be happy to have me." I shook my head incredulously. I could feel it, the connection to Papá. Yes, this was the right thing to do.

But that night, as I lay in the dark reflecting on our conversation, my excitement was tempered by a deep sadness. *Oh Rosa*, I whispered into the darkness, *I wish you were here. I wish you could meet her, too. We were supposed to do this together!*

And as with every night, I buried my face in my pillow and wept.

Before I left Nogales, there was one thing I wanted to do. Ana said a note would be sufficient, so I did write one just in case that would be my only resort. But I wanted something more personal; I felt he deserved that.

We got to the hospital quite early, but since Ana worked the evening shift, she wasn't certain when he arrived, or even if he came every day. She parked in a spot that gave us a view of the doctors' lot, and we just waited. We had been there well over an hour when Ana decided to get us some drinks. And that's when Dr. Ramírez pulled up in a sparkling silver sports car. My heart began to flutter, and I froze at first. But fortunately, he stepped out of the car and paused to smooth out his pants and tuck in his shirt, and then, walking around to the passenger's door, he reached in to get his suit jacket. That gave me time to work up my nerve and approach him.

He turned and looked at me quizzically. "Can I help you?" he asked. "Is something wrong? ¿Hay un problema?"

I swallowed hard. Suddenly I was at a loss for words. All I had planned simply escaped my mind.

"If you are in need of medical assistance, the emergency entrance is on the other side of this building. There are signs," he said, pointing with his small, clean hand.

I shook my head. "No, perdóname," I said softly. "No, I am here to say thank you. Gracias for your kindness."

Squinting his eyes, he tilted his head slightly.

I continued. "Your care and concern . . . brought me some comfort in a very difficult time." I stepped forward. "I was the girl . . . the girl who wouldn't talk."

I paused and waited to see if that meant something to him. Perhaps he dealt with other girls who would not talk. But it seemed to register, for his eyes widened and his mouth opened as if he were about to speak. But he didn't, at least not at first. He looked at my face closely and then a quick glance up and down. Finally, his face relaxed into a smile.

"You are well," he said with a degree of pleasure in his voice.

"Yes," I said. "Estoy bien. I have been fortunate enough to meet generous people, and my father always said to be sure to thank those who help us."

He nodded. "I feared you had met foul play . . . again. But I am happy to see you looking so well." His eyes lingered on my stomach.

"Yes," I nodded. "I am going to have this baby. In fact, I have family in Los Angeles, and I am leaving tomorrow. I wanted to thank you before I left." I wanted him to think I had a solid plan.

He reached out his hand. I slowly extended mine.

Dr. Ramírez squeezed my hand with both of his. "I can't tell you how pleased I am to see you. Thank you for coming today. And I wish you the best . . . you and your baby. Be sure to see a doctor about the baby. Take vitamins. Eat well . . . for two."

I nodded and stepped back. As the sun washed over me, I felt a surge of energy. I turned to walk away, but he held up his hand and said, "Wait! Un momento, por favor." Reaching in his pocket, he pulled out a black leather wallet. Removing the contents of green bills, he folded them neatly in half and handed them to me.

I shook my head, "No, it's not necessary. You've already done so much."

But he took my hand and placed the bills in my palm; then just as Señora Lopez had done with the crucifix, he folded my fingers over them. "Babies cost money." He smiled, then added, "Y los doctores también." Then gently touching my chin, he asked, "Your jaw? Is it healed?"

"Yes, it aches now and then, but it's okay. And thank you so much," I said, referring to the money in my hand. As I walked away, he called to me one more time.

When I turned, he asked, "Your name? ¿Cómo te llamas?"

"Alma," I said without hesitation. "Alma Cruz."

Ana was waiting behind a bush with two lemonades in her hand. "Is everything okay?" she asked.

I nodded, too choked up to speak. But as we drove on home, I composed myself enough to ask, "Could we stop somewhere first?"

She looked at me questioningly.

"I want to buy a book . . . a small notebook . . . and a pencil." And I proceeded to tell her about my little journal of math.

15

City of Angels

This van had seats. Three rows, in fact, with comfortable, plush cushions and armrests that folded down. Beside the middle seat sat a large cooler, which they had filled with ice and drinks and snacks. With loud music pumping, it was like a party on wheels—nothing like my van ride in Nogales.

We left in the evening to avoid traffic with the plan to drive right straight through, each student taking a turn at the wheel. That morning, Ana had given me a counterfeit social security card and a green card that she had purchased for $125—just in case we were stopped. If I were caught by authorities and my papers found to be fake, I would tell them I had lied to the students and that they were not aware I was undocumented. The last thing I wanted was to get them in trouble—or Ana for that matter.

None of this made sense to me. I could not enter el norte to search for my father without being a criminal of sorts. It wasn't enough that I had to sneak and hide, but anyone who helped me was put at risk as well. Borders and fences, quotas and visas, I did not understand. I simply wanted to find my father. I wouldn't harm anyone or take what was not mine. Why was my presence such a problem?

In an attempt to look like the students, I pulled my hair back into a long ponytail and wore a pair of jeans and one of their college T-shirts. I sat in the rear of the van with Eduardo, the Spanish speaking boy. He told me that if we got checked for IDs at any point to stay calm, pass up my papers, and then gaze out the window or pretend to sleep.

As it turned out, the ride was uneventful. I tried desperately to get some sleep, but my rising anxiety kept me wide awake. I hadn't realized how secure I felt at Ana's, but as the van sped further and further away, my hands turned cold and something in the pit of my stomach burned. Ana had made it clear that I could contact her at any time, and she would find me a ride back. She said we were family now, that I wasn't alone. I knew as I waved goodbye that I would always stay connected to them, no matter where I ended up.

How I ached for Rosa. She had always been my companion; I'd never gone anywhere without her. Those hazy weeks in the hospital and the months that followed at Ana's, I had been in a cocoon, incapable of thinking and feeling with any great depth, but now that I was moving forward again, my walls of protection had fallen away. I felt exposed and unprotected—and so very alone. Driving through Arizona in the dead of night, I felt the enormity of my life without Rosa. Trembling, I hugged myself and tried to stifle a sob.

Kind Eduardo may have sensed my restlessness, for he began to talk. He told me he wanted to be a doctor, like his father, and to travel to countries like Honduras, where his father's parents were born, or to Africa, where many children were starving. He wanted to work with the very poor, he said, where there was great need. I could tell by the way he spoke that he must be very smart. I asked him if college was difficult. He thought for a minute and then said it was probably like crossing the desert, one step at a time.

I gazed out the window at the passing darkness. That was my entire future now. One step at a time.

Los Angeles, like Mexico City, was terrifyingly huge—an endless maze of streets and freeways, with more vehicles than I had seen in my entire life. Houses, apartments, large buildings, small buildings stretched in all directions as far as the eye could see. It truly never ended.

"Is this still Los Angeles?" I asked again and again, as we wound our way through the early morning traffic, and they laughed and kept nodding yes.

Most of the students were dropped off on a busy corner near the college. Eduardo and Kelly, the girl whose father owned the van, would continue on with me to what they called the Valley, where Berta lived. Her address was neatly printed on a piece of paper beneath freeway numbers 405 and 101 and directions to the house in Canoga Park. Berta, who worked early morning hours at a bakery, would not be home until the afternoon; however, if I arrived before then, I was to go to the neighbor in the blue house on the left, and she would let me into Berta's house.

After driving down a very wide and busy street, we turned onto smaller ones lined with houses side by side. The van slowed down as we looked at street names and numbers. Some of the houses were nicely painted, with green lawns and colorful flowers, while others were faded, poorly tended, and overgrown with weeds. The one we finally stopped in front of was immaculate—yellow paint with white trim and several large bushes of red roses beneath the front window.

Eduardo walked me to the blue house next door and rang the doorbell. When a large dog appeared in the door's window growling like a ferocious wild boar, Eduardo set down the plastic bag containing my belongings and stepped forward, between me and the impending danger. My throat constricted remembering Manuel's futile attempt to protect me as well, so when a young woman balancing a baby on her hip shushed the dog away and flung open the door, I couldn't speak.

"You must be Alma," she said, speaking Spanish and eyeing Eduardo suspiciously.

"Yes," I finally blurted out. "And this is Eduardo, one of the college students who was kind enough to give me a ride."

She didn't seem impressed and continued to glare at him coldly. His eyes narrowed and he turned to me. "Will you be all right? Do you want us to stay until Berta shows up?"

Confused, I looked from Eduardo to the woman, wondering if they somehow knew each other. The tension was palpable. Then it occurred to me that maybe it was the color of his skin. Like me, she was brown, while Eduardo was darker, like afromexicanos in Oaxaca. I'd experienced this myself, some lighter Mexicans feeling they were better than darker Mexicans. It saddened me to think it might be the same here in el norte.

The woman shifted the baby to her other hip. "Berta didn't say to let anyone in, except you. If he waits, he waits outside."

Exasperated, Eduardo shook his head and rolled his eyes. Then with a deep sigh, he said, "Let me give you my number. If things don't work out here, just give me a call. We don't want you to end up on the streets." After writing his number on a piece of paper, he handed it to me and shook my hand. Casting a dark look toward the woman, he turned and walked to the car.

"Thanks again, Dr. Eduardo!" I shouted. He laughed as he climbed into the van. Kelly honked the horn as they sped away.

As I picked up my bag, the woman raised her eyebrows. "Be careful who you ride with. You never know in this city."

"You never know anywhere," I said softly as we walked toward the yellow house with two hanging pots of flowers on either side of the door. The red flowers and wrinkled leaves hung limply, begging for a drink of water. I made a mental note to tend to them as soon as I could.

As she unlocked the front door, she turned to me and said, "I'm Isabel. I went to school with Diego. When we were kids, I mean." Her nails were long with white tips and almost every finger had a silver ring.

I nodded and, holding out my stubby finger for the baby to grab, asked, "And what's his name?" His sleeper was blue with little trains, so I assumed he was a he.

"Paolo," she said without a glance at him. Then as an afterthought, "He's not mine; he's my sister's."

My gaze shifted to the interior as she swung open the door. The room we entered was dark until Isabel walked to the corner, reached behind the curtains, and pulled a long cord. Gracefully, the curtains glided open to a small yard with two large trees and a rusty swing set. Light swept through the room, revealing to the left a comfortable sofa and chair facing a TV and to the right a small round dining table with three chairs. But what made my heart race with anticipation were the dozens of framed photographs throughout the room. Some were on tables, some on shelves, and others were hanging on the walls.

Isabel sank onto the soft blue sofa, bouncing the baby on one thigh. "So, you're Diego's sister? Half-sister?"

I nodded.

"I didn't know he had any brothers or sisters."

I remained standing, shifting from one foot to the other, uncertain what I should do next. I bit my lip and decided to set down my bag and sit in the chair that matched the sofa.

As I settled in, it tipped back and swiveled to the left. Surprised, I giggled. It both rocked back and forth and turned in a complete circle. I could move it one way and watch the television, or I could swing the other way and look out into the yard. The arms themselves felt like plump pillows. I closed my eyes and settled back, feeling the soft fabric under my fingertips. When I opened my eyes, Isabel was looking at me with a crease down the middle of her forehead. My cheeks flushed, and I lowered my eyes.

"How long will you be staying?" she asked.

I shrugged. "I'm not sure yet." What could I say? I had no idea what was going to happen here. I would take one day at a time.

Isabel sighed and, gathering the baby, stood up. "Well, Berta said to call her when you got in. The phone number is out here in the kitchen."

I followed her back toward the front door and turned left into the small kitchen, which I hadn't noticed when we walked in. To the left was a washing machine and dryer like the Garcias had in Oaxaca. Beyond that a small table and two chairs, which Isabel motioned to, saying, "There's the number," pointing to a pad of paper, "and the phone" which hung on the wall. It was yellow like the walls.

"Anyway, give her a call. That's the bakery's number. And if you need anything, you know where I am. Berta comes home around one or two, I think." She walked to the door, opened it, then paused, "And I'll be home all morning, so . . . I'll be watching the house." She gave me a look of warning and then stepped out the door.

The silence that followed the click of the door was soothing. I glanced around the kitchen, bright with sunlight. Above the table was a clock in the shape of a sunflower. On either side hung figures of cows with large eyes. In fact, cows were everywhere. The salt and pepper shakers, the napkin holder, the dish towels that hung from the refrigerator. Little black and white cows smiled back at me throughout the room. I knew immediately that I would like Berta.

I sat down at the table and picked up the pad. ¡Alma, bienvenida! Welcome, in neat printing at the top, and then beneath that, Llámame, followed by a phone number. I glanced at the yellow phone and felt a twinge of nervousness. A bird cooed loudly outside. Glancing up, I noticed that above the sink, the window extended outward. Within it were three ceramic pots painted with sunflowers, each containing different herbs: basil, cilantro, and something unfamiliar. And all around these colorful pots were more little cows. One was standing on its hind legs, wearing a chef's hat and holding a rolling pin. Another was lying flat on its back wearing a bikini and sunglasses, and another, wearing a pink bonnet, was pushing a baby carriage with a calf peering out. I grinned and reached for the phone.

"Betty's Bakery," a voice said in English after three rings. I hesitated. "Hello," I said using the little bit of English that my father had taught us. "Please, Berta . . . Berta, please?" It occurred to me that I didn't even know her last name.

The woman said something and set down the phone. I could hear voices in the background, then footsteps. "Hello?" a woman's voice.

I responded in Spanish. "Is this Berta?"

"Sí. ¿Es Alma? You made it all right? You are there?" Her Spanish put me at ease.

"Yes, I am here in your happy kitchen . . . with the cows."

She laughed. "Listen, I am going to try and get out early, maybe by noon or so, but in the meantime, make yourself at home. There's food in the refrigerator—anything, eat anything. And you can settle into the bedroom on the left, at the end of the hall." She paused, "Let's see . . . anything else? How was your trip?"

"Fine, no problems. The students were very kind."

"¡Muy bien! Well, if you have any questions, just call. But I should get home in an hour or two. So, eat, take a shower, sleep if you are tired. Okay?"

My eyes welled up with gratitude. "Muchas gracias. You are so kind."

She was silent, then a quick, "Got to go. See you soon."

I hung up the phone and took a deep breath. Everything in the kitchen was dazzling and clean—sparkling sink, gleaming stove top and oven. I stood and ran my fingers along the beige tile counter. I curved around the kitchen table to another small doorway that led back to the room with the dining table, sofa, and swivel chair. And the photographs!

The photos were mostly of Diego. On the wall was a collage of baby pictures: asleep in a crib, on Santa's lap, surrounded by gifts beneath a Christmas tree, and in the arms of a young woman with a beaming smile, perhaps Berta? On a glass shelf mounted along one wall was a row of silver frames: a young boy in a baseball uniform, a gangly teenager beside a red car, a handsome young man in a tuxedo standing beside a girl in a long blue gown, and finally, a graduation photo in cap and gown. I could see a bit of my father in these later pictures, in Diego's high cheekbones, thick eyebrows, and dark eyes.

But it was as I turned that my heart stopped. Along the top of the oak piece that held the TV was a large photo of my father taken a year or two before he disappeared, for he looked exactly as I remembered him. He was standing proudly beside his son who towered above him by at least 12 centimeters, maybe more. Papá's eyes were soft, his chin lifted slightly, his smile full and warm. He was clearly happy to be there. I had never thought of that. That coming here was not just work, but a chance to see his American son. I gently touched the face smiling back at me. "Where are you?" I whispered.

Beside this photo were three others. One was perhaps of Berta's parents, an older couple—the woman seated, the man standing proudly beside her, his hand resting protectively on her shoulder. Then in a ceramic frame with sunflowers painted all around it, a pretty young woman with a twinkle in her eye grinned at the camera as if she'd just had a good laugh. I wondered if this was Berta, or perhaps, Berta's sister: Diego's mother, my father's first wife. On the other side of my father's picture was the third framed in black: a young man in a military uniform staring solemnly off to the side as if contemplating where he was headed. A brother perhaps?

I reached for my bag of belongings and walked down the hall: a small bathroom to the left, a bedroom to the right. I stopped and glanced in—Diego's room I guessed, with baseball posters, trophies on the dresser, and a blue plaid comforter on a large bed. At the end of the hall were two bedrooms and a larger bathroom. To the right, Berta's, with the bed unmade and the curtains closed. It was dark and I respected her privacy, so I entered the one on the left, the one I would sleep in while I was there.

A bed with a yellow and white flowered quilt sat along one wall beside a white dresser. And at the foot of the bed—a little white bassinet. I caught my breath. Did she know somehow? But how could she? I set down my bag and reached out to touch the lace edging. Inside sat two cloth dolls with flannel gowns and bonnets. Their braided hair of yarn was slightly faded and their faces soiled in spots. These dolls had seen better days, but they clearly had been well-loved. More photos on top of the dresser gave me a clue. Both were of the young woman in the sunflower frame. In one she was quite young, perhaps eight or ten, with the same teasing grin, her arm hooked around a smaller girl's shoulders. In the second photo, she was a young woman in a simple white dress, holding a bouquet of white roses, one flower behind her ear and one hand clutching the arm of a young Juan Cruz. My father was dressed in a suit that was much too large, clearly borrowed for the occasion. His handsome face glowed with pride and glee. Their wedding day.

I sank onto the bed as I realized that, of course, he had been here many times. He had been in this house and probably slept in this room, in this bed, for this had been *her* room: Berta's sister, my father's wife. I knew so little about this part of his life, only that he had lost her in childbirth and her sister had raised the baby. Beyond that nothing—not even her name. Lightly touching my abdomen, I thought, there was so much Berta could tell me, but first, I had to do the right thing. I had to tell Berta my truth, or at least a small part of it.

I awoke to find a large woman with very short salt and pepper hair standing above me. I sat up quickly, startling her. "Oh, I'm sorry," she said almost in a whisper, "I didn't mean to wake you. You must be exhausted."

"No," I said, rubbing my eyes. "I'm fine now. You're Berta?"

She nodded, "Yes, and you . . . you look so much like your father . . . and Diego."

"Do I? ¿Mi Papá?"

"Oh yes. The eyes, the nose, definitely."

I had never seen the likeness, but then my face had been much fuller until recently. I stood and looked in the mirror above the dresser.

"How long has it been . . . since you saw him last?" she asked gently.

My eyes met hers in the mirror. "June 1997. Almost three and a half years. He left after my brother's birthday." I sank back onto the bed. "We had had a party, and the next day he left." I remembered sitting with him the evening before, talking about how he wanted me to continue on to high school after I finished secundaria. I looked up at Berta, whose eyes had filled with tears.

"Do you have any idea where he might be?" I asked. "Any ideas at all?"

Closing her eyes, she took a deep breath and as she exhaled said, "Oh, m'ija. Come into the kitchen. Let's get some breakfast. I'm starving . . . and then we can talk."

Berta worked in a French bakery making breads and pastries with French names like batarde, and baguette, and croissant. "I love to cook, too, all kinds of food, not just Mexican. So, I hope you'll enjoy trying some new dishes." She moved swiftly about the tiny kitchen, pulling out a wooden board from one corner, some vegetables and eggs from the refrigerator, and a pinch of herbs from her window plants. "I hope you're a big eater—are you? With Diego gone, I always make too much, though I send it home with him when he stops by. Those boys sure can eat. ¡Grandes apetitos!" She chatted away as she laid out dishes and silverware, and though I asked if I could help, she shook her head and looked around. "Two cooks are one too many in this kitchen."

Fortunately, I was already halfway through my breakfast when she sat down to join me, for as she lifted her first forkful to her mouth, she said, "Now tell me about your journey across the border. Was it terribly difficult?"

The food stuck in my throat.

"Did you have a good coyote?" she continued, giving me a chance to catch my breath—and swallow. "Juan said the old routes were no longer good, that with the fences and alarms he was being pushed east into the deserts, and without a reliable guide, it was very dangerous." She paused and tore a piece of croissant.

"Did he?" I asked. "Did he use a guide?"

She frowned. "Not always. They cost so much money. But sometimes, yes."

"So . . . do you think that he . . . ?" My hands trembled, so I set down my fork and placed them in my lap. "Do you think he used one this last time?"

"I don't know," she said, lowering her eyes. "I hadn't spoken to him myself in months. He usually called us once he arrived in LA. Sometimes it was before he made his rounds in the fields, sometimes it was after, on his way back."

She took a few bites, while I played with my eggs, and then continued. "Diego spoke with him sometime that spring. He was finishing up his paramedic program, and they were going to celebrate on his next visit. Juan mentioned the summer, but he wasn't sure when." Her voice softened, "That's the last we heard from him, honey. Lo siento. I wish I knew more. Diego will tell you all about it. He contacted authorities, even went down to San Diego and El Centro. The firefighters and paramedics there were wonderful, so supportive and eager to help, but . . . not a trace." She sat for a moment, her eyes cast down, then stood with her dish and turned to the sink. I rose as well. In silence we washed and dried until, turning off the water, she turned to me and said, "Sweetie, to answer your question in the bedroom, I just don't know. He was so experienced at crossing and so careful. But he would have contacted us . . . if he was . . . okay. And yet, like you, I wonder." She smiled and stroked my cheek. "But you talk to Diego, tu hermano. He keeps hope alive, too."

My heart fluttered with those words.

She took my face in her hands and kissed my forehead. Then shaking her head, she said, "I can't believe how much you look like your father."

"Tell me about him," I said, squeezing her arms. "Tell me what you remember about Papá when he was young . . . about your sister and those early years."

Her face softened with tenderness as her eyes filled with tears. "Oh my," she said in a whisper. "Recuerdo."

16

Dar a Luz

(To give birth; literally, to give to the light.)

We settled into the living room, Berta in the big soft chair, and me, curled up in the corner of the sofa. She rocked as she talked, occasionally turning toward the window and gazing out beyond the yard to a time that was clearly still vivid in her mind.

Her name, I learned, was Lara, and she was born the same year as my father, 1950. And just like Rosa, she was the older sister by two years.

"It was just the two of us," Berta began. "My third sister died during delivery, and my mother lost her uterus as well. As it turned out, Lara was a handful anyway. Strong-willed and stubborn, muy terca, with a temper to match, yet she would fight to the death for you if needed," Berta said, shaking her head. "Oh, she gave my parents such a time—always. Not that she did anything bad, just that she was perpetually involved in some great drama. Bringing home abandoned pets one day and neglected kids another. She'd feed the whole damn neighborhood with what little we had, and no matter what my parents said to her, she wouldn't listen, scolding them as if they were the ones who were overstepping their bounds.

"When she was about sixteen years old," Berta continued, "one of the priests in our church spoke about the farm workers, how they were being exploited—low pay, terrible living and working conditions—so Lara and some of her friends got involved. They would go to grocery stores and tell people not to buy grapes. That's all she'd talk about day and night. Well, she heard that there was going to be a march from Delano to Sacramento, and she decided to go with some church members. I remember my parents trying to stop her, saying she would miss school, that she was too young even if a priest was going as well. But Lara always did what she wanted. And that's where she met your father. Or so he told me years later. Lara never spoke of that meeting. She claimed they met a couple of years after that at a rally for Cesar Chavez."

Berta paused and tilted her head to one side. "Now Juan's story was that he had fallen in love with her during that walk to Sacramento, but she wouldn't give him her number, saying if God meant them to be together, they'd meet again. And they did." Berta winked. "Of course, they met again! Your father wandered every corner of Los Angeles every chance he got during those two years trying to find her! He said he'd be working in Oxnard or Fresno, and he'd take a few days off, hitch a ride to LA, and wander a different part of the big city looking for her. He was close to giving up when he heard about a rally to support Chavez, who was ill from fasting. It was to be held at the old church in downtown Los Angeles. Convinced that Lara would be there—and that God meant them to be together—he made his way to LA. That was two years later, mind you, and this time when he found her, he got her phone number. After that, he came to LA as often as he could. ¡Tanto amor!" she sighed.

Berta swiveled the chair toward the photo above the TV, and the two of us sat staring at the smiling eyes of my father as she spoke. "My papá didn't like the fact that he was a migrant worker, traveling so much, but Lara kept telling him that there was nothing serious going on. They were just friends. And since Juan's visits were months apart, my dad eased up. But when he did finally come to see her, he'd always bring something for each of us. A cigar for my father, a basket of fruit for my mother, flowers for Lara, and even a little something for me—like a ribbon or a barrette for my hair, which was very long back then, very long." She smiled shyly and ran her fingers through her short hair.

I sank back into the cushion and sighed. I could see my father—the young Juan Cruz—with his arms full of gifts in the doorway, just as he would do years later for me. I wondered if he ever felt a pang of sadness standing at our door, yet remembering that earlier time. How humble I felt, realizing that his thoughts were not just of me—or even just our family.

Berta's voice brought me back to this doorway. "Soon all of us were looking forward to his visits, even Papá," she continued. "And of course, Lara fell in love. How could she not? He was so devoted to her."

"So, they married?" I asked, picturing my dad down on one knee—after getting her father's permission of course.

Berta sighed. "Oh no. Your father may have asked, but Lara had no such plans yet; she was going to college. She wanted to be a social worker. She worked part time and took two or three classes every semester. Nothing was going to stop her. That is, until she got pregnant. And oh, your father was so excited. The first thing he did was find a construction job nearby—and then he came to my father. Shortly after, they married and Juan moved in with us. Lara continued with school, and Juan went from job to job."

Berta grimaced, and I knew the love story was taking a fateful turn. "But then, one night, she awoke screaming. She was bleeding heavily, and sure enough, she lost the baby. It took her by surprise, I think. She hadn't realized how much she wanted that baby." Berta bit her lower lip and frowned. "It changed her a little. She wasn't as certain of everything anymore. And she began to lean on others, especially your father—and me. I guess she let herself need us. That's when we began to get really close, Lara and I. I had always been just her little sister, but after that, our relationship deepened. We became friends."

I was thinking of Rosa and struggling to hold back tears when I realized Berta was weeping softly.

Trembling, she said, "And then . . . Carlos died. *My* fiancé. In Vietnam. And I don't know what I would have done without Lara." She looked down at her empty hands with a puzzled expression.

My voice broke as I tried to say, "I'm so sorry." We sat in silence for a few minutes. Through the window I watched a little gray bird, hooded in black, land on an empty bird feeder and sway to and fro, pecking at the opening in search of one tiny morsel.

Berta reached for a tissue on the table and blew her nose. "Those years were such a struggle for me. But Juan and Lara kept me going. They continued to live here at the house. Juan worked at odd jobs—I remember that was always a struggle—and Lara tried desperately to get pregnant again. There were two more miscarriages, maybe more that I never knew about. She talked of adopting now and then and continued with college. Then in 1975, out of the blue, she got pregnant with Diego. Everyone tried not to get excited. We held our breath through the whole pregnancy, but there were no problems whatsoever—until the delivery."

Her lower lip quivered, and she lifted her chin. Then simply and quietly, Berta said, "Some freak thing with her uterus turning inside out after the delivery."

My dad had never spoken of any of this, just that Diego's mom had died in childbirth. I'd always pictured an older woman exhausted from labor, who simply drew her last breath, while all eyes were focused on baby Diego.

Berta leaned forward and, squeezing the arms of the chair, said, "It seemed impossible that she no longer existed. None of us could believe it. My parents were in shock that whole year. And Juan—oh your poor, dear father—was devastated. There was no consoling him. Even seeing little Diego only made him sob all the more.

"But for me," her eyes brightened as she continued, "Diego, mi bebé precioso, when I held him to my chest," she pressed her hands tightly to her bosom, paused, and then in a whisper that tugged at my soul, she said, "he soothed the pain in my heart."

I leaned back and pressed my hand over the spot where that ever-present heaviness weighed on my heart. My hand slid down to the rise of my abdomen. *"Soothed the pain in my heart."* I thought of Rosa modeling the rebozo for the couple in Oaxaca, of Manuel tearing pieces of his sweet bread for me, how his lips tasted like sugar when we kissed on the bench.

Then from somewhere far away, I heard my voice speak softly with a reverence saved only for prayers, "We were attacked during the crossing. Rosa, Manuel, and I. They are dead, I am certain. And I . . . I am going to have a baby . . . in the spring."

Her lips parted as she gasped, then settled into a frown. But her eyes, though full of sorrow, stayed bright.

If there had been any doubt whether I should have come there, it disappeared with the box of tissues we went through that day. It was as if I had always known her, that she'd been *my* Aunt Berta from birth. I found myself telling her things I would never have discussed with my mother. She didn't blink an eye when I told her I knew it was a girl; in fact, from that moment on, she referred to the baby as "Luz" as if she were nestled in my arms, not my womb.

The next day, she picked me up after work with her car full of bread and pastries for "the boys" as she called them, and we drove to the fire station. The garage door was open, so with our arms full of boxes and bags, we walked up the driveway. A tall, muscular man with a thick mustache approached from behind the ambulance to help, but when he smiled, I stopped abruptly, for a taller, fuller-faced version of my father stood before me. It took me a moment, but just as I was about to step forward to shake Diego's hand or accept a hug, a few men suddenly approached from the side, and I startled. Like a frightened cat, I jumped and let out a short, sharp cry. Diego's arm was around my shoulder in an instant, steadying me as I stumbled. I lowered my burning face and tried to calm my trembling hands. Then Berta was beside me rubbing my back and saying something in English to the men, who with eager nods headed toward the car and the rest of the bags full of baked goods.

I had had similar experiences when I was out with Ana, especially while waiting in lines: I broke into a sweat and couldn't catch my breath whenever people stood behind me.

Berta whispered something to Diego, who then led us into their kitchen where we all sat down at the table. Pouring me a glass of juice, Diego turned and said, "So I finally get to meet you, Alma—you are the smart one, right? Did you know that I helped pick out the calculator you once got for Christmas?" His Spanish was simple with an accent, but his smile was so like Papá's.

I tried to answer while a lump formed in my throat, "Really? Are you kidding? I didn't know."

His face became serious as he said somberly, "Your journey here must have been difficult."

Before I could speak, Berta interceded, and I held my breath. I had asked her not to tell anyone of my experience. She had argued that Diego should know some of it, he was family after all, and in addition, his experience as a paramedic had exposed him to all sorts of things. But I had begged her, saying in time perhaps, but not yet. I didn't want him looking at me and thinking . . . *that*.

She spoke to Diego softly, saying I was tired and it was something we could talk about another time, then she ended with something in English.

I began to fidget as the room filled with deep voices and the quick movements of his coworkers, who were reaching for éclairs, brownies, and bread. Berta stood and said, "Come for dinner, Sunday—you're off?"

He answered in English with what sounded like a long explanation etched in tones of uncertainty.

As she helped me to my feet, I glanced up in time to see Diego and Berta exchange a glance. "We'll talk Sunday," she said in English.

I understood those words clearly, as well as the sharp tone of her voice. He nodded and looked questioningly at me. I forced a smile as I squeezed past the men in the kitchen.

Once outside I took a deep breath and heard Berta say behind me, "I'm sorry, m'ija; we'll be more careful where we go. Okay?"

As she gently touched my arm, all I could think about was Rosa—how I wished she could have known the kindness of Berta.

That Sunday Berta made an Italian dinner, filling the house with glorious smells of tomato and garlic. My nausea disappeared just as she said it would with a warm piece of French bread. We set the table in the dining area with her good dishes, placed a vase of flowers in the center, and lit candles throughout the living room. When I asked if we shouldn't wait until Diego arrived, she said, "Heavens no! The party has already begun!" And with that she put on her favorite Beatles album and twirled me around the room. By the time Diego arrived, we were both flushed and giggling, and he didn't believe us when we said we hadn't been drinking at all.

After jokes and small talk, we sat down to dinner where Berta cleared her throat and told Diego my version of the story: I was pregnant, and the father was working in Temecula to save money for the baby, for us. He listened closely, asking some questions in English because, Berta said, his Spanish was not as good. Sometimes she answered in English, and I found myself frustrated by the sudden switch, relying on facial expressions and occasional translation, but all the more determined to learn the language as soon as possible. I saw doubt in Diego's eyes, perhaps questioning my story or the fidelity of my novio, but when we were finally alone in the living room with Mamá Berta (as he affectionately called her) singing loudly in the kitchen, he settled back into the sofa and smiled.

"Alma, you're an angel sent from heaven."

"¿Un ángel? ¿Por qué?"

He tilted his head toward the kitchen and began to speak, but Berta popped her head back in and shouted, "Alma! That's her song. Listen. 'Luz in the Sky with Diamonds!'" After a quick translation, she disappeared back into the kitchen, singing along with the Beatles.

Diego's eyes widened. "That's why. She's been pretty depressed since I moved out, but truth is she hasn't been quite this happy in years." He paused and looked out the window. "Maybe since, well, before Grandma and Grandpa died."

I'd forgotten about her parents. The story ended with Lara's death, and I hadn't thought to ask about them. This had been the family home; I knew that. "When was that? When did they die?" I asked, realizing how utterly alone she must have felt with their deaths.

He spoke slowly, pausing from time to time, perhaps to find the correct word. Though he struggled a bit with Spanish, I could understand him, and he seemed to understand me as well. "I was twelve and difficult. I remember being angry that everyone was always so sad, then angry that they died." He grunted in disgust. "Grandma had a stroke and was in a coma for a few weeks before she died. Grandpa just faded after that—died six months later. His heart." He glanced tenderly toward the kitchen. "She didn't touch their bedroom for over a year and then suddenly just emptied the whole thing. She was about to turn it into a weight room and game room for me, when the girls at the bakery came over and practically forced her to remodel both the bedroom and bathroom into a beautiful space for herself. They helped her paint and buy bedroom furniture. Then they gave her a party—and bought her purple sheets and a comforter and curtains and towels. Everything purple! She cried and laughed at the same time. I remember my adolescent brain thinking the whole thing was stupid, yet somehow touching, too."

"So, the room I'm sleeping in . . . it was her room, growing up? Not your mother's?"

He looked at me with a puzzled expression. "Yes, that was Mamá Berta's room. My room was where my mother grew up and later where she and . . . our papá lived . . . after they married . . . before I was born."

His voice softened and our eyes held fast. We hadn't yet spoken of him, but in that moment, we spoke volumes. There was no need for Spanish or English. What I saw in his eyes, I had seen before. The aching loss and deep sadness. The torment of not knowing. With the mention of my father, I had seen this response countless times in Rosa's eyes. And I began to weep.

He moved over closer to me and took my hand. "Berta said you came here to find him. Or to find out about him."

I nodded, still unable to talk.

"That year, that he disappeared, I contacted every agency on both sides of the border." He stopped and shook his head. "This is difficult for me in Spanish." He took a deep breath and began again slowly, struggling with his words. "I have a friend whose cousin works for the Border Patrol, and he did a lot of investigating for me. He also told me who to talk to both officially and unofficially. And since there's such a brotherhood amongst firefighters, I contacted several departments along the border. I've been at this a couple of years now." He stopped and pressed his lips tightly together.

I knew that what came next, he did not want to say, but the lips parted, "What everyone has concluded is that he probably died somewhere in the desert. That was a record-breaking summer of deaths. ¡Muertes innumuerables!"

I closed my eyes, but I could not block the image of the sun-bleached bones huddled together or the solitary skeleton prostrate in the sand. "But no body. No one found his body," I said evenly.

He sat back.

"No dead body was ever found," I repeated.

He studied me for a moment, and from the silence in the kitchen, I knew Berta was listening, too.

Diego cleared his throat, and then in an official voice—that of a man who knew how to deal with people in an emergency situation— he spoke. "Alma, there is a cemetery near the border in a little town called Holtville. And in the back, in a field of mud, there are many bodies buried—unidentified bodies—of men and women and even children who have died crossing the border. Their families will never know. Nunca. They will never see a body. Nunca. Perhaps his body rests in peace in such a place."

"Or perhaps," I began and stopped. He wrinkled his forehead and waited. "Perhaps there is some reason, some other reason." I left it at that.

"Like?" he asked impatiently.

I shrugged, and with that movement, I saw him dismiss my reasoning.

I sat up. "You don't know everything about me. And I don't know everything about you."

"What does that mean? We hardly know each other at all."

"Does Berta know everything about you? Have you no secrets? Do you think you know everything about her?" He startled for a moment, and I saw his eyes take focus again. I continued. "Our father lived two lives that we know of, and even then, we know so little about each of those. How do we know anything for certain—except that he is missing?"

Berta had slowly entered the room and sat on the arm of the sofa. "Alma, what are you getting at? What is behind this?" she asked.

I thought of the letter in his wallet, the elegant curve of the script, "Forgive me," tucked so tenderly away.

I thought of the hands that touched my body in the moment Luz was conceived. Were they greedy and cold, or loving and warm? Cruel and rough, or soothing and soft? Anything could happen in this world. Nothing was certain. ¡Nada!

"We don't know," I said firmly. "We don't know anything for sure."

Berta rose and approached me with a sadness in her eyes. "Then why are you so certain . . . about Rosa?" she asked gently.

"What about Rosa?" Diego asked, puzzled.

I looked away. My heart began to race. My stomach burned. My face flushed, as my skin prickled all over. I could barely catch my breath.

I was certain because I *knew* about Rosa. I had always known, but I wouldn't let myself go there. At least not until now, in this room, with these two particular people who knew and loved Papá. It was almost like he was here. I could *feel* him. Here, where I felt as safe as I could ever feel again. I closed my eyes and remembered . . .

I was being lifted into the air. The sky, a vivid blue. The sun, so bright it blinded my eyes for a moment. Then my body hoisted over a shoulder. My head hanging down. Scattered amongst the gravel and brush, a shoe, a torn shirt, a trail of blood. My head bounced as I was shifted on the shoulder. And then . . . Rosa, stretched out on the ground, her head tilted back. Unaffected by the brilliant sun, her lifeless eyes were open wide, as wide as the scarlet gash across her neck, a flood of blood down her chest. Rosa! I tried to scream, but the sound I made vibrated inside my head until a thousand tiny lights exploded into darkness.

I knew Rosa was dead. But of Manuel, I had no memory. My brief glimpse was of only Rosa and her vacant, lightless eyes. Trembling, I tried to reach out toward Berta, but suddenly the room began to spin until only a pinpoint of light closed into blackness.

I awoke on the sofa, my legs elevated and a cool washcloth across my forehead. Berta was stroking my hair, and Diego was taking my pulse.

"I'm sorry, m'ija," Berta said. "I told Diego everything. It's good that he knows. He is your brother."

Then squeezing my arm and cooing in a deep, soothing, familiar voice was a young man so like my father, my heart fluttered with both sorrow and joy.

The months that followed would have filled me with utter delight if they were not a daily reminder of all that Rosa would never know—a sense of family with Berta and Diego complete with Sunday dinners, a glorious Christmas, and a surprise birthday party for Diego; a way of life full of promise that opened doors I would never have found in Chiapas; and a belief that I was closer to Papá here than I ever could be in Mexico.

I gradually overcame my apprehension to venture out alone and became familiar with the bus lines, traveling to the bakery where I worked three days a week, to the market, and even to adult school for English classes, although Berta insisted on picking me up after dark. I spent every spare moment studying English in my books or by listening to the television, especially the news and the talk shows. I insisted on speaking English to Berta and the others at the bakery, and eventually I began to take orders from customers. But most exciting was when I began to work the cash register. I would compute the totals in my mind and even figure out the change back before checking the machine to see if I was right. And one night, on my way to English class, I walked by a room where a young man was teaching math, and I stood beside the doorway and watched him work a problem on the board. My heart raced with excitement. Perhaps one day, I could take a math class again.

All of this was more than I deserved. That I knew. My penance was not sharing it with Rosa. Every potentially happy moment was accompanied by a jolt of remembrance that pierced my soul. As for

Manuel, try as I might, I found myself straining to remember his face, his voice. Only fragments of that short time with him remained— and I feared they would fade as well.

Yet one beautiful morning in May, after seventeen hours of labor, with Berta rubbing my back and cheering me on, I am told that I called for Manuel as Luz finally made her way into the light. Berta says I shouted his name three times, though I do not remember. Nor do I remember that when the doctor said, "It's a girl," I responded in Spanish, "Well, of course she is! ¡Idiota!" I only recall the tiny balled fists swinging, the feet kicking, and that furious scream that told me my little Luz de Rosalba was here to fight her way beside me in this dark world.

17

For Love

My favorite time of the day was just after sunrise. Luz, who would be sleeping in bed beside me since her 2:00 a.m. feeding, would stir when the bright rays would begin to light our room. Then I'd carry her to the patio where we would settle into a rocking chair and enjoy the early morning's cool air. The summer was unbearably hot in the San Fernando Valley, so these quiet mornings, with Berta still at work and Luz groggy with sleep, were a peaceful beginning to each day. The birds would begin their chatter, and I would listen and rock and gaze at my daughter tugging gently at my breast. Soon enough the oppressive heat, Luz's waking demands, and Berta's hovering presence would drain my energy and deflate my enthusiasm. But for these few minutes—sometimes close to an hour—I would feel a quiet joy and be grateful for what my life had become.

One such morning in August, in the midst of my reverie, I found myself thinking about the last time I had seen my mother. It would have been about one year before, the morning of that awful fight over Tito. I remembered feeling a tug as she threw those blankets at my feet, as if a taut rope that connected us was strained to its limit. But as she fled through the doorway, her long braid swinging as if waving goodbye, I felt that rope snap so close to my heart that nothing was dragging behind me when I left.

I kissed Luz's forehead thinking how I would never let her break that tie. I would always make sure that we were connected no matter what differences we had. As if to defy me, she fidgeted and released my breast, wiggling in my arms until a juicy burp settled her and she latched on again. Eyes wide, she gazed up at me as she suckled, and I stroked her cheek with my thumb.

Rosa and I had discussed many times our mother's lack of affection. Neither of us could recall being rocked in her arms, or tickled, or comforted. She would tug at our hair as she brushed it or tell us to brush each other's. Any sentence that began with "Alma?" was always followed by some set of instructions of what I was supposed to do—or a scolding for what I neglected. She didn't abuse us in any way, but neither did she caress us. And while I cannot remember her laughing or singing, neither can I remember her sobbing, for she simply withdrew.

So different from my father.

What was it about her that attracted Papá, especially after Lara? I wished there was someone who could tell me her story, like Berta had told me Lara's. All I knew was that they'd met at a wedding in Oaxaca in 1980, four years after Lara died: four years of Papá working the fields in California and visiting his son; four years of returning to this little house that held so many memories of Lara.

I don't even know whose wedding it was that led Papá to return to Mexico. He would have been thirty and Mamá only seventeen. She had come to Oaxaca years before to help an uncle whose wife was ill, but the woman had died earlier that year. Whatever ignited between them kept my father there as well. They were married within the year.

I had never once asked my mother about her childhood or about her and Papá. It was only now that I found myself aching with curiosity, so when Berta wearily pushed open the door with her arms full of groceries, I offered to trade bundles—an offer that I knew would energize Berta despite hours of baking. She adored Luz and loved nothing more than rocking her, even when I had just put her down for a nap. The minute she would as much as gurgle, Berta would snatch her up. So once Berta had settled into the rocking chair, cooing and making faces at Luz, I quickly put away the groceries and joined them in the living room.

I knew exactly what Berta's first response would be, so I addressed that point immediately. "Please don't start in again about me trying to contact my mother, please . . . but I was wondering . . . what do you know about her? Did Papá ever talk about her at all?"

Berta's startled face settled into a puzzled squint, though I may have caught a brief wince in the middle, but she averted her eyes as she shifted Luz over her shoulder, and said, "Flora?"

My mother's name floated between us for a moment. Even Luz seemed to lift her little head, briefly, in response.

"Yes," I answered.

Berta rubbed the baby's back in small circles. "Well, your father and I had a falling out of sorts, and I didn't see much of him for a while, but . . . ." She sighed. "It was a difficult time for both us, m'ija."

I couldn't imagine my father quarreling with anyone. "A falling out? What do you mean?"

Luz began to fuss, grunting and squirming, so I reached for her just as Berta started to get up. "I've got her!" Berta snapped, swinging to the side and standing with the baby in her arms. She turned, and we looked at each other for a moment until I stepped back, letting her pass. She jiggled Luz as she walked, talking softly in her ear.

After a few paces back and forth, she stopped and said, "No, Alma, he didn't talk about Flora. I'd been telling him to get on with his life for so long, and that's what he did. Went down to Mexico to find a young wife, got married—and then called for his son." Her eyes glazed with tears. "He called and said he decided he wanted to raise his son in Mexico. But we both knew what that meant. Without papers . . . I'd never see Diego again."

"Without papers?" I asked, confused.

"I wasn't a U.S. citizen then. My parents and I . . . we didn't become citizens until the amnesty of 1986, so I couldn't travel back and forth easily. And though Diego had dual citizenship, Juan didn't, so he wouldn't be able to bring him here for visits. There was no easy answer, so I . . ."

She began to shake, trembling so much that when I reached for Luz, she let me take her. Then she eased herself back into the chair.

"Alma, if anyone can understand, it is you."

I sank onto the sofa and held Luz so tight she didn't budge. We both seemed to hold our breath.

Berta exhaled. "Diego was my life. He was my son for five years, day and night. I had just enrolled him in kindergarten when Juan called. Everyone assumed that I was his mother, only family and close friends knew the truth. And Juan had agreed—all those years, he had agreed that this was the best for Diego—my parents, me, and the schools here in the United States. There had never been any question until that year that Juan went down to Oaxaca. He said he found a job as a manager or foreman on a plantation. A few months went by, then a few more. He'd call to talk to Diego, but no mention of when he'd return."

She closed her eyes for a moment and then continued, "A part of me was relieved, thinking he had finally turned him over completely to me. But then I'd worry; what if he changed his mind? What if he wanted his son? And then it happened. He called to say he was married and wanted me to send Diego down with a cousin who would be traveling through Los Angeles."

Her chin lifted, and she looked at me squarely without saying a word. I hugged Luz even tighter.

"He was his son," she said in a whisper, "but he was my son, too." Tears streamed down her round cheeks. "You understand, don't you?"

I nodded.

Berta leaned forward. "What would you do? If you were me, what would you have done then?"

"I don't know," was all I could manage, but I knew. I too had lost a sister. I too had lost someone I loved who might have been my future. Luz had become my reason for living again. I knew exactly what I would do.

She echoed my thoughts in cold, crisp words. "I fled with Diego north to a place appropriately called Lone Pine. My father had an old fishing buddy who offered us his cabin. But before I left, I sat down and wrote a letter. I poured my heart out to Juan, begging him to have mercy and let me keep his precious son as my own."

Berta began to sob, the pain on her face as fresh as if she were sitting in that cabin in Lone Pine. "Bless his soul, Alma. He consented, though not at first. He told me later how he agonized, how he read my letter over and over . . . until he was finally able to let Diego go."

She continued talking about how long she stayed in Lone Pine afraid to return to Los Angeles, even after Juan had agreed. How even once she returned, she held her breath each time she dropped Diego off at school, fearing that Juan would appear to sweep him up and off to Mexico. How it took more than a year for her to finally relax and believe that Diego was hers to raise and love for the rest of her days. She talked in a rush of words, her eyes flooded with tears, her hands moving nervously in explanation.

But my mind was not there in Los Angeles with Berta and Luz. Nor was it in Lone Pine with Diego playing near a stream as Berta anxiously glanced around with every crack of a twig. I was sitting in Oaxaca in our tiny house, and in my hands was my father's wallet, soft black leather that folded twice, one he bought in the United States. Curiously leafing through, I found a letter, wrinkled and worn. Slowly I unfolded it, furtively reading words not meant for my eyes: *"Forgive me, Juan, I am so deeply sorry. There is no easy answer for us. What else can I do? I never thought I was capable of such a thing, but love can overpower our reason and lead us down unexpected paths."*

I closed my eyes and thought of Berta's grocery lists, the small, perfectly rounded script: *milk, eggs, brown sugar,* evenly spaced beneath the smiling cow pictured on the memo pad.

Papá's secret letter was from Berta. And the love that he ached for, the love that he kept folded secretly away, was the same love that kept him crossing the border back and forth, year after year. The love for all of his children.

There was no secret lover, no other life that he might have escaped to; my father had disappeared in the summer of 1997 while crossing the border to see his son. My outburst of tears startled Berta until I unburdened my long-held secret belief—all based on what I thought was a clandestine love letter.

She was deeply moved that my father had carried this letter with him throughout his life, yet she was concerned that it may have been due to profound guilt. "Over the years I made a point of conveying how grateful I was, how well Diego was doing, how Lara would have been so pleased," she said anxiously. "He would always murmur, 'Yes, it was best for Diego. I know it was,' but perhaps he was trying to convince himself." She sighed, "But in the end, he was proud of what Diego accomplished. I think, in the end, he was okay with it."

In the end. I sat rocking Luz, tears sliding down my cheeks.

"Oh Alma," she said, sitting beside me and rubbing my back. "So that's why you believed so strongly that he was . . . somewhere else."

I nodded.

She pulled my head down onto her shoulder, and I nestled in, Luz lying on both of our laps. We sat together in silence for several minutes.

He was gone. I now knew that for certain. For if Papá were alive, he would find his way home . . . to his children. To me. To Diego.

Maybe he was with his Rosa. Sobbing, I pulled Luz up and buried my face in her neck.

Later that evening, after hours of heartfelt discussion, Berta left me
in the cool comfort of her room, so I could make some important
phone calls in private, using her purple bedroom phone. I sat on the
edge of her bed, the lilac comforter plush and soft beneath me. The
air conditioner hummed from the window, drowning out any dis-
tractions that Luz might create beyond the bedroom door. While I
had been in touch with Ana and her mother a few times and shared
the latest news of my life, there were those I knew I needed to connect
with; it was time. I took a deep breath and smoothed out the papers
that I had prepared containing the phone numbers of the Garcias in
Oaxaca and the Mendozas in Chiapas, Mamá's relatives who might
be able to find her and Tito. The Garcias' number I was certain of, the
Mendozas' I was not—those were foggy in my memory, since they
came from somewhere in my childhood.

I began with Maestra Garcia, whose genuine joy at hearing
my voice made my story all the more difficult to tell, but I felt she
deserved the truth. We talked and wept for almost an hour, each
of us comforting the other. She said her father wasn't well, for he'd
had another heart attack and now slept a good part of the day. For
many reasons, she would not tell him what happened. When we had
exhausted our talk of heartbreak, we spoke at length of my new life,
of Berta, Diego, and especially of my Luz. Before we said our goodbyes, she said something that made me sit up and think; she said that
perhaps I'd come close to what I was searching for—some answers
about my father and a sense of family again. But at what cost! The
truth was I still felt there was something more to find. I couldn't put
my finger on what, but I wasn't finished.

She then asked if there was anything more that she could do on
her end. Contact authorities or family? I hesitated and thought if she
could find my mother and arrange for her to receive a call, this way
she'd be prepared and, perhaps, we could talk without too much hys-
teria in between. I told her about the Mendozas.

She said she'd be happy to do that and ended with, "And please, Alma, call me Elena."

When I stepped back into the living room, Luz was lying in Berta's arms, gazing at a little doll that she jiggled above her. Luz kicked her legs in excitement and grinned until a little squeal filled the room, sending Berta and me into girlish giggles. I knelt beside them and kissed Luz's little fist.

"Is everything okay?" Berta asked.

I nodded, too exhausted to explain.

"Well, I need to get ready for work," Berta said, handing Luz to me.

As I settled into the warm chair, bouncing Luz on my knee, I looked up at Berta, who had paused in the hallway. "This feels like home, Berta. Is that okay?" I asked.

Her face relaxed into a youthful smile. "Oh yes, honey. It most certainly is."

"Next week, I want to talk to Betty about work again, and I'd like to go back to adult school this fall."

She nodded. "Sounds like a plan."

As sounds of the shower water echoed down the hall, I settled back and swiveled the chair to the left, until, building momentum, Luz and I twirled in a full circle. Round and round we went until the room was spinning even once we stopped. Leaning back, I closed my eyes until things settled, and then opening them, I saw my father's loving gaze, his hand resting on the curve of Diego's shoulder. He looked both proud and content, clearly at peace with his choices in life. That letter would have been safely tucked away in his pocket, a reminder of what he had lost and why, of the sacrifices life sometimes demands, and the peace that can be found in acceptance.

I looked deep into the warm familiar eyes. "I love you, Papá," I said, as Luz reached up and touched my cheek.

A few nights later, I heard my mother's voice on the phone, small and soft, saying my name several times, "Alma, Alma, Alma."

All I could respond was, "I'm sorry, lo siento," to each sound of my name.

"Tell me," she finally said, struggling to keep her voice even. "Tell me about Rosa? It is true? ¿Está muerta? Tell me."

I could only weep and continue to beg for her forgiveness.

"No, no," she said in a tight, high voice. "It is not your fault. I shouldn't have let you go. I should have stopped you—two young girls. No, no, you are just a child yourself." Then as if remembering, with a catch in her voice, she said, "A baby? ¿Una niñita?"

My heart burst and in a flood of words I said, "Oh Mamá, she is so beautiful! She is strong and loud and full of spirit!"

My mother laughed a soft trickle of warmth across the kilometers, "Just like you! So full of life. So independent. You needed no one, Alma—except your father's undying approval."

I could not speak.

"You are not alone? ¿Estás bien?" She hesitated, "Do you want to come home?"

Home. I looked about Berta's purple room where I once again sought refuge to talk in privacy on Berta's purple bedroom phone; Luz's blanket in a heap where the three of us had napped earlier; photos of Berta with Diego neatly spaced along her dresser, and square in the center, a photo of Diego, Luz, and me, taken a month ago.

"It is good for Luz here, Mamá. And for me." I paused. "I can go to adult school and work with Berta at the bakery."

"School. That is good for you. You were always a good student."

"And the boys? They're okay?"

"Oh yes. They've asked about you often." Her voice broke for a moment. "I must tell them . . . about Rosa . . . but they will be so happy about you and the baby."

"Luz. Luz de Rosalba."

"Luz de Rosalba," she repeated softly. Then she added, "And Alma? I am . . . I am also going to have a baby." Her voice sounded weary.

"¡Estupendo!" I tried to sound hopeful, then I remembered. "Wait. Weren't you pregnant when we left?"

She was silent for a while, then softly, "I lost it. It wasn't meant to be."

I thought of her life with Tito and my heart ached. I wanted to give her some words of comfort, but I came up empty. Instead I said, "I have the Mendozas' address now, so tell the boys I will write and send pictures and surprises." And money, I thought, suddenly eager to return to work. Then with a bit of effort, "Te quiero, Mamá."

Silence until I heard a muffled sob, then, "Yo también, Alma."

My latest math problems, which I will number as if I still had my precious Math Journal.

Math Problem #7
The drive from Nogales, Arizona to Los Angeles, California, was 551.39 American miles.
If five of the seven passengers planned to drive an equal distance, how long would they each have to drive if they traveled at an average of 65 miles per hour?

Math Problem #8
Betty's Bakery received the following order:
25 plain croissants @ $1.75
25 chocolate croissants @ $1.75
25 Napoleons @ $1.95
25 chocolate éclairs @ $1.95
25 brioches @ $1.85

Compute the total cost in American dollars and cents.

Then compute the change for this purchase if given two $100 bills and a $50 bill. (Explain what American bills and coins you would choose as change.)

*Do not use a calculator! It's important to keep your basic skills sharp!

Math Problem #9

A recipe for Berta's Sugarbaby Cookies calls for ½ kg of sugar. How many times can she make these cookies before she uses up a 6 kg bag of sugar?

18

Dolores

About one month after I learned about Berta's letter and confronted the reality of my father's most likely death, another tragedy of horrific proportions stopped us all in our tracks: 9/11. That morning, as I clutched Luz to my chest, I sat cross-legged in front of the TV and watched the horrors unfold. How much cruelty and senselessness was there in this world? I found myself sinking again, only this time I wasn't alone. Everyone, everywhere, was feeling the depths of this despair. Strangers on the bus would nod in acknowledgment of the grief we shared. Even Luz seemed more subdued. I struggled to get my momentum back, but I felt weighed down by so much sadness.

Then one evening, Berta pointed out a photo of Dolores Huerta in the newspaper. She had attended a prayer vigil at La Placita in downtown Los Angeles honoring the victims of 9/11. I grabbed the paper and stared at her familiar face. Knowing that she had recovered from her aneurysm and was well enough to venture out into the world again filled me with such encouragement and reassurance. That she was here in the city, so close, thrilled me beyond words. I felt a rush of emotions and an acute sense of connection. Manuel had spoken once of los nahuales, a spirit that guides or shadows us on our journey. I began to wonder if Dolores and I shared similar nahuales in spirit, for our journey back to life followed a common road. "God has a plan for me. My work is not done." I was determined to get back to work.

But it was the following year that I began to see this connection as something more, something that held a meaning I should respect. After a year of night school, where I had greatly improved my English, I was finally convinced by both Berta and Diego to enroll in a couple of classes at the community college. My English teacher at adult school had given me a math workbook with a teacher's edition so I could check my work, and I had pored over that book faster than Berta read a *People* magazine. At the bakery, I worked the cash register regularly, and Betty was beginning to show me how to keep the books. But it was Diego who took me over to the college on his day off to help me fill out papers and show me around.

We walked the length of the campus, stopping by a field where a few horses were grazing—part of their equine program, we were informed. My heart rose to my throat as I thought of Manuel's grin as he led those sorry beasts to me and Rosa. I gazed up at the blue sky and took a deep breath. It was peaceful here at Pierce Community College. I could see myself hurrying to class, maybe even studying on the grass with Luz by my side.

Math Problem #10: Math Placement Review!

1. Change to Mixed Numbers: 9/4

2. Change to Improper Fractions: 7 ¾

3. Simplify (reduce to lowest terms): 32/68

4. Multiply: 1 ½ x 2 ¾

5. Divide: 4 3/5 ÷ 2 ½

*6. Berta and I have the combined age of 66. Berta is 32 years older than I am. **How old is Berta? How old am I?***

On the evening before I was to take the placement tests in English and math, I began to panic. How could I do this? I had never even gone beyond what they considered middle school here. I could not measure up to what would be expected. I was feeling so low, I almost didn't turn on the news, which I faithfully watched in English every night as part of my adult school assignment. But finally, in part as a distraction, I closed my review books and switched on the TV.

And there she was again. Dolores. She had marched for ten days, one hundred and fifty miles, from Bakersfield to Sacramento in support of a bill for farm workers. In fact, she claimed that if the governor didn't sign the bill, she would begin a fast in his office. There she stood behind the banner ("March for the Governor's Signature"), so small, between two tall men, a straw hat shading her face. Dolores, who two years before had lain in a hospital bed just as I had, uncertain of her future; yet here she was, as determined as ever to take on this mighty feat.

The next day, I paid Itzel, the teenaged girl next door, sister to Isabel, twenty American dollars to watch Luz while I rode a bus to Pierce College to take the placement tests. I did so well on the math test that I was enrolled in college level math. Nothing was going to stop me, not even my daily struggle trying to decipher the meaning of rapidly spoken English.

A few months later, my math professor announced to the class that the highest score on our mid-term exam was mine—96%. I carried that exam home with great pride, placing it in the second-best place to my treasured box of stars—on Berta's fridge. She boasted as much as Papá would have and made me feel like I had won a major award. The next week I awoke to find hanging beside my exam a news article with a beaming Dolores, hands clasped, her face lit with joy. Once again, she was in Los Angeles for a ceremony that honored her work and announced that she was the winner of the 2002 Puffin/

Nation prize of $100,000. I sank onto the kitchen chair and gazed into her warm face. I felt such an intense connection, such a deep desire to meet her after all, to speak to her about Papá. I wasn't sure what I would say, but I wanted so to see her. She had met Papá—and Lara—in their passionate youth. Her eyes had met theirs; I wanted ours to meet as well.

Berta and I followed her trail in Los Angeles, made a few phone calls, but she had already left.

More than a year later, this chance was placed in my hands, literally—by Diego. He and his new fiancée Julie had come over for Sunday dinner in mid-March. Luz, almost three years old now, flew to the door, throwing herself at him as usual. "Tio Day-go!" she squealed, as he scooped her up and tossed her in the air. Once safely nestled in his arms, she began to explore his pockets where she knew some treat was hidden.

So, by the time the leaflet got to my hands, it was wrinkled and torn. It announced a march for Cesar Chavez in a park in the northeast San Fernando Valley on a Sunday morning in two weeks. As I smoothed out the wrinkles, Diego leaned over my shoulder and pointed to the words, "Guest Speaker: Dolores Huerta."

He offered to take the day off. Berta said she would go as well. But this had been our destination—Rosa and I—so I felt a strong need to go on my own, with only Luz.

That morning I woke early with an awed excitement that a bride must feel on her wedding day. *Oh Rosa, be with me*, I thought, squeezing my eyes shut and wishing hard. *See through my eyes and share this end to our journey.*

Berta drove me to the park, chatting to Luz but allowing me my silence. As we pulled to the curb, she reached over and took my hand. "You sure you don't want me to go? I could help with Luz."

A marching band not far from the car began to assemble in lines; beside them Aztec dancers adjusted their costumes. At the other end of the park, hundreds of people were gathered around a platform. I shook my head.

In my hand she placed her cell phone. "Call me when you're ready. I'll be waiting at home." Then she leaned across and kissed my cheek. "Don't be afraid to speak to her. Just push your way through the crowd."

I smiled, thinking of the box cars, the Mexican officials, Señor José, and the blazing desert. If I had gotten this far, a friendly crowd would not be a barrier.

I stepped out of the car and eased Luz out onto the grass. After smoothing out her pink sweatshirt and straightening the bows in her hair, I took her hand and began to walk toward the platform. Fascinated by the feathers of the headdress, Luz stretched her arm toward the dancers.

"No, m'ija, not now. Later. We'll see them later. Right now, we have to go over there," I said, pointing toward the crowd.

She continued to watch the dancers as I dragged her along, finally forcing me to pick her up and carry her across the large field.

By the time I approached the rear of the crowd, I was sweating and short of breath. Luz felt like three times her weight. A woman was speaking but I could not see beyond the crowd, so I circled around to the far left and found myself on the side of the stage not far from the steps. I heard "¡Viva!" as the crowd responded to the speaker's cheers.

And then I saw her.

After so many years and so many miles; each campesino, each

weary traveler whose lined face spoke of sun, sweat, and struggle; each with a story about her that further piqued my curiosity or bolstered my fading strength: "What cojones, that woman! What determination and fire." And just as I heard, first from my father years ago and repeatedly as I inquired throughout my long journey north, she was dressed in red. Bold. Determined. Red.

Dolores Huerta descended the podium and walked within arm's reach. My heart raced, and I wanted to stop her. I wanted to take her arm and say, *Dolores, because of you I stand here with my little daughter, Luz, squirming in my arms.*

As if on cue, Luz arched her back and howled, "Down! Get down!" in loud, defiant English. But Dolores was walking away through the crowd of outstretched hands, her back obscured by dark-suited men, only flashes of red between them. The sun beat down with the fierceness of the desert sun that Rosalba and I endured. And I thought of the miles I journeyed, of the Guatemalan boys, the night of the blinding stars, the woman with the eyes of a saint, and, of course, of Manuel and Rosa. But mostly, I thought of my father, whose laugh was as clear in my mind as Luz's face before me now.

I stepped forward.

"Dolores!" I said, my voice straining somewhere between a command and a plea.

As she turned, her smile was full and warm, like the sun breaking through a cool morning mist. Her eyes fell on Luz still struggling in my arms. Then she was beside me, the red sleeves reaching out, gathering my daughter to her hip, relieving me, for a moment, of my burden.

I paused, my heart racing; then she leaned forward slightly, her dark eyes fixed firmly on mine. She was listening, waiting, for me to speak.

"My name," I faltered, "is Alma, and my father . . . he said . . . he said you were the fiercest woman ever to walk this earth." Then I took a deep breath and began.

19

Waiting for Alma

I sat on the grass, watching Luz devour a blue snow cone. It dripped and splattered an elaborate design on her new pink sweatshirt, but it was the least I could do after our walk. We had marched the short distance between two parks with Dolores, trailing the Aztec dancers that kept Luz spellbound. During the walk, I poured out much of my story, and to my surprise it was she, not I, that asked most of the questions. We spoke mostly in English, with occasional Spanish for flavor, as Berta was fond of saying. I had become quite comfortable with my new language. After the march, Dolores had asked me to wait on the grass while she signed posters and T-shirts. When she was finished, she walked toward us, shaking hands along the way with her endless admirers.

"Can you manage a bit of a walk again? Let's get beyond this crowd." She reached down and helped Luz up as I stood. Together we walked again, the three of us hand in hand, Luz skipping between us.

We found a spot behind a tent where she managed to borrow two folding chairs. We settled ourselves and watched Luz gather tiny stones.

"Alma," she said with such gentleness it touched my heart. "I am sorry to say I do not remember your father or Lara. I've met so many wonderful people throughout these years. But I think you expected that now, didn't you?"

I nodded and added shyly, "I guess I just wanted to meet you—after

all that's happened—and to tell you my story." I was slightly embarrassed, yet also comforted by her presence.

She sighed and seemed to tremble at the same time. "Well, Alma—
there is more to it than that. Much more, I think." She leaned forward and took my hand, her face aging a bit as the warm smile was
replaced with a no-nonsense set of the lips. There was business to
tend to, her steady eyes told me, get ready.

She held my hand tightly as she said in a firm, even tone, "I have
heard your story before—at least part of it." She paused. "The first
half." Then she sat up straight, keeping a grip on my hand. "Over a
year ago, perhaps two, in San Diego, I was approached by a young
man who asked if I'd met a young woman looking for her father—a
young woman named Alma Cruz."

I gasped.

She took my hand now in both of hers. "Manuel, tu novio," she
said gently, the face softening again. "He said his name was Manuel,
and he was trying to find you. He thought that perhaps—since you
were looking for me—that I might have some knowledge of you, of
where you were. What city at least."

"Manuel is alive?" My hands burned cold, as if I had placed them
on a slab of dry ice. "¿Está vivo?" My mind whirled. How many years
had it been? "San Diego? He is in San Diego?"

She shook her head. "No, he had only come there because he knew
I was speaking at a rally. A priest had told him, I believe. No, he was
working somewhere else, with a brother, I think. But sweetie," she
began, as I interrupted.

"Temecula? Was it Temecula?"

She reached up and took my face in her hands. "Listen to me.
I have a number. He gave me a number in case you found me. He
insisted." She laughed. "Oh, he was as passionate as you—he insisted
that you would find me one day, and when you did, he wanted me to
give you this number."

I could barely catch my breath. Manuel, alive. I could call him, speak to him . . . see him?

Dolores continued, "It is in my purse, which I'm afraid I left at my friend's house. I didn't want to carry it on the march. But it is here in Los Angeles, and I'll find it for you this evening. Don't worry. I'll get it to you tonight." Her eyes were narrow slits as she smiled, her dark lashes glistened with tears. "I put it behind a photograph of my mother in my wallet. I told her to keep it safe." She shook her head. "I haven't thought of that paper in months, but I'm sure it's still there," she reassured me.

"I can't believe he's alive. I thought . . ." I stopped, unable to speak beyond the image that formed in my mind.

She held her hands open as Luz approached and began placing stones, one by one, in Dolores's palm. "I can add a few details to your story, if I remember correctly."

I held my breath.

"*He* is the one who carried you to the hospital, leaving you at the entrance and then hiding in the shadows. That night, while sleeping in a parking garage, he was caught by authorities and eventually deported—all the way back to Guatemala."

Poor Manuel! After all of that. Guatemala! But the look on Dolores's face spoke of even more misery. I placed my hand over my heart and listened.

She was frowning as she said, "He spent time in the hospital, for his lungs, I think. He wasn't well for many months, he said. Then, I believe, a brother helped get him over the border again. They were working together somewhere in Southern California." She stopped and turned to me, "This was a while ago, remember—one year, maybe close to two."

I took this in, imagining the torment of his journey south and the numbness of his journey north again. "How did he look?" I asked, hungry to be in that moment.

She looked down at the stones, rolling them between her fingers.

"He was thin—tall and thin, I remember that. His hair cut close to his head—almost in what we used to call a crew-cut. And a scar," she said gently, "along the side of his face." Her fingers closed over the tiny stones as she lifted her hand to her face and traced a line straight down from temple to chin.

It didn't sound like Manuel—tall, thin, no mass of hair over his brow, but then it had been a few years—and I no longer looked like the Alma he knew. And the scar . . . we were both scarred, that was certain.

Suddenly Dolores's face lit up. "Oh yes, I remember something else! I was to tell you that he has . . . a little book of math?" She looked at me questioningly. "Does this mean something?"

I couldn't answer, for my breath wouldn't come, but I nodded furiously as tears streamed down my face. Gathering a puzzled Luz to my chest, I rocked her and finally managed to whisper to Dolores, "Gracias. Gracias. Gracias."

The number that Dolores gave me reached someone Manuel had once worked for in Temecula. His name was Nuñez, no first name offered. He stated simply that the brothers worked the area often, but they weren't there just now. He'd put my message on the board; I was welcome to keep checking in.

I was not disappointed. Julie and Diego kept at me, suggesting we drive down and ask around, but I smiled at their impatience and shook my head. "There is no hurry. It will happen," I said.

Diego thought I was shy or perhaps worried that Manuel had found someone else. Julie thought I was afraid I wouldn't know him anymore. But they didn't know yet what it is to share a journey, and they didn't understand the comfort in just knowing.

What I knew for certain was that distance is never a barrier, nor time, for love keeps multiplying even when miles—or borders—divide.

Epilogue
The Writing Journal of
Luz de Rosalba Cruz

Los Angeles: August 2017

I am not like my mother; I do not like numbers. For me, it is words that are magical, for they help me create something solid and lasting out of my tangled mess of emotions. With words I can make sense of the anger and fear, the love and the longing, which are fiercely twisted together in my relationship with my mom, like the braid she yanks together so tightly every morning in her attempt to tame my thick, wild hair. I let her do it because later, when I set it free, I love the kinky waves that cascade over my shoulders. So do the boys.

But that's not what I want to write about today. There are two things, and again they are stubbornly intertwined. The first is that my mother drives me crazy. She thinks I am stupid. Not student, school stupid. She knows that I am very smart in that department. Teachers are already talking to us about universities and full scholarships. In fact, my dream is to learn the Tzotzil language of my mother's indigenous family in Chiapas, so I can study Mayan Tzotzil poetry one day. No, when I say stupid, I mean my mom thinks I don't know the truth about her life, especially the years before she came to live with Berta. But they all forget that I am good at reading between the lines. I've heard enough times from Berta that I don't know all

227

of my mother's suffering. When I talk back to my mom in front of
Uncle Diego, he gets as close as is possible to something like anger
toward me, and I am reminded that my mother deserves my undying
love forever. But it's his pause, his look, and their implications that
speak volumes. And then there is the simple fact that I have lived
with my mother my whole life and heard the piercing screams in the
middle of the night, the cries for Rosa and Manuel, that she always
blames on something she ate that evening, too much garlic or too
many habaneros. I am no fool.

Sometimes I am angry with her. Why can't she trust me with
the truth? I'm not a child anymore. I am the same age she was
when she made her journey. I am the age that her father was when
he worked the fields and walked the picket lines with Cesar Chavez
and Dolores Huerta. There is some dark secret that she doesn't
want to share with me, especially about her sister Rosa. I don't
believe that she died in a car accident on her way home to Oaxaca,
though this could explain my mother's guilt that she continued
on with my father to Los Angeles, while Rosa headed back. Still, I
can feel it; there is something she does not want me to know. But
I have to be honest with myself, and this is where writing helps
me see clearer: Do I want her to know everything about my life?
Absolutely not.

And yet, twisted up with all of these feelings of anger and frustra-
tion are an underlying awe and respect. My mother has accomplished
so much with her determination and hard work, mastering English
and completing her associate's degree in math. She now works as an
assistant to an accountant, and she tutors kids in math in our community, but she hopes one day, when I am finished with college, to
return to school to become a teacher. I know she will.

She has always given me a good life. We have lived in our own
apartment ever since Berta started doing foster care and I begged
Mom to get our own place, which she did. And then, of course,

there's the way she has persevered on her own, especially after losing my father a second time.

I have fleeting memories of those few months that he was in our life. Though I was only about three or four years old, I remember a sadness about him from the start. He spoke little and coughed a lot. I didn't like to be held by him. I would fidget and run to Mom. He told me to call him Papá, but I don't think I did. I don't think I called him anything. Since then, I've always thought of him as Manuel. That's how Mom refers to him, with a soft, faraway look in her eyes.

At that time, we all took a trip together to the San Diego Zoo and the next day to a cemetery, where we put colorful paper flowers on graves marked John and Jane Doe. I now know that cemetery is in Holtville, where Mom imagines her father is buried with other unidentified souls who died in the desert trying to cross the border. She was both happy and sad that day; it was hard to tell if her tears were from joy or grief. I guess both. I remember being jealous because she kept holding his hand and leaning her head on his shoulder.

A few months later, after he left for a job in Central California, Mom got a call from his brother, and I heard her make a sound like an animal. Apparently, Manuel collapsed while working in the fields and died a few hours later in an emergency room. Cause of death: strep throat and severe pneumonia. My mother sat on the kitchen floor, sobbing and stroking the thick pink scar on her thigh, until Berta got home. I remember sitting there with her as she cried, while Berta's smiling cows looked down at us. Even now when I see those silly figurines, I feel a deep sadness.

Consequently, every time I get a sore throat, Mom takes me to the clinic to check for strep, that is if I tell her anymore. She hovers so, sometimes makes me feel like I can't breathe. But then I ask myself, *Can you blame her? You're all she has left.* Only now, I am the one who wants to hover. I am terrified I might lose her. With this new president, I live in daily fear of my mom being deported. I just can't understand why. She has not harmed anyone, has suffered enough, and has worked so hard in this country, which is our home. She has so much more to give here in America. Uncle Diego looked into getting her legal papers, but it's tricky, I guess, and very risky. I was just a baby then, and they feared it might backfire, and she'd be sent back, so they left it alone.

I need her now more than I ever realized. I wish there was something I could do. At school, we have groups that write letters or march in the streets to speak out and let our voices be heard. Sometimes I feel powerless, but other times, when we come together as one, I feel confident and strong.

That's what my mother said Dolores Huerta accomplished. She helped the farm workers come together and speak in one loud voice. Mom is taking me to see a documentary about her. *Dolores* opens in a few weeks, and the woman, Dolores, will actually be there. Mom wants to get a picture of the three of us together. Again, I am so afraid for her to go anywhere in public. What if someone grabs her and takes her away from me? She tries to reassure me that we are safe, but I can see in her eyes that she knows otherwise. Then I remember something she said that used to annoy me. "Distance is never a barrier, nor time, for love keeps multiplying even when miles—or borders—divide."

I pray we will never be divided by borders, but just as that sentence weaves together my love of words and hers of numbers, I now know that my mother and I will always be tightly intertwined—and this is one braid I will never set free.

Math Journal of Alma Cruz:
Problems and Solutions

Math Problem #1

In Chiapas, 75 people sneak onto the train. At Checkpoint One, 64 people run into the fields, 33 are caught, the rest hide and manage to re-board the train. At Checkpoint Two, half of those now on the train are stopped and asked for money. One-third have nothing and are taken into custody to be deported. The rest pay and are allowed to re-board. How many of the 75 make it to Oaxaca?

Solution: 35

After Checkpoint One: Since 64 ran, 75 − 64 = **11 stayed on the train.**

Of the 64, 33 are caught. 64 − 33 = **31 re-board train.**

Therefore 11 + 31 = **42.**

After Checkpoint Two: 1/2 of 42 = 21

21 are stopped and asked for money;

21 stay on the train.

1/3 of 21 are taken into custody, leaving **14 to re-board** with the other **21** still on the train. (14 + 21 = 35)

Therefore 35 make it to Oaxaca.

Math Problem #2

Two trucks leave for Oaxaca. One breaks down in Tehuantepec, 250 km from Oaxaca at 12 noon. The first truck continues on at 50 km/hour, makes one 30-minute stop, then a second 10-minute stop. The second truck is repaired in 45 minutes, travels at 50 km/hour, makes one 40-minute stop only. What time does each truck arrive in Oaxaca?

Solution: 1st truck arrives at 5:40 p.m.
2nd truck arrives 6: 25 p.m.

At 50 km/hour, it would take 5 hours to reach Oaxaca with no stops.

250 km ÷ 50 km/h = 5 hours

The first truck adds two stops: 30 min + 10 min = 40 min.

12 noon + 5 hours + 40 min = **5:40 p.m.**

The second truck is delayed 45 minutes and makes one 40 min stop: 45 + 40 = 85 min or 85 min = 1 hour 25 min

12 noon + 5 hours + 1 hour + 25 min = **6:25 p.m.**

Math Problem #3

Señor Garcia, who is 68 years old, has read, on the average, 8 books every month for the last 47 years. If he continues this pace, how many more years must he live to reach his goal of 10,000 books?
If this is not possible, how many books must he read each month to achieve this goal by the age of 90?

Solution: He must live another 57 years and 2 months or read 21 books/month by age 90.

8 books/month = 8 × 12 months = 96 books/ year
96 books × 47 years = 4,512 books read so far

10,000 − 4,512 = 5,488 books needed to read to achieve 10,000

5,488 books ÷ 96 books/year = **57 years 2 months**

Since Mr. Garcia is 68, this is not possible, as he would have to live to be 125 years old.

If he lived to be 90 . . .

90 years − 68 years = 22 years left to read

5,488 books ÷ 22 years = 249.5 each year

249.5 ÷ 12 months = 20.8 or **21 books/month**

Math Problem #4

Three hundred people set out from Delano, California, heading for the state capital of Sacramento. By the time they reach their destination, they have grown to ten thousand strong.

Consider the numbers 300 and 10,000. What are their common factors?

* A common factor is a whole number that will divide exactly into two or more given numbers without leaving a remainder.

Solution: 2, 4, 5, 10, 20, 25, 50, 100.

The factors of 300 are 2, 3, 4, 5, 6, 10, 12, 15, 20, 25, 30, 50, 60, 75, 100, 150.

All of these numbers can be divided into 300 with a remainder of zero. Of these numbers, 2, 4, 5, 10, 20, 25, 50, 100 are also factors of 10,000. These shared numbers are called common factors.

Math Problem #5

The temperature in the Arizona desert climbed to 47° Celsius.
Convert this to Fahrenheit.

The ground temperature is reported to be 140° Fahrenheit.
Convert this to Celsius.

Solution: 47° Celsius = 116.6° Fahrenheit
            140° Fahrenheit = 60° Celsius

Formula for Celsius to Fahrenheit: **(Celsius × 9/5) + 32 = Fahrenheit**
47°C × 9/5 = 84.6   84.6 + 32 = **116.6°F**

Formula for Fahrenheit to Celsius: **(Fahrenheit − 32) × 5/9 = Celsius**
140°F − 32 = 108   108 × 5/9 = **60°C**

Math Problem #6

(Chart on wall of Border Patrol waiting room.)
According to Mexico's Foreign Relations Office:
In 1995, **61** border deaths along the Mexico/Arizona border.
In 1996, **87**
In 1997, **149**
In 1998, **329**
In 1999, **358**
In 2000, to date mid-August, **401** written in, crossed out, replaced
with **411.**
(This wouldn't include the bodies seen in the desert or all those unaccounted for throughout the years.)

What is the average number of deaths per year since Operation
Gatekeeper in California, Operation Safeguard in Arizona, and
Operation Rio Grande in Texas began in 1994?

Solution: 61 + 87 + 149 + 329 + 358 + 411 = 1,395
1,395 ÷ 6 years = 232.5 deaths/year

Consider just the most recent three years, 1998–2000. What is the average number of border deaths each day?

Solution: 329 + 358 + 411 = 1,098
1,098 ÷ 3 years = 366 deaths/year or ~1 death/day

Math Problem #7

The drive from Nogales, Arizona to Los Angeles, California, was 551.39 American miles.

If five of the seven passengers planned to drive an equal distance, how long would they each have to drive if they traveled at an average of 65 miles per hour?

Solution: 1 hour and 42 minutes each

551.39 miles ÷ 5 drivers = 110.3 miles each

110.3 miles ÷ 65 miles per hour = 1.7 hours

7/10 of 60 minutes = 42 minutes

Therefore 1 hour and 42 minutes each

Math Problem #8

Betty's Bakery received the following order:

25 plain croissants @ $1.75

25 chocolate croissants @ $1.75

25 Napoleons @ $1.95

25 chocolate éclairs @ $1.95

25 brioches @ $1.85

Compute the total cost in American dollars and cents.

Then compute the change for this purchase if given two $100 bills and a $50 bill. (Explain what American bills and coins you would choose as change.)

*Do not use a calculator! It's important to keep your basic skills sharp!

Solution: Total cost is $231.25 Change back is $18.75

(One $10 bill, one $5 bill, three $1 bills, and three quarters.)

$50 \times \$1.75 = 87.50$

$50 \times \$1.95 = 97.50$

$\underline{25 \times \$1.85 = 46.25}$

Total cost $231.25

Change back: $250.00 − 231.25 = $18.75

$10.00 + $5.00 + (3 × $1.00) + 3 quarters @ 0.25 cents each = $18.75

Math Problem #9

A recipe for Berta's Sugarbaby Cookies calls for ½ kg of sugar. How many times can she make these cookies before she uses up a 6 kg bag of sugar?

Solution: 12 times

$6 \text{ kg} \div \tfrac{1}{2} \text{ kg} = 6 \times 2/1 = 12/1 = 12$

Math Problem #10: Math Placement Review!

1. Change to Mixed Numbers

   9/4

   Solution: $9 \div 4 = 2\,\frac{1}{4}$

2. Change to Improper Fractions

   7 ¾

   Solution: 31/4 $(4 \times 7) + 3$ over 4 or $(28 + 3) =$ **31/ 4**

3. Simplify (reduce to lowest terms)

   32/68

   Solution: 8/17 (divide each by 4) $32 \div 4 =$ **8** $68 \div 4 =$ **17**

4. Multiply

   1 ½ x 2 ¾

   Solution: 4 1/8

   First change to improper fractions: $1\,\frac{1}{2} = 3/2$; $2\,\frac{3}{4} = 11/4$

   $3/2 \times 11/4 = 33/8 =$ **4 1/8**

5. Divide

   4 3/5 ÷ 2 ½

   Solution: 1 21/25

   First change to improper fractions: $4\,3/5 = 23/5$; $2\,\frac{1}{2} = 5/2$

   Then invert the second fraction and multiply: $23/5 \times 2/5 = 46/25$

   $=$ **1 21/25**

6. Berta and I have the combined age of 66. Berta is 32 years older than I am.

   How old is Berta? How old am I?

   Solution: Berta is 49. I am 17.

   If $x =$ my age $x + 32 =$ Berta's $x + (x + 32) = 66$

   $2x + 32 = 66$ $2x = 66 - 32$ $2x = 34$ $x = 34 \div 2 =$ **17**

   $x = 17$ **My age** $17 + 32 = 49$ **Berta's age**

Author's Note
Bearing Witness to *Luz*

Since I first began working on this novel in 2004, I've been asked many times what led me to write about a young Mexican immigrant girl's experience. In truth, I think the real question was: Am I qualified, and do I have a right to tell this story? I have worked with the immigrant community in Southern California for decades; I've heard numerous stories of the dangers of border crossings and the struggles faced once here; and I've been an immigrant rights activist—but I am not Latina.

Initially, I assumed that to write about the issues at the heart of this book, I should take what I called a Barbara Kingsolver approach: In her novel *The Bean Trees,* her main character is a young, white southern girl who sets out on a journey of her own, which is the center of the novel, but she also meets a couple fleeing the civil war in Guatemala and conveys their story, too, as well as Native American concerns associated with the baby that the protagonist finds. My first attempt at a novel, *Blue Flags,* was about an Italian-American woman who moves to Southern California to help her brother after a family tragedy, and while there, she learns about migrant deaths in the desert near the border.

After finishing a draft, I set the novel aside and took a writing class with author Gayle Brandeis, winner of Barbara Kingsolver's Bellwether Prize for Fiction of Social Engagement. In response to one of Gayle's assignments, I began writing in the voice of a young Mexican girl who was searching for her missing migrant father. It was just an assignment, so I didn't worry that maybe I shouldn't or couldn't. As a result, Alma's story poured out of me. I couldn't stop writing. I knew it came from somewhere genuine and true. I trusted that feeling and just kept going.

In the months leading up to the publication of Alma's story, now titled *Luz*, a controversy broke out that spoke to the very heart of the concerns I harbored about my own book. *American Dirt*, the novel by Jeanine Cummins about a middle-class Mexican woman's harrowing border crossing with her young son, was criticized for stereotypical portrayals of Mexicans and Mexican culture and for not having offered an accurate depiction of the issues at the heart of her story.

As writers, we all stretch our imagination in order to climb into each character's skin and walk around in it, as Atticus Finch taught us about understanding another person's point of view. If we didn't, we'd only be writing about our own very narrow experiences. I examined myself, my motivations, and my research carefully in the wake of the *American Dirt* scandal. My publisher reread the manuscript. We decided that Alma's journey felt true. I had settled into Alma's skin along the way. I went on her journey with her, and she is as true a character to me as many of the real-life women who've endured equally horrifying situations or the characters portrayed in other excellent novels and memoirs on this topic—and there are several. For me, Alma's story told one truth, one single experience among many.

What led to my passionate connection to the immigrant experience began in the 1990s. As a young adult, I had moved from a small town in upstate New York to Los Angeles. At the time, I was an RN specializing in intensive care, but my real love was writing. In fact, I took fiction writing classes at UCLA Extension Writers' Program while I worked at the medical center as a nurse. When my children were school-age, I went back to college full-time to study literature and creative writing. Once I graduated, my first job was teaching English as a Second Language to adults. Many of my students were Mexican and Central American. Their language, food, music, and religion took me back to my early childhood growing up in an Italian neighborhood in Binghamton, New York. Ranchera music reminded me of my Grandpa playing the "squeezabox," as he called it. Reverence for the Virgin Mary (la Virgen de Guadalupe) and the strong central role of the mother were so familiar. All of this gave me great comfort for at the time my marriage was headed for divorce, and I was three thousand miles away from family.

I loved going to work. My students inspired me. If they, at sixteen, thirty-six, or seventy, could begin again in a new country and with a new language, well, I certainly could in my own country with my own language. I saw how hard they worked and how family-centered they were. I suppose I also saw my own extended family in their stories. My Italian grandparents were immigrants. My grandfather worked construction, and my grandmother worked in a cigar factory. I remember my father telling me how he was punished for speaking Italian in kindergarten. For these many reasons, I felt a fierce connection.

Once divorced, I needed a full-time job with benefits (ESL was part-time), so I began teaching at a Los Angeles public high school. Many of my students were from Mexico and Central America, so stories I had heard from adults, I was now hearing from their children. It was a difficult time with focus on test-taking, which was terrible for the kids. I chose literature that they could relate to, writers like Sandra Cisneros, Jimmy Santiago Baca, and especially Luis Rodriguez, who had a wonderful bookstore nearby, Tia Chucha's, that we visited. My students would read their poetry for Luis, and he would talk with them about his gang life and how education and poetry saved him.

I also showed them a documentary called *¡Chicano!* so they could learn about the discrimination so many faced before them, about the walkouts in 1968, and the changes that resulted: bilingual classes, Latinx counselors, Chicano history, no more corporeal punishment. I encouraged them to be proud of their heritage. I told them how lucky they were to be able to learn their family's language, to watch TV in their language, to go to stores that catered to their food. My Italian neighborhood back home had disappeared completely. They were fortunate to have all of this at their fingertips.

At the same time, I was upset by the anti-immigrant sentiment sweeping our country. Even some of my own family in upstate New York would argue with me about undocumented immigrants, insisting that they were breaking the law and asking why they didn't stay in their own country. I would tell them my students' stories about poverty in Mexico and war and violence in Central America, pointing out that they might do the same thing to help their families. I'd heard and read so many stories of the dangers of border crossing—dehydration and death, criminals waiting to take advantage of the vulnerable, the horrors of Ciudad Juárez. As a result, I became involved with Amnesty International, focusing on refugee and immigrant rights. Our group toured what was then the Terminal Island Immigration Detention Center in San Pedro (closed in 2007 after being deemed unsafe). With BorderLinks of Tucson, we spent time in Nogales, Arizona and Mexico, talking with people on both sides of the border, including border patrol agents, maquiladora (factory) workers and their foreman, and a family in Los Encinos Colonia, a squatters' community in Mexico. The matriarch of the family generously fed us lunch and spoke of how we were all one America—North, Central, South—all one.

I had written since I was in my twenties, but at this point in my life I wanted to write about the undocumented immigrant community in a way that others could see through their eyes and experience and understand why they were driven to leave their homes and risk their lives to come to our country. I started with *Blue Flags*, as mentioned above. In this novel, a woman ends up on a journey that exposes her to the horror of migrant deaths in the desert, as well as the beauty of the blue flags placed as markers by containers of water left by compassionate volunteers.

While researching this novel, I met three remarkable men: Father Richard Estrada, a tireless defender of the rights of immigrants and refugees, most especially, homeless migrant youth; Enrique Morones, founder of Border Angels, an organization that focuses on immigrant rights and reform, while also preventing deaths along the border; and John Hunter, scientist and humanitarian, who believed in putting people before politics. With them, I took part in Water Stations Project in the Imperial Valley's desert east of San Diego, where we placed jugs of water in simple cardboard boxes marked by a blue flag. Afterwards, we had a ceremony at Terrace Park Cemetery in Holtville, about 125 miles east of San Diego, where unidentified migrants' remains were buried in a dirt lot in the back. We left paper flowers and No Olvidados (Not Forgotten) signs beside the John and Jane Doe bricks that marked their graves. I had the honor that day of reading a passage about blue flags from my novel:

> She could still see the blue flag flowing limply in the breeze. Most certainly, it was a marker of sustenance in the midst of an indifferent and barren landscape, but it was more than that. It was also a symbol to Josie of the fragile possibilities of hope, of man's tenacious belief that life holds endless opportunities for those who try, risk, change, and persevere, though sometimes at great cost. But what soothed her most, after this heart-wrenching day, was the fact that the blue flag stood tall as a symbol of man's potential for love and compassion, reaching up and out to those in need.

That was the first time I felt like an authentic writer, reading words that were written from the depths of my emotions, words that moved others that day as we stood together in a circle, heads bowed, to honor those who had perished in the desert unidentified and to remember, for the families who would never know their loved one's fate.

Not long after this, I began Gayle Brandeis's class. Alma began to speak, and I began to write.

Upon completing *Luz*, I decided to contact Latina writer Alma Luz Villanueva, winner of the American Book Award for her novel *The Ultraviolet Sky*. I wanted to be certain that my novel rang true in the eyes and heart of a woman so familiar with both the United States and Mexico. After reading an email that included my experiences described above and then the manuscript of my novel, she responded with overwhelming support and encouragement. She left comments throughout my manuscript that told me she got every little moment that I had hoped my reader would get, expressing joy and heartbreak as she read, and bringing me to tears that someone I so admired loved my characters and my novel. Ultimately, she suggested that I include this author's note and left me with this final blessing: "You aren't Latina, but you have borne witness to La Luz." This in itself meant the world to me, for it has many layers of meaning.

In the novel, Luz is the name of Alma's daughter. In Spanish, luz means light. Alma gives her this name for a special reason, as those of you who have read the novel are aware. In addition, the phrase "dar a luz" literally means "to give to the light," but it also means "to give birth"—such a beautiful concept. Luz/light has always been an important symbol to me. While teaching high school, I formed a club called Students In Action, only we used a candle as the "I": Students ⚡n Action. Our motto was, "It is better to light a candle than to curse the darkness." Students could team up and choose any issue—animal rights, homelessness, bullying, veterans' rights, immigrant rights, etc. —and try to make a difference. The candle is also the symbol used by Amnesty International. ⚡ **AMNESTY** INTERNATIONAL And finally, I have always loved and, therefore, chose as my epigraph to this novel, Martin Luther King, Jr.'s well-known quote, "Darkness cannot drive out darkness, only light can do that. Hate cannot drive out hate, only love can do that." So, to be told by Alma Luz Villanueva that I have borne witness to La Luz was truly a blessing to me. I am not Latina, but my soul is Alma, my light is Luz, and love is the source of why I wrote this novel.

Acknowledgments

I am profoundly grateful to so many who contributed to the birth of this novel. First and foremost, to my midwives: Gayle Brandeis, whose overwhelming encouragement from the earliest stages kept me writing, rewriting, and believing; and Alma Luz Villanueva, whose praise and final blessing gave me the courage to push this novel to the light. I am so fortunate to have worked with both of them.

The seeds of this novel began in my ESL classes at Reseda Adult School, as I met people from Mexico and Central America and heard countless stories about their lives before, during, and after their travels to el norte. Their stories of courage and perseverance inspired me on so many levels, both personally and professionally. I later heard similar stories, from a different perspective, at James Monroe High School, as my Latinx students wrote about their parents or grandparents. What touched me most was to read their essays about the American Dream, often concluding that they hoped one day to buy a house—not for themselves, but for their hardworking, self-sacrificing parents.

I am also grateful to Amnesty International and BorderLinks of Tucson for the life-changing experience of visiting both sides of the border, where we spoke with Border Patrol, toured a battery factory in Mexico, and ate lunch with a community leader in Los Encinos Colonia. Hearing varying viewpoints on the complex issues at the border broadened my knowledge and opened my heart even more.

I was so fortunate to meet Father Richard Estrada, John Hunter, and Enrique Morones, three compassionate men, whose focus on saving lives with Water Stations Project put people before politics. I'm grateful to have been a part of that special day of honor in 2002 for those unidentified souls buried in the back of Holtville's Terrace Park Cemetery.

To Dolores Huerta, a role model for social justice activism on all fronts, your spirit guided my Alma on the page, as in real life you have inspired so many for decades—and your legacy will continue to guide and inspire for many more.

I would also like to acknowledge the influence of an amazing, Pulitzer Prize winning, six-part series in the *Los Angeles Times*, "Enrique's Journey," written by Sonia Nazario and photographed by Don Bartletti, later expanded and published in book form. This work had a powerful effect on me, ultimately finding its way into Alma's journey in the form of Manuel.

I would also like to thank the following: writer/editor Elizabeth McKenzie, whose insights and suggestions, after reading an early draft of this novel, helped me enormously in the confusing stages of revision; Professor Jayne Howell, Department of Anthropology and Co-Director, Latin American Studies, Cal State University, Long Beach, for her helpful email correspondence regarding the education of young girls in Oaxaca; Leticia Mendoza, for patiently checking my use of Spanish throughout the novel; Patricia Daniels, for her thorough proofreading of my final copy; and finally, Carrie Barnett and Alma Villegas Torres, colleagues and math teachers extraordinaire, for taking the time to check *my* Alma's math problems and solutions for any errors.

To my She Writes Press and BookSparks team: Brooke Warner, Samantha Strom, and Crystal Patriarche, this novel could not have found a better home and, literally, would not have seen the light without you.

And most especially, to my family. I'd like to thank my mom and dad, Alice and George DiFulvio, for showing me what love of family truly means. How I wish you could have seen this book in print! To my sister, Dee Osier, whose love and devotion touch all those around her. To my soul-sister, Margaret Walsh, how I treasure our special friendship. To my son and daughter, Dean and Claire Daniels, thank you for giving me the greatest joy in my life—simply loving you both, and to their partners in life and love, Megan Daniels and Wayne McClammy. To Calvin and Max Daniels, you fill my heart to bursting. And finally, to my husband, Bruce Thomas: thank you for believing in my writing and encouraging my passion; it was your love that gave this book life.

Reading Guide
Topics and Questions for Discussion

1. Alma states that she has given her daughter Luz the safer story, rather than the truth. What do you think about this decision? Is it possible that, one day, she will tell Luz the truth/la verdad? How might Luz react to this?

2. Discuss the many ways that Alma's father's disappearance changes her life.

3. What is your opinion of Alma's mother? What were her choices, and what decisions did she ultimately make? What might you have done in her place?

4. How are Alma and Rosa alike? How are they different?

5. What options did Alma and Rosa have after fleeing Chiapas? Discuss the possible consequences of each. Was heading for el norte a good decision? How was it any better, or worse, than the other options?

6. Discuss the secret letter. What did it represent to Alma? Why do you think she didn't tell Rosa about the letter? Once she has fallen in love with Manuel, in what ways has her belief in the letter intensified?

7. Why does Alma feel responsible for Rosa's fate? Is she? Discuss.

8. Discuss both Ana and Senorita Garcia. What motivates each to help Alma in her journey?

9. Who did you connect with the most in this novel? Explain.

10. What does the image of one white calla lily on a deep blue background, found on both Alma's little box of stars and her math journal, represent to you?

11. Discuss the math problems that Alma creates on her journey. What role did they play?

12. Consider Berta's story: the loss of her fiancé, her sister's death, her role in Diego and Juan's life. What do you think of her decision regarding Diego and the truth about the secret letter?

13. What role does Dolores Huerta play in the novel? How does she influence Alma's decisions along the way or boost her spirits during difficult times, and, finally, in what ways does she help bring closure to Alma's journey?

14. Discuss *Luz* as a coming of age novel. How does Alma change from the time her father disappeared until her meeting with Dolores?

15. Discuss Luz's journal entry at the end. How does it bring closure to the novel?

16. Discuss the possible meanings of the title, *Luz*.

About the Author

© Bruce Thomas

Originally from Binghamton, New York, Debra Thomas has lived in Southern California for most of her adult life. She holds both a bachelor's and a master's in English from California State University, Northridge, and attended the UCLA Extension Writers' Program. She has taught literature and writing at a Los Angeles public high school and English as a Second Language to adults from all over the world. Her experience as an advocate for immigrant and refugee rights led her to write *Luz*. She is currently at work on her second novel.

SELECTED TITLES FROM SHE WRITES PRESS

She Writes Press is an independent publishing company founded to serve women writers everywhere. Visit us at www.shewritespress.com.

In a Silent Way by Mary Jo Hetzel $16.95, 978-1-63152-135-5
When Jeanna Kendall—a young white teacher at a progressive urban school—becomes involved with a community activist group, she finds herself grappling with issues of racism, sexism, and oppression of various shades in both her professional and personal life.

Profound and Perfect Things by Maribel Garcia $16.95, 978-1631525414
When Isa, a closeted lesbian with conservative Mexican parents, has a one-night stand that results in an unwanted pregnancy, her sister Cristina adopts the baby—but twelve years later, Isa, who regrets giving up her child, threatens to spill the secret of her daughter's true parentage.

The Rooms Are Filled by Jessica Null Vealitzek $16.95, 978-1-938314-58-2
The coming-of-age story of two outcasts—a nine-year-old boy who just lost his father, and a closeted young woman—brought together by circumstance.

American Family by Catherine Marshall-Smith $16.95, 978-1631521638
Partners Richard and Michael, recovering alcoholics, struggle to gain custody of Richard's biological daughter from her grandparents after her mother's death only to discover they—and she—are fundamentalist Christians.

The Belief in Angels by J. Dylan Yates $16.95, 978-1-938314-64-3
From the Majdonek death camp to a volatile hippie household on the East Coast, this narrative of tragedy, survival, and hope spans more than fifty years, from the 1920s to the 1970s.

Shelter Us by Laura Diamond $16.95, 978-1-63152-970-2
Lawyer-turned-stay-at-home-mom Sarah Shaw is still struggling to find a steady happiness after the death of her infant daughter when she meets a young homeless mother and toddler she can't get out of her mind—and becomes determined to rescue them.